RAILWAY TO THE GRAVE

by

Edward Marston

Magna Large Print Books
Long Preston, North Yorkshire,
BD23 4ND, England.

British Library Cataloguing in Publication Data.

Marston, Edward
    Railway to the grave.

    A catalogue record of this book is
    available from the British Library

    ISBN   978-0-7505-3248-8

First published in Great Britain in 2010 by Allison & Busby Limited

Copyright © 2010 by Edward Marston

Cover illustration by arrangement with Allison & Busby Ltd.

The moral right of the author has been asserted

Published in Large Print 2010 by arrangement with
Allison & Busby Ltd.

Magna Large Print is an imprint of Library Magna Books Ltd.

Printed and bound in Great Britain by
T.J. (International) Ltd., Cornwall, PL28 8RW

RAILWAY TO THE GRAVE

Yorkshire 1855. Colonel Aubrey Tarleton is well respected by his neighbours in the village of South Otterington, so the community is stunned when he deliberately walks into the path of a speeding train. Pinned to his chest is a note for his friend, Superintendent Tallis of Scotland Yard. Then Tallis receives a letter from Tarleton stating he no longer wishes to live without his beloved wife, who has vanished. Was Tarleton responsible for his wife's disappearance and was his suicide the act of a guilty man? Tallis, accompanied by Inspector Robert Colbeck, the famous Railway Detective, sets out for Yorkshire determined to uncover the truth.

RAILWAY TO THE GRAVE

In loving memory of
Raymond Allen
uncle, friend and engine driver

CHAPTER ONE

1855

Colonel Aubrey Tarleton led an orderly existence.
Born into a military family and subject to the
dictates of a martinet father, he'd been educated
at a public school that prided itself on its strict
regime. When he joined the army, therefore, he
was already accustomed to a life within pre-
scribed limits. He felt supremely comfortable in
uniform and, as succeeding promotions came, he
gloried in his position. His father had never risen
above the rank of major. To acquire a colonelcy
and thereby better the man who'd sired him was,
to Tarleton, a source of intense satisfaction. He
carried that satisfaction into his retirement,
finding, in civilian life, the deference to which he
felt entitled.

'Is that all you want, Colonel?' asked his housekeeper, softly.

'That is all, Mrs Withers,' he replied.

'As a rule, you have such a hearty breakfast.'

'I don't feel hungry this morning.'

'Shall I make you some more coffee?'

'No, thank you.'

'Very good, sir.'

With a respectful nod, Mrs Withers backed out
of the dining room. She was a handsome woman
of middle years with an ample frame held firmly

in place beneath her dress by steadfast stays. Retreating to the kitchen, she waited until she heard Tarleton ascending the staircase, then she snapped her fingers at the girl who was cleaning the knives with emery powder. Subdued in the presence of her employer, the housekeeper now became peremptory.

'Clear the table,' she ordered.

'Yes, Mrs Withers,' said Lottie Pearl.

'And be quick about it.'

'Did the colonel eat anything today?'

'That's none of your business, girl.'

'I was only wondering.'

'You're not paid to wonder.'

'No, Mrs Withers.'

'Now do as you're told.'

Lottie scurried out with a tray in her hands. She was a scrawny girl of sixteen and, as maid-of-all-work, was a relative newcomer to the house. In awe of Colonel Tarleton, she was frightened of the stern housekeeper and of her curt reproaches. Creeping tentatively into the dining room, she looked at the untouched eggs and the half-eaten piece of bread on the plate. Only a few sips had been taken from the cup of coffee. The sound of heavy footsteps in the bedroom above made her glance warily up.

Tarleton was on the move, crossing to open the wardrobe in order to examine its contents before walking to the window to look up at the sky. When he'd taken his usual morning walk with the dog before breakfast, there'd been more than a hint of rain in the clouds but they seemed to have drifted benignly away, allowing the sun to come into view. On such an important day, he was determined to dress well. After removing the well-worn corduroy suit he kept for his rambles through the countryside, he changed his shirt and put on his best trousers, waistcoat and frock coat. Shining black shoes, a fob watch and a cravat completed the outfit. Tarleton studied himself with care in the cheval mirror, making a few adjustments to his apparel then brushing back some strands of thinning white hair.

Taking a deep breath, he crossed to the door that led to the adjoining room and tapped politely on it. Though there was no response from within, he opened the door and gazed wistfully around. Everything in the room was a cherished keepsake. His eyes took in the paintings, the vases, the plants, the ornaments, the jewellery box, the furniture, the Persian carpet and the more functional objects before lingering on the double bed. On the wall above it was a beautiful Dutch tapestry that set off a surge of fond memories and he permitted himself a moment to savour them. After bestowing a wan smile on the room, he withdrew again and closed the door gently behind him as if not wishing to disturb its occupant. Then he collected his wallet, his spectacles and a folded sheet of paper. The last thing he picked up was a large safety pin.

Mrs Withers was waiting for him in the hallway, holding his top hat. As he took it from her, she indicated the letter on the table.

'The postman came while you were upstairs, Colonel,' she said.

'I've no time to read the mail now, Mrs Withers.'

'But there might be *news*.' She quailed slightly as he turned to stare at her with a mingled anger and pain. Writhing under his glare, she gestured apologetically. 'Forgive me, sir. I spoke out of turn. You know best, of course.'

'Of course,' he emphasised.

'Do you have any orders for me?'

'Remember to feed the dog.'

'I will, Colonel.'

'Goodbye, Mrs Withers.'

'What train will you be catching back from Doncaster?'

'Goodbye.'

It was a brusque departure. He didn't even wait for her to use the clothes brush on his coat. Putting on his hat and picking up his walking stick, he let himself out of the house and strode off down the drive. Face clouded with concern, the housekeeper watched him through the glass-panelled door but Tarleton did not look back. His tall, erect, still soldierly figure marched briskly away towards the main gate as if on parade before royalty.

South Otterington was a pleasant, scattered village on the east side of the River Wiske, large enough to have a railway station, three public houses, two blacksmiths and a cluster of shops, yet small enough for each inhabitant to know everyone else in the community. Colonel Tarleton was a familiar sight there, a member of the gentry held in high esteem as much for his heroic feats in the army as for his social position. When he'd walked the mile or so from his home, he entered

14

the main street to be greeted by a series of ingratiating smiles, polite nods and obsequious salutes. He acknowledged them all with a lordly wave of his walking stick. Nan Pearl, returning from the butcher with scraps for her mangy cat, all but curtsied to him, desperately hoping for a brief word of praise for her daughter, Lottie, now in service at the Tarleton household. Instead she got an almost imperceptible nod. Mrs Skelton, the rector's wife, on the other hand, merited a tilt of his top hat and a cold smile that flitted across his gaunt face.

Though he seemed to be heading for the railway station, he walked past it and continued on until he'd left the village behind him and was out into open countryside. Fields of wheat and barley lay all round him. Sheep were grazing contentedly on a hillside. There was fitful birdsong but it only increased the extraordinary sense of peace and tranquillity. Tarleton had always loved his native Yorkshire and never tired of roaming the North Riding on foot. This time, however, he took no pleasure from the surroundings. His mind was concentrated on a single goal and nothing could distract him from it.

He kept on until he judged himself to be mid-way between the village and Thirsk to its south. At that point, he clambered over a gate and picked his way across a wheat field until it dipped down towards the railway line. He was still spry enough to climb over the dry-stone wall without difficulty, straightening his hat when he reached the track then slipping a hand inside his pocket. He took out the sheet of paper and used the

15

safety pin to secure it to his coat like a medal. A glance at his watch told him that he had timed his arrival perfectly. Dropping the watch back into his waistcoat pocket, Tarleton took a deep breath and inflated his chest.

He was ready. Keeping between the rails, he walked over the sleepers with a measured tread. He was quite untroubled by fear. When he heard the distant noise of an approaching train, he sighed with joy. His ordeal would soon be over.

Halfway between Thirsk and South Otterington, the train was travelling at full speed. Standing on the footplate, the driver and the fireman were chatting happily together. The journey had passed without incident and they could congratulate themselves on their punctuality at each stage. When they came round a long bend, however, their good humour vanished. The driver saw him first, an elderly gentleman walking uncaringly towards them on the track as if out on a morning stroll. The fireman could not believe his eyes. Cupping his hands, he yelled a warning at the top of his voice but it was drowned out by the frenzied panting of the locomotive and the ear-splitting rattle of the train. Even the shrill blast of the whistle did not deter the oncoming walker. His gait remained as steady as ever.

Shutting off steam, the driver applied the brakes but there was no hope of stopping in such a short distance. All that they could do was to watch in horror as he strode deliberately towards the hurtling train. They had hit animals before when they'd strayed on the line but this was a very different matter. Here was a flesh and blood human being – a man of substance, by the look of it – advancing towards them with an air of challenge about him. It shook them. At the last moment, both driver and fireman turned away. The impact came and the train surged on, carriage after remorseless carriage rolling over the mangled, blood-covered corpse on the track.

Shocked by what had happened, the fireman emptied the contents of his stomach over the footplate. The driver, meanwhile, feeling some-how guilty at the hideous death, closed his eyes and offered up a prayer for the soul of the victim. When the squealing train finally ground to a halt amid a shower of sparks, the driver was the first to jump down from the locomotive and run back up the track. He kept going until he reached the lifeless body, buffeted into oblivion and spread untidily across the sleepers. The face had been smashed to a pulp and the walking stick split into a dozen pieces. What caught the driver's atten-tion, however, were not the gaping wounds and the misshapen limbs. It was a piece of paper, pinned to the man's coat and flapping about in the breeze.

He bent down to read Colonel Tarleton's last request.

'Whoever finds me, notify Superintendent Tallis of the Detective Department at Scotland Yard.'

CHAPTER TWO

Detective Inspector Robert Colbeck liked to make an early start to the working day but the cab ride to Scotland Yard showed him that London had already been wide awake for hours. The pavements were crowded, the streets thick with traffic and the capital throbbing with its distinctive hullaballoo. Glad to reach the restorative calm of his office, he was unable to enjoy it for even a moment. A constable told him to report to Superintendent Tallis immediately. There was a note of urgency in the man's voice. Colbeck obeyed the summons at once. After knocking on Tallis's door, he let himself into the room even though he was given no permission to do so. He soon saw why.

Wreathed in cigar smoke, the superintendent was leaning forward across his desk, supporting himself on his elbows and staring at some invisible object in the middle distance. Beside him was a bottle of brandy and an empty glass. Colbeck knew that something serious had happened. Consuming alcohol while on duty was anathema to Edward Tallis. He'd dismissed several men from the Metropolitan Police Force for doing just that. Strong drink, he argued, only impaired the mind. If he was ever under pressure, he would instead reach for a cigar. The one between his lips was the third that morning. The blackened vestiges of its two predecessors lay in the ashtray. Tallis was in pain.

'Good morning, sir,' said Colbeck.

The superintendent looked up. 'What?'

'You sent for me, I believe.'

'Is that you, Inspector?'

'What seems to be the problem?'

Tallis needed a moment to compose himself. Taking a last puff on his cigar, he stubbed it out in the ashtray and waved a hand to disperse some of the fug. Then he pulled himself up in his chair. Noticing the bottle, he swept it off the desk and put it away in a drawer. He was plainly discomfited at being caught with the brandy and tried to cover his embarrassment with a nervous laugh. Colbeck waited patiently. Now that he could see his superior more clearly, he noticed something that he would not have believed possible. Tallis's eyes were moist and red-rimmed. He'd been crying.

'Are you unwell, Superintendent?' he asked, solicitously.

'Of course not, man,' snapped Tallis.

'Has something upset you?'

The explosion was instantaneous. 'The devil it has! I'm in a state of permanent upset. How can I police a city the size of London with a handful of officers and a woefully inadequate budget? How can I make the streets safe for decent people when I lack the means to do so? Upset? I'm positively pulsing with rage, Inspector. I'm appalled by the huge volume of crime and by the apparent indifference of this lily-livered government to the dread consequences that it produces.

In addition to that...'

It was vintage Tallis. He rumbled on for a few minutes, turning the handle of his mental barrel organ so that his trenchant opinions were churned out like so many jangling harmonies. It was his way of establishing his authority and of trying to draw a veil over the signs of weakness that Colbeck had observed. The inspector had heard it all before many times but he was courteous enough to pretend that he was listening to new-minted judgements based on sound wisdom. He nodded earnestly in agreement, watching the real Edward Tallis take shape again before him. When he'd regained his full confidence, the superintendent extracted a letter from his pocket and handed it over. It took Colbeck only seconds to read the emotive message.

'Goodbye, dear friend. Though her body has not yet been found, I know in my heart that she is dead and have neither the strength nor the will to carry on without her. I go to join her in heaven.'

Colbeck noticed the signature – Aubrey Tarleton.

'Is the gentleman a relation of yours, sir?' he asked.

'We were comrades-in-arms,' replied Tallis, proudly. 'Colonel Tarleton was an exemplary soldier and a treasured friend.'

'I take it that he's referring to his wife.'

'They were very close.'

'When did the letter arrive?'

'Yesterday morning,' said Tallis, taking it from him and reading it once more with a mixture of sadness and disbelief.

'Then we may still be in time to prevent any-thing untoward happening,' suggested Colbeck. 'I see from his address that he lives in Yorkshire. Trains run regularly from King's Cross. Would you like me to catch the next one to see if I can reach your friend before he does anything precipitous?'

'It's too late for that, Inspector.'

'Oh?'

'This telegraph was on my desk when I arrived.' He indicated the piece of paper and Colbeck picked it up. 'As you see, it tells of the death of a man on the railway line not far from Thirsk. A note was pinned to his coat, saying that I should be contacted.'

'Yet no name of the man is given,' said Colbeck, studying it. 'The victim may be someone else altogether.'

'It's too big a coincidence.'

'I disagree, sir. Colonel Tarleton was an army man, was he not?'

'To the hilt - he came from a military family.'

'Then he probably has some firearms in his possession.'

'He has quite a collection,' recalled Tallis. 'Apart from various shotguns, he has an exquisite pair of duelling pistols.'

'Isn't that a more likely way for him to end his life? If, that is, he's actually done so, and we've no clear proof of that. A bullet in the brain is a much quicker and cleaner way to commit suicide than by means of a railway.'

Tallis snatched back the telegraph. 'It's him, I

tell you. And I want to get to the bottom of this.'

'Sergeant Leeming and I can be on a train within the hour.'

'I know, Inspector, and I will accompany you.'

'Is that necessary?'

'I owe it to Aubrey – to Colonel Tarleton. There has to be an explanation for this tragedy and it must lie in the death of his wife.'

'But that's only conjectural,' Colbeck reminded him. 'The letter says that she's disappeared but no evidence is given of her demise. That's an assumption made by the colonel. He could be mistaken.'

'Nonsense!' snarled Tallis.

'There are other possibilities, sir.'

'Such as?'

'Well,' said Colbeck, meeting the blazing eyes without flinching, 'the lady might have been injured while out walking and unable to get back home. She might even have been abducted.'

'Then a ransom note would have been received. Clearly, it was not, so we may discount that hypothesis. Only one possibility therefore remains – Miriam Tarleton has been murdered.'

'With respect, Superintendent, you are jumping to conclusions. Even if we suppose that Mrs Tarleton *is* dead, it doesn't follow that she must have been killed. Her death might have been accidental or even as a result of suicide.'

'She'd have no call to take her own life.'

'Can you be sure of that, sir?'

'Yes, Inspector – it's inconceivable.'

'You know the lady better than I do,' conceded Colbeck. 'Given your knowledge of the marriage,

22

is it also inconceivable that Mrs Tarleton is still alive and that she's simply left her husband?'

Tallis leapt to his feet. 'That's a monstrous allegation!' he yelled. 'Colonel Tarleton and his wife were inseparable. What you suggest is an insult to their memory.'

'It was not intended to be.'

'Then waste no more of my time with these futile arguments. You read the letter. It's a plea for my help and I intend to give it.'

'Sergeant Leeming and I will be at your side, sir. If a crime has indeed been committed, we'll not rest until it's solved.' Colbeck crossed to the door then paused. 'I take it that you've visited Colonel Tarleton at his home?'

'Yes, I have.'

'How is he regarded in the area?'

'With the greatest respect,' said Tallis. 'Apart from being a magistrate, he holds a number of other public offices. His death will be a terrible blow to the whole community.'

Lottie Pearl was stunned. The news of her employer's gruesome death had left her speechless. She could not begin to comprehend how it had come about. Nothing in the colonel's manner had given the slightest indication of what he had in mind. On the previous morning, he'd gone through his unvarying routine, rising early and taking the dog for a walk before breakfast. He'd eaten very little food but loss of appetite did not necessarily equate with suicidal tendencies. Lottie was in despair. Within weeks of her securing a coveted place there, she'd seen the mistress of the

23

house vanish into thin air and the master go to his death on a railway line. Her prospects were decidedly bleak. When she finally recovered enough from the shock to be able to focus on the future, one question dominated. What would happen to her?

'Lottie!' called the housekeeper.

'Yes, Mrs Withers?'

'Come in here, girl.'

'I'm coming, Mrs Withers.'

Lottie abandoned the crockery she'd been washing in the kitchen and dried her hands on her apron as she made her way to the drawing room. As soon as she entered, she came to a sudden halt and blinked in surprise. Seated in a chair beside the fireplace, Margery Withers was wearing a faded but still serviceable black dress and looked more like a grieving widow than a domestic servant. She used a handkerchief to stem her tears, then appraised Lottie.

'You should be in mourning wear,' she chided.

'Should I, Mrs Withers?'

'Do you have a black dress?'

'No, I don't,' said Lottie, self-consciously.

'Does your mother have one?'

'Oh, yes, she does. She dyed an old dress black when Grandpa passed away.'

'Then you must borrow it from her.'

'What will I tell my mother?'

'You must wear it out of respect. She'll understand.'

'That's not what I mean, Mrs Withers,' said Lottie, uneasily. 'What am I to say to my mother about me?'

The housekeeper was puzzled. 'About *you?*'

'Yes, what's to become of me now?'

'Good heavens, girl!' exclaimed the older woman in disgust. 'How can you possibly think of yourself at a time like this? The colonel's body is barely cold and all you can do is to flaunt your self-ishness. Don't you *care* what happened yesterday?'

'Yes, Mrs Withers.'

'Don't you realise what the implications are?'

'I'm not sure what you mean,' said Lottie, re-gretting her folly in asking about her future. 'All I know is that I was so hurt by the news about the colonel. He was such a decent man. I cried all night, I swear I did. And, yes, I will get that black dress. Colonel Tarleton ought to be mourned in his own home.'

Her gaze shifted to the portrait above the mantelpiece. Tarleton and his wife were seated on a rustic bench in their garden with the dog curled up at their feet. It was a summer's day with every-thing in full bloom. The artist had caught the strong sense of togetherness between the couple, of two people quietly delighted with each other even after so many years. Lottie winced as she saw the smile on Miriam Tarleton's face.

'This will be the death of her,' she murmured.

'Speak up, girl.'

'I was thinking about the mistress. If ever she does come back to us – and I pray daily for her return – Mrs Tarleton will be upset beyond bearing when she learns about the colonel.'

'Don't be silly,' said Mrs Withers, rising to her feet and looking at the portrait. 'There's no earthly chance of her coming back.'

'You never know.'

'Oh, yes, I do.'

The housekeeper spoke with such confidence that Lottie was taken aback. Until that moment, Mrs Withers had always nursed the hope of a miraculous return or, at least, had given the impression of doing so. There was a whiff of finality about her comment now. Hope was an illusion. Husband and wife were both dead. The realisation sent a cold shiver down Lottie's spine.

'We must prepare the guest bedrooms,' continued Mrs Withers. 'Word has been sent to the children so they will soon be on their way here. The house must be ready for them. Everything depends on their wishes. If one of them decides to move in here then there may be a place for you in due course, but only,' she added, pointedly, 'if I recommend you. So until we know what the future holds, I urge you to get on with your chores and forget about your own petty needs. Do you understand?'

'Yes, Mrs Withers,' said Lottie, recognising a dire warning when she heard one. 'I do.'

Victor Leeming's dejection sprang from three principal causes. He disliked train travel, he hated spending nights away from his wife and family, and he was intimidated by the proximity of Edward Tallis. The village of South Ottering-ton sounded as if it was in the back of beyond, obliging the sergeant to spend hours of misery on the Great Northern Railway. From what he'd gathered, he might be away from home for days on end and his loved ones would be replaced by the spiky superintendent. It was a daunting prospect. All that he could do was to grit his teeth and curse inwardly.

Colbeck sympathised with him. Leeming was a man of action, never happier than when struggling with someone who resisted arrest or when diving into the Thames – as he'd done on two occasions – to save someone from drowning. Being trapped in the confines of a railway carriage, albeit in first class, was agony for him. Colbeck, by contrast, had found his natural milieu in the railway system. He took pleasure from each journey, enjoying the scenery and relishing the speed with which a train could take him such large distances. He tried to cheer up his sergeant with light conversation but his attempts were in vain. For his part, Tallis went off to sleep, snoring in unison with the clicking of the wheels yet still somehow managing to exude menace. Leeming spent most of the time in a hurt silence.

When they reached York ahead of schedule, there was a delay before departure. Tallis was one of the passengers who took advantage of the opportunity to visit the station's toilets.

'That's a relief,' said Leeming when they were alone. 'I've never spent this long sitting so close to him. He frightens me.'

'You should have overcome your fears by now,' said Colbeck. 'The superintendent poses no threat to you, Victor. He's racked by grief. Colonel Tarleton was a very dear friend.'

'I didn't know that Mr Tallis had any friends.'

'Neither did I. He's always seemed such a lone wolf.'

27

'Why did he never marry?'

'We don't know that he didn't. In view of his deep distrust of the opposite sex, I agree that it's highly unlikely, but even he must have felt the rising of the sap as a young man.'

'He never *was* a young man,' said Leeming, bitterly. 'In fact, I don't believe he came into this world by any normal means. He was hewn from solid rock.'

'You wouldn't have thought that if you'd seen him earlier. Solid rock is incapable of emotion yet Superintendent Tallis was profoundly moved today. We've been unkind to him, Victor. There is a heart beneath that granite exterior, after all.'

'I refuse to believe it. But talking of marriage,' he went on, glancing through the window to make sure that nobody was coming, 'have you told him about your own plans?'

'Not yet,' confessed Colbeck.

'Why not?'

'I haven't found the right moment.'

'But it's been weeks now.'

'I've been waiting to catch him in the right mood.'

'Then you'll wait until Doomsday, sir. He's never in the right mood. He's either angry or very angry or something far worse. I tell you, I'd hate to be in your position.'

'The appropriate time will arrive one day, Victor.'

It was during a previous investigation that Colbeck had become engaged to Madeleine Andrews, proposing to her in Birmingham's Jewellery Quarter and buying her a ring there and then to seal their bond. While the betrothal had been formally announced in the newspapers, Tallis had not seen it. All that he ever read were court reports and articles relating to the latest crimes. Colbeck was biding his time until he could break the news gently. He knew that it would not be well received.

'He never stops blaming me for getting married,' complained Leeming. 'He says that I'd be a far better detective if I'd stayed single.'

'That's not true at all. Marriage was the making of you.'

'It's having a happy home life that keeps me sane.'

'I envy you, Victor.'

'Have you set a date yet, sir?'

'Oh, it won't be for some time yet, I'm afraid.'

Colbeck was about to explain why when he saw Tallis coming along the platform towards them. Grim-faced and bristling with fury, the super-intendent was waving a newspaper in the air. When he got into the carriage, he slammed the door behind him.

'Have you seen this?' he demanded.

'What is it, sir?' asked Leeming.

'It's a report about Colonel Tarleton's death in the local newspaper,' said Tallis, slumping into his seat, 'and it makes the most dreadful insinuations about him. According to this, there are strong rumours that he committed suicide because he felt guilty over the disappearance of his wife. It more or less implies that he was responsible for her death. I've never heard anything so malicious in my entire life. The man

29

who wrote this should be horsewhipped.'

'Does he offer any evidence for the claim?' wondered Colbeck.

'Not a scrap – well, see for yourself.' He thrust the newspaper at Colbeck and remained on the verge of apoplexy. 'This puts a wholly new complexion on our visit to the North Riding. The colonel has not only lost his life. He's in danger of losing his impeccable reputation as well. He must be vindicated, do you hear?'

'Yes, sir,' said Leeming, dutifully.

'Slander is a vicious crime. We must root out those with poisonous tongues and bring them before the courts. By Jove!' he added, seething. 'We're going to tear that damned village apart until we find the truth. Mark my words – someone will suffer for this.'

CHAPTER THREE

For most of its existence, South Otterington had been largely untouched by scandal. It was a relatively safe and uneventful place in which to live. Petty theft and being drunk and disorderly were the only crimes to disturb the even tenor of the village and they were occasional rather than permanent features of its little world. The disappearance of Miriam Tarleton from 'the big house' was a different matter altogether. It concentrated the minds of all the inhabitants and set alight a roaring bonfire of speculation. The grotesque suicide of the colonel only served to add fuel to the flames. There was a veritable inferno of gossip and conjecture. Precious little of it, however, seemed to favour the dead man.

By the time that the detectives arrived, rumour was starting to harden into accepted fact. Alighting from the train, the first person they sought out was the stationmaster, Silas Ellerby, a short, slight, middle-aged man with protruding eyes and florid cheeks. When the visitors introduced themselves, he was suitably impressed.

'You've come all the way from London?' he asked.

'There are personal as well as professional reasons why I want a full investigation,' explained Tallis. 'The colonel and I were friends. We served together in India.'

31

'I thought you had the look of an army man, sir.'

'Who's been put in charge of this business?'

'That would be Sergeant Hepworth of the railway police.'

'I'll need to speak to him.'

'He lives here in the village.'

'Mr Ellerby,' said Colbeck, taking over, 'the colonel's death is clearly linked to the disappearance of his wife. How long has Mrs Tarleton been missing?'

'It must be all of two weeks now,' replied Ellerby.

'Was an extensive search undertaken?'

'Yes, the colonel had dozens of people out looking for her.'

'He'd have led the search himself,' said Tallis.

'He did, sir – day after day, from dawn till dusk.'

'Were no clues found?'

'Never a one – it was baffling.'

'Let's go back to the events of yesterday,' suggested Colbeck. 'Where exactly did the suicide take place?'

'It was roughly midway between here and Thirsk.'

'That's south of here, then.'

'Correct, sir,'

'According to the superintendent, the colonel's house lies due north. If he wanted to throw himself in front of a train, he could have done so without coming through the village at all.'

'Sergeant Hepworth had the answer to that.'

'I'd be interested to hear it.'

'The line to Northallerton is fairly straight. The

driver would have had a better chance of seeing someone long before the train reached him. He might even have been able to stop in time. The colonel chose his spot with care,' Ellerby went on. 'He picked the sharpest bend so that he wouldn't be spotted until it was far too late. Hal Woodman said there wasn't a hope of missing him.'

'Was Mr Woodman the driver?'

'Yes, Inspector, and it turned him to a jelly. When the train pulled in here, Hal could hardly speak and his fireman was in an even worse state. I'll wager they're both off work today.'

'You talk as if you know them, Mr Ellerby.'

'I should do. I've had many a pint with Hal Woodman and Seth Roseby over the years. It wasn't an express between London and Edinburgh, you see. It was a local train that runs between York and Darlington.'

'Where does Mr Woodman live?'

'He's just over four miles away in Northallerton.'

'Sergeant,' said Colbeck, turning to him. 'I think that you should pay him a visit. Take the next train.'

'But we've only just got here,' protested Leeming.

'It's important to have a clearer idea of what actually happened.'

'I can give you Hal's address,' volunteered Ellerby.

'Then it's settled,' said Tallis, taking control. 'Leave your bag with us and catch the next train to Northallerton.'

'Yes, Superintendent,' said Leeming with a

grimace. 'Where will I find you when I come back?'

'They have two rooms at the Black Bull,' said Ellerby, pointing a finger, 'and George Jolly lets out a room at the rear of the Swan, if you don't mind cobwebs and beetles.'

'That one will do for you, Sergeant,' decided Tallis. 'We'll probably be at the Black Bull. Meet us there. When we've booked some rooms, we'll be going out to the colonel's house. The first person I want to speak to is Mrs Withers.'

Margery Withers let herself in and crossed to the window. It was the biggest and most comfortable bedroom in the house, commanding a fine view of the garden and of the fields beyond. She spent a few minutes gazing down at the well-tended lawns and borders, noting the rustic bench on which her employers had once posed for a portrait and the ornamental pond with its darting fish. She was torn between anguish and elation, grief-stricken at the colonel's suicide yet strangely excited by the fact that she – however briefly – was now the mistress of the house.

After looking around the room with a proprietorial smile, she did something that she had always wanted to do. She sat in front of the dressing table and opened the jewellery box in front of her. Out came the pearl necklace she'd seen so many times around the throat of Miriam Tarleton. The very feel of it sent a thrill through her and she couldn't resist putting it on and admiring the effect in the mirror. Next came a pair of matching earrings which she held up to

34

her lobes, then she took out a diamond bracelet and slipped it on her wrist. It had cost more than her wages for a year and she stroked it jealously.

On and on she went, working her way through the contents of the box and luxuriating in temporary ownership. Mrs Withers was so caught up in her fantasy that she didn't hear the sound of the trap coming up the gravel drive at the front of the house. It was only when the dog started yapping that she realised she had visitors. Skip, the little spaniel who'd been moping all day, scurried to the door in the hope that his master had at last returned. When he saw that it was not the colonel after all, he retreated to his basket and began to whine piteously.

Mrs Withers descended the stairs in time to see Lottie Pearl conducting two men into the drawing room. Going in after them, she dismissed the servant with a flick of her hand.

'Thank you, Lottie,' she said. 'That will be all.' As the girl went out, the housekeeper looked at Tallis. 'I wasn't expecting you, Major. I fear that you've come at an inopportune time.'

'We're well aware of that, Mrs Withers. We're here in an official capacity. You only know me as Major Tallis but, in point of fact, I'm a superintendent of the Detective Department at Scotland Yard.'

She was astounded. 'You're a *policeman?*'

'Yes,' he replied, indicating his companion, 'and so is Inspector Colbeck.'

'I'm pleased to meet you,' said Colbeck, 'and I'm sorry that it has to be in such unfortunate circumstances. You must feel beleaguered.'

35

'It's been an ordeal, Inspector,' she said, 'and there's no mistake about that. However, I must continue to do my duty. The colonel would have expected that of me.' She waved an arm. 'Please sit down. Can I get you refreshment of any kind?'

'No, thank you, Mrs Withers,' answered Tallis, lowering himself onto the sofa. 'What we'd really like you to do is to explain to us exactly what's been going on.' She hovered uncertainly. 'This is no time for ceremony. You're a key witness not simply a housekeeper. Take a seat.'

Mrs Withers chose an upright chair and Colbeck opted for one of the armchairs. The housekeeper was much as she'd been described to him by Tallis. She looked smart, alert and efficient. He sensed that she had a fierce loyalty to her employers.

'In your own words,' coaxed Tallis, 'tell us what you know.'

'It's the things I *don't* know that worry me, Major – oh, I'm sorry. You're Superintendent Tallis now.'

'Start with Mrs Tarleton's disappearance,' said Colbeck, gently. 'We understand that it was a fortnight ago.'

'That's right, Inspector. The colonel and his wife went for a walk with Skip – that's the dog. I think he *knows*, by the way. Animals always do. He's been whining like that all day long. Anyway,' she continued, 'Colonel and Mrs Tarleton soon split up. She was going off to see a friend in Northallerton. It would have been quicker to go by train or to take the trap but she loved walking.'

She paused. 'Go on,' urged Colbeck.

36

'There's not much more to say. She was never seen again and I haven't the slightest idea what happened to her. Some people claim to have heard shots that afternoon but that's not unusual around here.'

'I'm sure it isn't, Mrs Withers. Farmers will always want to protect their crops and I daresay there are those who go out after rabbits for the pot.' He noticed the hesitant look in her eyes. 'Is there something you haven't told us?'

'Yes,' she replied, blurting out her answer, 'and it's best that it comes from me because others will make it sound far worse than it is. They have such suspicious minds. On the day that his wife vanished, the colonel was carrying a shotgun. He very often did.'

'I can vouch for that,' said Tallis. 'On the occasions when I've been here, we went out shooting together. I can't believe that anyone would think him capable of committing murder.'

'Oh, they do. Once a rumour starts, it spreads. And it wasn't only the nasty gossip in the village,' she said, ruefully. 'There were the letters as well.'

'What letters?'

'They accused him of killing his wife, Superintendent.'

'Who sent them?'

She shrugged. 'I've no idea. They were unsigned.'

'Poison pen letters,' observed Colbeck. 'What did the colonel do with them, Mrs Withers?'

'He told me to burn them but I couldn't resist reading them before I did so. They were foul.'

'Were they all written by the same hand?'

37

'Oh, no, I'd say that three or four people sent them, though one of them wrote a number of times. His comments were the worst.'

'How do you know he was a man?'

'No woman would use such filthy language.'

'It's a pity you didn't keep any of them,' grumbled Tallis. 'If anyone is trying to blacken the name of Colonel Tarleton, I want to know who they are.'

'Well, there was the one that came yesterday,' she remembered. 'When I pointed it out to the colonel, he said he didn't have time for the mail. I think he couldn't bear to read any more of those vile accusations. In my opinion, they drove him to do what he did.'

'Could you fetch the letter, please?'

'I'll get it at once, Superintendent.'

As soon as her back was turned, Tallis glanced meaningfully at Colbeck and the latter nodded his assent. The superintendent felt that Mrs Withers might be more forthcoming in the presence of someone she already knew rather than when she was being cross-examined by the two of them. Getting to his feet, Colbeck went into the hall and asked where he could find the servant who'd opened the door to them. Mrs Withers told him, then she went back into the drawing room with the letter, her black taffeta rustling as she did so.

'Here it is, sir,' she said, handing it over.

'How can you be sure that it's a poison pen letter?'

'I recognise the handwriting. It's from the man who's already sent more than one letter. The postmark shows it was posted in Northallerton.'

Tallis scowled. 'That means it came from a local man.' He opened the envelope and read the letter with mounting horror. 'Dear God!' he exclaimed. 'Is this the sort of thing people are saying about the colonel? It's utterly shameful.'

Lottie Pearl was in the larger of the guest bedrooms, fitting one of the pillowcases she'd just ironed. Even though it was too big for her, she was wearing the black dress that she'd borrowed earlier from her mother. There was a tap on the door and it opened to reveal Colbeck. When she saw his tall, lean frame filling the doorway, she moved back defensively as if fearing for her virtue.

'I'm sorry to startle you,' he said. 'Lottie, isn't it?'

'That's right, sir.'

'I'm Inspector Colbeck and I'm a detective from London.'

'I haven't done anything wrong,' she cried in alarm.

He smiled reassuringly. 'I know that you haven't, Lottie. Look, why don't we go downstairs? I think you might find it easier if we had this conversation in the kitchen.'

'Thank you, sir.'

Glad to escape from the bedroom, she trotted down the steps and went into the kitchen. Sitting opposite her, Colbeck first explained what he and Tallis were doing there but he failed to remove the chevron of anxiety from her brow.

'Do you like working here?' he asked.

'Yes, I do, sir. There's a lot to do, of course, but

39

I don't mind that. My mother always wanted me to end up here in the big house.'

'It is a big house, isn't it?' said Colbeck. 'I would have thought it needed more than two of you on the domestic staff.'

'There used to be a cook and a maidservant, sir.'

'Do you know why they left?'

'No, that was before my time. Mrs Withers took over the cooking and I was expected to do just about everything else. The girl who had my job was dismissed for being lazy.'

'How did you get on with your employers?'

'I didn't see much of them, sir, but they never complained about my work, I made sure of that. Mrs Tarleton was a nice woman with a kind face. The colonel was a bit strict but Mrs Withers told me that that was just his way. She spoke very highly of both of them.'

'How long has she been here?'

'Donkey's years, said Lottie. 'She came as house-keeper and her husband was head gardener. He died when he was still young and Mrs Withers stayed on. And that's another thing,' she added. 'There used to be three gardeners but there's only one now.'

'I see.'

She drew back. 'Have you come to arrest some-one, sir?'

'Only if it proves necessary,' he said. 'Neither you nor Mrs Withers have anything to fear. All we're after is guidance.'

'I can't give you much of that.'

'You may be surprised. Tell me what happened

40

on the day that Mrs Tarleton went missing.'

Pursing her lips, she gathered her thoughts. 'It was a day like any other day,' she said. 'The colonel went for his usual walk before breakfast with Skip, then his wife joined him for the meal. Later on, he took her part of the way along the road to Northallerton then he went off shooting. He brought back some pigeons for Mrs Withers to put in a pie. I had to take the feathers off.'

'When did it become clear that Mrs Tarleton was missing?'

'It was when she didn't turn up at the railway station. She walked to Northallerton but was going to come back by train. The colonel was very worried. He drove over there in the trap and called on the friend his wife went to see. Mrs Tarleton had never been there. The friend had been wondering where she was.'

Lottie rambled on and Colbeck encouraged her to do so. Much of what she told him was irrelevant but her comments on the village and its inhabitants were all interesting. It was clear from the way that the words tumbled out that the girl had very little chance to express herself at the house. Colbeck had unblocked a dam and created a minor waterfall.

'And that's all I can tell you, sir,' she concluded, breathlessly. 'Except that I feel as if it's something to do with me. I mean, none of this happened until I came to work here. It's almost as if it's my fault. Deep down, that's what Mrs Withers thinks. I can see it in her eyes. Mind you,' she went on, philosophically, 'there's some as are worse off than me.'

'What do you mean?'

'The engine driver is the one I feel sorry for, Inspector. He killed Colonel Tarleton. That'll be on his conscience for the rest of his life. Poor man!' she sighed. 'I'd hate to be in his shoes.'

'How fast was the train travelling?' asked Victor Leeming.

'Fast enough – almost forty miles an hour.'

'And where exactly on the line did you hit him?'

'The spot will be easy to find, Sergeant,' said Hal Woodman. 'I'm told that some people have put flowers there.'

'It must have been a shock to you and the fireman.'

'It were. We sometimes have children playing on the line – daring each other to stand in front of a train – but they always jump out of the way in plenty of time. The colonel just marched on.'

'Didn't he just stop and wait?'

'No, he seemed to be in a hurry to get it over with. It were weird. When we hit him, like, Seth – he's my fireman – spewed all over the footplate. But we left an even worse mess on the line.'

Leeming had been in luck. Expecting a long search in the town, he was relieved to discover that Woodman lived within easy walking distance of the railway station. It took the sergeant only five minutes to find him and to acquaint him with the reason they'd come to the area. Woodman was a thickset man in his thirties, with a weather-beaten face and missing teeth. He was still patently upset by the incident on the previous day and went over it time and again.

'Did you know Colonel Tarleton beforehand?' said Leeming.

'Everyone knows the colonel. The old bastard sits on the bench in this town. They reckon he's a tartar. I'm glad that I never came up before him.'

'Did you recognise him at the time?'

'Of course not,' said Woodman. 'When you're on the footplate, you're staring through clouds of smoke and steam. All we could make out was that it was a man with a cane.' He pulled a face. 'It fair turned my stomach, I can tell you. There was simply nothing we could do.' He rallied slightly. 'In a sense, I suppose, I shouldn't feel so bad about it, should I?'

'Why not?' asked Leeming.

'Well, I was doing everyone a favour, really. We all know that he shot his wife. He got himself killed on purpose before the law caught up with him. Yes,' Woodman continued as if a load had suddenly been lifted from his shoulders, 'you could say we were heroes of a kind, me and Seth Roseby. We gave that bugger what he deserved and did the hangman's job for him.'

CHAPTER FOUR

Before they left the house, Colbeck asked if he could see the room where Colonel Tarleton had kept his firearms. Mrs Withers led them down a long corridor until they came to a brick-built extension at the back of the property. Edward Tallis had been there before but it was new to Colbeck and he was impressed by its array of weaponry. It was less of a room than an armoury. No fewer than six shotguns stood side by side in a glass-fronted cabinet. Also behind glass was a magnificent pair of duelling pistols with ivory handles. In a separate cabinet were two long-barrelled matchlock pistols, a flintlock musket and a Spanish blunderbuss. An old fowling piece rested on two pegs driven into a wall. Boxes of ammunition were neatly arranged on a shelf.

Evidently, Tarleton had been a collector. Colbeck counted four sabres, six pikes, eight daggers of varying sizes and an assortment of clubs, maces and axes. There were even suits of armour and a lance. What they were standing in the middle of was a history of warfare.

'I don't like seeing all this,' admitted Mrs Withers, eyeing a spiked iron ball on the end of a chain, 'but I was the only member of the staff allowed in here because the colonel wanted it kept clean and tidy. I didn't touch the guns, of course. They're under lock and key.'

'That was his favourite,' said Tallis, pointing at a shotgun in the cabinet. 'You can see his initials carved into the stock. It was made by James Purdey himself. The duelling pistols were the work of Joseph Manton, who perfected the percussion cap principle. Gunsmiths worldwide owe a real debt to Manton.'

'James Purdey is one of them,' noted Colbeck. 'He learnt his trade under Manton.' Looking around, he took a swift inventory. 'The contents of this room are worth a pretty penny.'

'He built up the collection over many years,' said Tallis.

'It's a real museum.'

'Well, it won't stay like this,' said Mrs Withers. 'Neither of the children has the slightest interest in guns and swords. Whoever inherits the house will want to get rid of these things.'

Tallis shook his head. 'They won't be able to do that.'

'Oh?'

'Inspector Colbeck will explain. He's well versed in the law. Before he joined the police force he was a barrister.'

Her eyes widened. 'Really?'

'Yes,' said Colbeck. 'The law regarding suicide – or *felo de se* - is very specific. In taking his own life, Colonel Tarleton has dispossessed his children to some extent. Under the terms of a statute of 1823, his goods and chattels are forfeit to the Crown.'

'That's cruel,' she cried.

'It's the law, as it stands, Mrs Withers.'

'I've never heard that before.'

'You've probably never heard of someone committing suicide before either,' said Colbeck.

'No, sir, that's true.'

'Fortunately, it's a rare occurrence. As for the way the colonel took his own life, it was unique.'

Mrs Withers was aghast. 'Are you telling me that the children will get *nothing?*'

'They'll retain the land. It's only the goods and chattels that are forfeit and they, alas,' he said with a gesture to take in the whole room, 'include everything in here.'

'I had no idea of any of this,' said the house-keeper, quivering all over. 'I'd hoped that one of the children would take over the house and that we'd carry on as before. The colonel promised me that I had a job for life. This has been my only real home. I'd hoped that I could *stay.*'

Fearing for her future, she suddenly burst into tears and rushed out of the room. When Colbeck tried to go after her, he was restrained by the firm hand of Tallis.

'Let her go, Inspector.'

'I wanted to console her,' said Colbeck.

'When all is said and done, Mrs Withers is of no consequence. She's only a servant. We can forget about her.'

'That's rather harsh, sir.'

'I'm being practical. As for the children, there's something you should know. Colonel Tarleton was not their father. When he married her, his wife was a widow with two young children – a boy and a girl. He brought them up as his own and they took his surname.'

'I see.'

'The son, I regret to say, is something of a wastrel. He was still single when I last heard of him. The daughter, Eve, is married and has been more of a credit in every way. She'll be absolutely horrified at the turn of events – as am I,' said Tallis, soulfully. 'The colonel was my friend but I can't condone his suicide. In my view, it's a sin as well as a crime. It always appals me.'

Colbeck remembered how distressed Tallis had been by the suicide of Leonard Voke, a silver-smith they'd encountered during another investigation. The superintendent had no personal connection with the man yet had been badly shaken when he heard that Voke had shot himself. The fact that a friend of his had now committed suicide – and done so in the most extraordinary manner – disturbed Tallis at a deep level. He was still dazed by the news. Colbeck tried to offer the consolation that he'd intended to give to the housekeeper.

'All may not yet be lost, sir,' he said.

'What are you talking about?' grunted Tallis.

'Colonel Tarleton's earthly possessions. They will only be forfeit to the Crown if the inquest rules that he took his life while of sound mind. The technical conditions of murder apply to suicide, namely, if a person commits any un-lawful, malicious act, the consequences of which is his or her own death, then that person must be deemed to be a self-murderer. That's what *felo de se* means.'

'I know that, man.'

'Then you must also know that the law permits the deceased some leeway. If it can be shown that

47

someone committed suicide while the balance of his mind was disturbed, then he will be considered to have been insane and therefore not responsible for his actions. That being the case, nothing will be surrendered to the Crown. Don't you see, sir?' asked Colbeck. 'That may well be the outcome here.'

Tallis was outraged. 'Aubrey Tarleton was not insane.'

'Look at the facts, Superintendent.'

'The only fact that interests me is that I knew this man for almost thirty years. As a soldier and as a friend, he was above reproach. He was the sanest man I ever met in my whole life.'

'That may have been so,' said Colbeck, 'but I ask you to gaze around this room. A man could choose dozens of different weapons with which to kill himself here, yet Colonel Tarleton preferred to walk along a railway line in the path of an oncoming train. Does that sound like the action of someone in full possession of his faculties?'

'How dare you even suggest it?' howled Tallis, caught on the raw. 'You're talking about someone you never met.' He reached into his pocket for an envelope. 'You read the letter he sent me. Did that sound like the ravings of a lunatic?'

'No, Superintendent, it was a sad but rather dignified letter.'

'You heard the housekeeper. She noticed nothing unusual in her employer's behaviour. Even under the intense stress of losing his wife, he bore up well and showed the resilience that I'd seen him display on the field of combat. He was a man of iron self-control. Frankly,' said Tallis, 'I deplore what he did but he conceived and followed a definite plan. That was the action of a sane man.'

'Then I must beg to differ.'

'You can do what you like, Colbeck. But don't you dare have the audacity to say in my hearing that Colonel Tarleton was of unsound mind. That's a slur on his character that I simply won't permit.'

Tallis spent most of his life in a state of permanent ire but his fury had reached a new and more dangerous pitch. Colbeck was tactful. He tried to reduce the intensity of the superintendent's rage.

'I defer to your superior knowledge of the gentleman,' he said with a note of apology. 'It's not my place to form a judgement of him. That must be left to the inquest. I'd rather turn my attention to the event that provoked his suicide. Foul play must be suspected and that leaves us with one question – what happened to his wife?'

It fell to Victor Leeming to be the first to make the acquaintance of Eric Hepworth. Entering the Black Bull in search of his colleagues, Leeming was immediately confronted by the imposing figure of the railway policeman. Sergeant Hepworth was in uniform, his long black coat patently worn with pride, his boots gleaming. The low ceiling had obliged him to remove his top hat, revealing a large head that was rapidly balding. As if to counter the dramatic loss of hair, he'd grown a thick, dark beard out of which came a deep, accusatory voice.

'Are you one of the people trying to take over

my duties?' he challenged. 'You got no right to do that.'

'You must be Sergeant Hepworth,' said the newcomer.

'That's right.'

'I'm Detective Sergeant Leeming of Scotland Yard.'

'I don't care if you're the Emperor of China. Nobody pushes me aside.'

'That's not what we're trying to do.'

Leeming took a step towards him and promptly lost his hat as it collided with a beam. Showing quick reactions, he managed to catch it. Hepworth laughed derisively.

'A fine bleeding detective you are,' he said. 'You couldn't even detect a beam above your head.'

'Maybe not,' riposted Leeming, squaring up to him, 'but I can detect hostility when I find it. If you value your position, Sergeant, you'd better learn to show some respect.'

'You have no jurisdiction over this stretch of line. It's my patch and I look after it well.'

'Then you should patrol it more effectively so that people don't get killed by a train.'

Hepworth was indignant. 'That wasn't my doing!' he bellowed. 'If someone is stupid enough to walk on the track, that's his funeral. My job is to clear up the mess afterwards. I won't listen to threats. You have no authority over me.'

'Inspector Colbeck does.'

'Colbeck?' The name jolted him. 'Are you talking about the Railway Detective?'

'That's the man. His reputation goes before him. The inspector has solved crimes for most of the railway companies in this country and they've been extremely grateful. He will doubtless have influence with your employers and won't hesitate to use it. If, that is,' Leeming went on, 'he meets with the same boneheaded resistance that I did.'

'Who are you calling boneheaded?'

Hepworth took a combative stance but soon thought better of actually exchanging blows. Leeming stood his ground fearlessly. He was a solid man with the powerful fists and battered face of someone who'd survived many brawls. Ten years younger than Hepworth, he also looked much fitter. Realising that he'd met his match, the railway policeman resorted to a companionable chuckle. He patted Leeming's shoulder.

'There's no call for us to fall out,' he said, genially. 'After all, we're in the same business, really. If you've come all this way, Sergeant, you must have built up a thirst. What can I get you?'

Leeming asked for a pint of beer and the two of them were able to have a conversation instead of an argument. It was not long before Colbeck came into the bar, doffing his hat as he did so.

'There,' said Hepworth, approvingly. 'That's what I call a real detective. He spotted that beam at once.' Leeming introduced the two men and they shook hands. The debonair Colbeck looked rather incongruous in the rough-and-ready surroundings of a rural pub but he was completely at ease. Having heard of his reputation, Hepworth regarded him with wonder.

'You actually saw the body, then,' said Colbeck.

'I saw what was left of it, Inspector,' replied Hepworth. 'It was a sorry sight. His own mother wouldn't have recognised him. I had the remains taken to an undertaker in Northallerton.'

'Mrs Withers told us that. Superintendent Tallis is on his way there right now by train. He wants to see the body for himself.'

'That's more than I'd want to do,' said Leeming.

'He's acting out of a sense of duty.'

'Then he's in for a nasty shock,' warned Hepworth. 'That train broke almost every bone in his body.'

'The superintendent was in the army. He must have seen some hideous things on the battlefield. He won't blench.'

'I would,' confessed Leeming. 'I felt sick when our cat was crushed to death under the wheel of a coal haulier's cart.'

Hepworth insisted on buying Colbeck a pint of beer, then the three of them moved to sit down at one of the tables. The railway policeman took a long sip from his tankard.

'This is my first suicide,' he said. 'I don't count the sheep and cows that wandered onto the line and got themselves smashed to smithereens. That's not suicide – it was plain stupidity.'

'It's the duty of farmers to keep their stock fenced in,' said Colbeck. 'When there are accidents, it's not only the animal that suffers. Locomotives have sometimes been derailed by the impact.'

'Fences cost money, Inspector, and there are farmers who resent having track across their land. They defy railways.'

'They stand to profit by it. They can move their stock to market far quicker by rail than by driving them there overland.'

'This is Yorkshire. Old ways die hard.'

'I've no complaints about the beer here,' said Leeming, quaffing his pint then licking his lips. 'I like it.' He glanced at Hepworth. 'The sergeant is afraid that we want to do his job for him.'

'Not at all,' soothed Colbeck. 'The most needful thing has already been done and that was to clear the remains from the track. The colonel is dead. Our interest shifts to his wife and we may be forced to tread on a few toes there. I take it that the search was conducted by police from Northallerton.'

'What few there are,' said Hepworth. 'Most of those who went out were villagers recruited by the colonel. I was glad to help myself when I was off duty, and not only because we were paid.'

'How far afield did you search?'

'We went for miles, Inspector. We combed every inch between here and Northallerton because that's where Mrs Tarleton was going when she disappeared.' He hunched his shoulders. 'There was no trace of her.'

'Do you know whom she was going to see in the town?'

'Oh, yes, it was Mrs Reader. She's the wife of a banker and was very friendly with Mrs Tarleton. They often visited each other's houses. So did their husbands. The four of them played cards together.'

'We'll need to speak to Mr and Mrs Reader,' said Colbeck.

'He's easy to find. His bank is in the High Street.'

'Thank you for telling me.'

'I'm always available, if you need help, sir,' said Hepworth. 'Policemen are few and far between in the North Riding. It would be a feather in my cap if I could assist the famous Railway Detective.'

'The best way to assist me is to tell me what your own opinion is, Sergeant. Some unpleasant rumours are circulating, I hear.'

'Not only in South Otterington,' Leeming put in. 'When I spoke to Hal Woodman in Northallerton, he claimed that everyone there knew for a fact that the colonel had murdered his wife.'

'What evidence did he put forward, Victor?'

'None at all, really – he seemed to think it was so obvious.'

'You can tell me later about your visit to him. What about you, Sergeant?' asked Colbeck, looking into Hepworth's eyes. 'Do you subscribe to the notion that it's so obvious?'

'No, sir, I don't,' replied Hepworth, seeing a chance to impress. 'I'm a policeman. I like to study all the facts before I make any decision. On the other hand,' he said, thoughtfully, 'the suicide *could* have been some kind of repentance for a heinous crime.'

'It could equally well have been the action of a loving husband, driven to desperation by the disappearance of his wife.'

'You'll not find many people around here who agree with that.'

'Why is that?'

'Colonel Tarleton was a peppery character. He was the sort of man who has to have his own way no matter how much offence that might cause. Everyone here respected him but few of us liked him. Fewer still would have called him a loving husband.'

'How would you describe him?'

'He was a crusty old stick. He did some good things – giving to charity and suchlike – and I admire him for that. But I resented the way that he threw his weight around.'

'So you think he's a murderer, do you?' said Leeming.

'The honest answer is that I don't know.'

'What's your guess?'

'Oh, it's a bit more than a guess,' confided Hepworth, checking that nobody else was within earshot. 'I have this theory, you see.'

'Well?'

'I don't think that Mrs Tarleton is dead.'

'Then where is she?'

'Who knows? She's a long way away, probably.'

'That's an interesting theory,' said Colbeck. 'Why did you take part in the search for a woman you thought had simply left the area?'

'It was because of the way that the search was conducted by the colonel that I began to think. He made us go over and over the same ground as if he was trying to convince himself that she was there when, in his heart, he knew that she'd simply run away from him. That's what played on his mind and drove him to suicide. He was too proud to admit that Mrs Tarleton had deserted him.'

'Was he such a dreadful husband?'

'All I can tell you is that he was difficult to live with.'

'How do you know that?'

'My daughter used to work at the big house.'

'Ah, I see.'

'Ginny was shocked when she first went there,' said Hepworth. 'The colonel and his wife had separate bedrooms. Ginny thought that was unnatural. It's something my wife and I would never dream of doing. Married people should sleep together.'

'That's what I believe,' said Leeming, stoutly.

Hepworth confided an intimate detail. 'I wouldn't get a wink of sleep without my wife beside me. I need to feel her there.'

'Separate bedrooms are not that unusual in some marriages,' Colbeck pointed out, 'and the arrangement may suit both partners. If one of them snores all night, for instance, I can imagine them sleeping apart, and there are lots of other innocent reasons why they might not wish to share a bed.'

Hepworth leant forward. 'Ginny still thought it was odd.'

'It's downright peculiar,' muttered Leeming.

'What else did your daughter think was a little odd, Sergeant Hepworth?' asked Colbeck.

'Lots of things,' said the other. 'One of them was that the colonel and his wife didn't seem to spend much time together. He was always out shooting, sitting on the bench in Northallerton or going off somewhere by train. And Mrs Tarleton was always visiting friends.'

'I can't see anything odd in that, Sergeant,' said Colbeck. 'You've just described a lot of marriages. Some couples prefer to rub along amiably instead of living in each other's pockets. What I haven't heard so far is any motive for desertion. When I was at the house earlier, the housekeeper was at pains to tell us that the colonel and his wife were devoted to each other.'

Hepworth curled a lip. 'Mrs Withers would say that.'

'You dispute the fact?'

'My daughter does. Ginny heard them arguing more than once. She saw Mrs Tarleton run off to her room in tears one evening.'

'Did she know why?'

'She thinks so.'

'What did she tell you?'

'Ginny believes the argument was over Mrs Withers. My daughter was only a slip of a girl when she was there but she's got sharp eyes and she senses things.'

'And what did she sense?'

'That something was going on between Mrs Withers and Colonel Tarleton. It was nothing she could put her finger on but it was sort of in the air, if you know what I mean.'

'So there's no actual proof of any attachment between them?'

'There is now, Inspector.'

'Well, I certainly don't see it,' said Leeming, scratching his head. 'All you've told us so far is that your daughter senses things.'

'She worked beside Mrs Withers every day.'

'Did she actually catch the two of them together?'

'No,' conceded Hepworth, 'not exactly.'

'Then where is the evidence?' pressed Colbeck.

'It's in the suicide, Inspector. That's what gave him away. My belief is this. The colonel and Mrs Withers started carrying on together and his wife found out about it. When she could stand it no longer,' said Hepworth, developing his theory, 'Mrs Tarleton ran away and is probably living somewhere under an assumed name. To cover his shame, the colonel organised that long search for her when, all the time, he knew what had really happened. To a man of his standing, it must have come as a thunderbolt. Think of the scandal he'd have faced. Knowing that the truth was bound to come out one day,' he concluded, 'the colonel took his own life in order to escape the humiliation.' Hepworth grinned and sat back as if expecting applause. 'You see? I've solved the case for you. I can always work things out when I put my mind to it.'

The undertaker lived over the premises. He was annoyed when someone called so late that evening but was soon mollified by the information that his visitor was a senior detective from London. He conducted Tallis to the room where the coffin was resting on trestles. The lid was on it but had not yet been nailed down.

'Do you really want to put yourself through this?' he asked.

Tallis nodded. 'He was my dear friend.'

'Then you have my sympathy, sir.'

The undertaker removed the lid so that the corpse could be viewed. Even though herbs had been used to sweeten the atmosphere, the stench of death rose swiftly up into Tallis's nostrils and made him retch. He gaped in horror. The shroud failed to conceal the broken limbs and the ugly distortions of the body, but it was the head that really shocked him. Colonel Tarleton's face had been smashed to a pulp and the bare skull cracked apart. What dismayed Tallis, however, was something else. Head and body were quite separate. When the locomotive struck him with such force, his friend had been decapitated.

Closing his eyes to shut out the pain, Tallis began to pray.

CHAPTER FIVE

Sergeant Hepworth was a mine of information about the area but his comments about those who lived there were liberally salted with spite and prejudice. The inhabitants of the village and its neighbouring communities were either his friends or his enemies. There seemed to be no intermediate ground between the two groups. While they were grateful to learn so much from him, Colbeck and Leeming found his loquaciousness wearing and his pomposity irritating. When it was time for the railway policeman to leave, therefore, neither of them tried to detain him. They were glad to be left alone so that they could compare notes about what each of them had so far discovered. They were still deep in discussion when Tallis came in. He took only a few halting steps into the room then stood there with a look of utter bewilderment on his face as if he had no idea where he was. Colbeck beckoned him over.

'Come and join us, Superintendent,' he said, rising to his feet. 'You look as if you might need a stiff drink, sir.'

'Yes, yes,' said Tallis. 'Thank you, Colbeck.'

'Brandy?'

'Excellent.'

Colbeck went across to the bar counter and Tallis sat down at the table with Leeming. The superintendent still looked distracted. It was only when he'd taken a sip of the double brandy that was put before him that he came out of his reverie.

'That's better,' he said.

'You obviously viewed the body.'

'I did.'

'It must have been a gruesome experience,' remarked Colbeck.

'It was. I'd hate to have to go through that again.'

'Why did you force yourself to do it, sir?' asked Leeming.

'It was my duty. He'd have expected it of me.'

'Colonel Tarleton is dead. He'd never have known if you viewed his corpse or not.'

'*I'd* have known, Leeming. It would have made me feel guilty.'

'Then it's as well you went, sir,' said Colbeck, quietly. 'While you were away, we met Sergeant Hepworth, the railway policeman in charge of clearing the remains from the line. He's very well informed about life in this little corner of the North Riding.'

'What did he tell you?'

'What *didn't* he tell us?' said Leeming, rolling his eyes.

'The sergeant talked our ears off. Much of what we heard was irrelevant to our investigation but he did come up with one interesting notion.'

Tallis's eyebrows lifted. 'Oh? And what was that?'

'He believes that Mrs Tarleton is still alive.'

'That's ridiculous!'

'Well, we have no actual evidence of her death.'

'There's no other way to explain her disappearance, man,' said Tallis, roused. 'When a devoted wife goes missing for such a long period, she has to be the victim of foul play.'

'Sergeant Hepworth doesn't agree, sir.'

'What, in God's name, does *he* know about it?'

'His daughter worked at the house,' said Colbeck, 'and was able to see at close quarters how the marriage operated. She came home with tales of dissension in the house – though I'm inclined to question the girl's truthfulness. According to the girl who succeeded her, Ginny Hepworth was dismissed as maid-of-all-work because she was lazy, so she may well have an axe to grind.'

Tallis was impatient. 'Come to the point, Colbeck.'

'The girl alleges that the colonel and his wife were estranged.'

'That's absurd!'

'She claims to have overheard arguments.'

'Then she suffers from hallucinations.'

'When were you last there, Superintendent?' asked Colbeck. 'When did you last visit them in their house?'

'What difference does that make?'

'Had you been there in the last year, for instance?'

'Of course not,' said Tallis, tetchily. 'How could I spare time from my work to see friends who live so far away? Since I took over my present post, I've been slaving away at my desk seven days a week.'

'That means you haven't been here for over five years,' Leeming calculated. 'A lot can happen in

62

that time, sir.'

'The colonel and I kept up a regular correspondence.'

'But I doubt if he'd have said much about his wife in his letters. He must have known that you hold peculiar views about marriage.'

'My views are not peculiar,' retorted Tallis, reddening. 'They are based on observation. Marriage, in most cases, serves to emasculate a man and divert him from his true purpose in life. That was not the fate of Colonel Tarleton. His was a rare example of how marriage can help a husband to explore his true potential.'

'My wife has done the same for me, sir.'

'That's a moot point, Leeming. What I see in you is a man whose attention is occasionally diverted by the demands of his family. Look to the inspector. Bachelors like Colbeck are far more effective upholders of the law. Now, will one of you please tell me exactly what this railway policeman is claiming, based on the dubious evidence of his daughter?'

'In essence,' said Colbeck, 'his theory is this. Mrs Tarleton was alienated from her husband because she believed that he'd developed an interest in another woman. After a series of rows, she fled the house and – rather than admit the embarrassing truth – the colonel gave out that she had gone missing.'

'That is preposterous!' exploded Tallis.

'It's only a theory, sir.'

'It's a pack of damnable lies.'

'The sergeant's daughter did work there,' Leeming reminded him. 'And we do know that the colonel and his wife had separate bedrooms.'

'That's none of your business!' howled Tallis.

Leeming cowered. 'No, no, I agree, sir.'

'Colonel Tarleton would no more look at another woman than he'd fly to the moon on the back of a brown cow. He observed his marriage vows to the letter. He'd never bestow his affections on another woman. To start with, he'd never let her anywhere near him.'

'He did in this instance,' said Leeming. 'She worked there.'

Tallis was open-mouthed in astonishment. 'Mrs *Withers?*'

'They spent all their time under the same roof, sir.'

'Good God, man! Have you taken leave of your senses? Mrs Withers is a *servant*. Colonel Tarleton would never dream of even looking at her in the way you imply. She's beneath him. I'll hear no more of this nonsense,' he went on, getting to his feet and picking up his glass. 'I'm going to bed.'

'Aren't you hungry, sir?' asked Colbeck.

'I couldn't touch a thing – especially after listening to the arrant nonsense that you've just told me. Colonel Tarleton loved his wife dearly. I'll trouble you to remember that from now on.'

After taking a long sip of his brandy, he stalked off. Colbeck was relieved that there were so few people there to witness Tallis's volcanic loss of temper and he regretted passing on Hepworth's theory about the missing wife. Something else worried him.

'This case is arousing too many emotions in him,' he observed. 'I think his personal involvement is a handicap to his judgement. He has an image of the perfect marriage that existed when he was last here a number of years ago. Since then, a great deal has happened. To begin with, the size of the domestic staff at the house has been reduced and the garden is no longer maintained to such a high standard. Something very serious must have happened yet there seems to have been no hint of it in the letters sent from here to the superintendent.'

'What do you think we should do?'

'Persuade him to leave the investigation to us.'

'It will not be easy.'

'I realise that, Victor.'

'I wouldn't fancy going anywhere near him when he's in this state. What about you, Inspector? Why don't you go up to his room this minute to put the idea to him?'

'I'm not that brave,' said Colbeck with a grin, 'or that foolhardy.'

'Go on,' teased Leeming. 'You can mention your engagement while you're up there. He's in the ideal mood to talk about marriage.'

Happy by nature, Madeleine Andrews now took even more pleasure out of each day. The moment she woke up, she rolled over in bed to look at the engagement ring that stood in its open box on the bedside table. It symbolised her delight. She'd met Robert Colbeck under difficult circumstances when her father had been badly injured during the robbery of a train he was driving. What had begun as a chance meeting had slowly matured into a friendship before developing into

65

something far deeper. Yet she'd never really believed that it would lead to holy matrimony. Given the difference in their social positions, she'd never dared to think that she'd be an acceptable wife for him.

Colbeck, however, had seen her true qualities. In his view, Madeleine was much more than merely the daughter of a widowed engine driver. She was a beautiful, intelligent, resourceful young woman who'd given crucial help during some of his investigations. Apart from reading voraciously the books she'd borrowed from his extensive library, Madeleine had also developed her artistic talents to the point where she could sell her work. Colbeck's encouragement had been decisive and, unlike most people, he didn't think that her subject matter was unfeminine. Because she celebrated railways to such startling effect in her paintings, he'd found one more reason to love her. Over breakfast that morning, her father was curious.

'When will you be seeing him again, Maddy?' he asked.

'I don't know,' she replied.

'I called on your mother regular before we were married. It's what men are supposed to do when they're betrothed.'

'Robert is a very busy man. According to the note he sent me yesterday, he had to catch a train to Yorkshire.'

'Yorkshire!' said Caleb Andrews with disgust. 'That means he'll have travelled on the Great Northern Railway. I wouldn't use one of their trains if you paid me.'

'It has a good reputation.'

'The only company worth its salt is the one I work for.'

'Mr Brunel would have something to say about that.'

'You can forget him, Maddy. The Great Western Railway is a complete mess. Brunel can't even use a proper gauge on his track. As for the GNR, it's in an even worse state.'

Having worked for the London and North Western Railway since it came into existence, Andrews treated its competitors with routine contempt and he was always annoyed when Colbeck's work took him on lines operated by its rivals. Madeleine continued eating her breakfast in amused silence. She knew better than to argue with her father because it would only prolong his attack on other railway companies. Her task was to feed him well at their little house in Camden before sending him off to Euston on the early shift.

Short, wiry and with a wispy beard, Andrews was a man of truculent disposition. Workmates feared his sharp tongue and took care not to provoke him. His daughter, however, had learnt how to cope with his irascibility and had been a tower of strength to him since the death of his beloved wife. Andrews was very conscious of what she'd done for him over the years.

'I'll miss you, Maddy,' he said, munching some bread.

'I haven't gone yet, Father,' she pointed out, 'and it may be some time before I do so. Robert warned me about that.'

'Sooner or later, you'll be off. I won't have to worry about you.'

She smiled. 'I thought I was the one worrying about *you.*'

'I can look after myself. And now that you're settled, I can start thinking about retirement.'

'You'll never retire. The railway is in your blood.'

'It's in my lungs as well,' he said, coughing and beating his chest by way of testimony. 'That's what you get for breathing in smoke all day long. I'm not as young as I was, Maddy. I can't go on for ever.'

'You wouldn't know what to do with yourself if you retire.'

'I'll find someone I can beat at draughts.' They shared a laugh. Ever since he'd taught her the game, she'd been able to win against him nine times out of ten. 'Who knows?' he added, mischievously. 'I might even consider walking down the aisle myself.'

She was shocked. 'You'd get married at *your* age?'

'I need some companionship. Oh, I know you think that I'm sinking slowly into dotage but there are still certain ladies who'd look upon me as a catch. You should see some of the warm glances they give me in church.'

'That's the last place you ought to be getting glances of any kind,' she said with mock disapproval.

'London is full of desirable women.'

'Father!'

'All that I have to do is to take my pick.'

'What you have to do is to remember how old you are.'

'Many a good tune played on an old fiddle.' Cackling wickedly, he got up from the table, downed the remains of his tea in one mouthful and beamed at her. 'You'd better tell Inspector Colbeck to get a move on,' he said, 'or I'll be hearing wedding bells before he does. Make him name the day, Maddy.'

'I'll do nothing of the kind,' said Madeleine, firmly. 'Robert's work comes first and we have to plan our lives around that. And I don't care which railway company took him to Yorkshire as long as it brings him safely back home to me.'

Breakfast at the Black Bull was served in a little room adjoining the kitchen. The food was good, the portions generous and the tea exceptionally strong. Colbeck tried to make conversation but Tallis was distrait. After a sleepless night, agonising over the death of his friend, he looked pale and weary. The visitor brought him fully awake. They were just about to leave the table when the Reverend Frederick Skelton burst into the room like an avenging angel.

'I am the rector of St Andrew's Church,' he declared, striking a pose, 'and I understand that you are here in connection with this ugly stain that's been left on the village.'

'We're here to look into the circumstances of Colonel Tarleton's death,' said Colbeck, levelly, 'and to find his missing wife. We've yet to notice any stains here, ugly or otherwise.'

'That's because you don't have to live here, sir.'

The rector was a tall, slim, thin-lipped man in his forties with a smooth, colourless face and flowing brown locks of which he was so inordinately proud that he stroked them as if caressing a favourite cat. Sizing him up, Colbeck introduced himself and Tallis. Skelton went on the attack at once.

'I wish to make one thing crystal clear,' he boomed, addressing an invisible congregation. 'There is no place for that criminal in my churchyard. He does not deserve to lie in consecrated ground.'

'That's a matter for the archbishop to decide,' said Tallis.

'I'm in charge of what happens in my parish.'

'Colonel Tarleton is not a criminal.'

'Suicide is a crime, Superintendent. Surely, a man in your position must know that. There was a time when those who took their own lives were buried on a public highway with a stake through their bodies. If it were left to me, that practice would be revived.'

'Fortunately,' said Colbeck, sharply, 'it is not left to you or to anyone else enamoured of such medieval brutality. Parliament has shown due mercy to those unfortunate people compelled by the sheer misery of their lives to commit suicide. The Burial Act of 1823 gives them the right to lie in consecrated ground as long as the body is interred between the hours of nine o'clock in the evening and midnight. What the Act does not authorise is the performance of any of the rites of Christian burial.'

'I care nothing for the Act,' said Skelton, dismissively.

'Then it will give me pleasure to arrest you for contravening it,' said Tallis, wagging a finger. 'You have a very short memory, sir. The church of St Andrew, as I recall, was rebuilt almost ten years ago. I know that the major costs were borne by Mr Rutson of Newby Wiske, but a handsome donation to erect a stone cross in the churchyard came from my good friend, Colonel Tarleton. Is that not so?'

'Yes, it is, but I regard that as irrelevant.'

'He worshipped regularly in your church.'

'All the more reason for him to set a good example to the rest of my flock,' said the rector. 'Instead of that, he causes distress in the mind of every true Christian by his abominable act.'

'Is suicide *always* abominable?' asked Colbeck.

'It's abominable and unforgivable.'

'Then I'm surprised that you haven't been to Westminster Abbey to open the tomb of Viscount Castlereagh. He slit his own throat with a letter opener yet he was given a Christian burial there. He was a peer of the realm and held some of the highest offices of state. Would you have him disinterred so that he could lie beneath a public highway with a stake through his body?'

'That was a different case,' said Skelton, irritably, 'and bears no parallel to this one. Viscount Castlereagh, poor man, committed suicide in a fit of madness. That's an extenuating factor.'

'Could it not also be an extenuating factor here?'

'No,' Tallis interjected. 'Colonel Tarleton was as sane as I am.'

'My wife can bear witness to that,' asserted the rector. 'She actually met him when he was on his

71

way to commit the vile act. In fact, she may have been one of the last people to see him alive. That thought has troubled her beyond measure.'

'What exactly happened?'

'He strolled through the village as if on one of his normal perambulations. He raised his hat to my wife and smiled at her. In short, he behaved as he would always have done and that, I may tell you, is my definition of sanity.'

'The inquest may decide otherwise,' said Colbeck.

'Not when Mrs Skelton gives her evidence.'

'The coroner will not reach a verdict on the basis of a brief encounter in the village with a single individual. Testimony will be taken from everyone who saw Colonel Tarleton that day. And whatever the outcome, his right to be buried in consecrated ground remains.'

'I intend to enforce that right,' cautioned Tallis.

'You can do as you wish,' said the rector, 'but I repeat what I came here to inform you. No suicide will lie within the precincts of my churchyard. Law or no law, I'll not let it be corrupted.'

Without waiting for a reply, he turned on his heel and swept out of the room, brushing back his luxuriant hair before putting on his hat. Tallis was fuming. Colbeck sought to reassure him.

'Nobody can deny him the right of burial, sir,' he said.

'He'll have that right,' said Tallis, hotly, 'even if I have to dig the grave with my own bare hands.'

'I appreciate your feelings but you can't usurp the privileges of the children. They are his heirs, Superintendent. We must bow to their wishes. It's up to them to make the funeral arrangements.'

Wearing mourning attire and with her face hidden behind a black veil, Eve Doel embraced Mrs Withers with an amalgam of fondness and grief. They wept copiously on each other's shoulders. Adam Tarleton, meanwhile, supervised the driver who was unloading their luggage before carrying it into the house. When that was done, the man collected his fare, tugged his forelock in gratitude then climbed back up on the seat of his carriage. As the vehicle rumbled away, Tarleton looked with disapproval at the two women.

'That's enough of that,' he said, brusquely. 'We can't stand out here all day.'

'No, no, of course not,' said Mrs Withers, disentangling herself and dabbing at her eyes with a handkerchief. 'Welcome back, sir. It's been a long time since we saw you.'

'It's been far too long.'

'Do come inside.'

She stood back to let the brother and sister go into the house. Waiting in the hall was a tremulous Lottie Pearl, her mother's black dress looking baggier than ever. Not knowing whether to speak or to curtsey, she opted for a nervous smile that neither of them even saw. Ignoring her completely, they went through to the drawing room. The housekeeper followed and took a close look at them. Eve Doel had been there during the search for her mother but Adam had not been to the house for a long time.

Dark-haired and elfin-faced, Eve was still the same petite beauty as ever. Two children had robbed her of none of the bloom that came into view as she removed her hat. Her brother, on the other hand, was showing even more obvious signs of dissipation. He was of medium height with a sallow complexion and with dark bags beneath his watery eyes. At thirty, he was four years younger than his sister but he looked much older. He, too, was in full mourning wear, sweeping off his top hat as if it were an imposition and handing it to Mrs Withers.

'It's been a long journey,' he said. 'We'll need refreshments.'

'I'll see to it at once, sir,' said Mrs Withers.

'I'd have been here earlier,' explained Eve, 'but my husband is abroad at the moment and I had to wait for Adam to come for me.'

'I'm so sorry that this has happened, Mrs Doel.'

'When I read your letter, I was in despair.'

'So are we all.'

'Everyone has to die sooner or later,' remarked Tarleton.

'Adam!' reproved his sister.

'Well, it's true. I'd have preferred it to have been by natural means, of course, but he had other ideas and he's left us to face the scandal. That was typical of him.'

'I dispute that, sir,' said Mrs Withers, loyally.

'I thought you were fetching refreshments.'

'Colonel Tarleton always tried to spare people any trouble. He was a very considerate man.'

'We can do without your opinion, thank you.'

'Excuse me.' Hurt by his manner, the house-keeper went out.

74

'There's no need to be so rude to her, Adam.'

'I hate the way that she *dithers*.'

'She's served the family faithfully and she's as distressed as any of us over what happened to Father.'

'He was never my father, Eve.'

'That was your fault. You never accepted him.'

'He kept badgering me to go into the army. Why? I loathed the very idea. If I'd been stupid enough to agree, I'd probably be in the Crimea right now getting shot at by those bloodthirsty Russians.'

'At least you'd have done something honourable.'

'We can't all marry and have children the way that you did. I value my freedom and our so-called father let me have very little of that in this house. I'll not weep for him.'

'That's a terrible thing to say.'

'I'm only being honest, Eve. I never understood why Mother consented to marry him in the first place and I still think that he had something to do with her disappearance.'

'Adam! You can't believe that, surely?'

'I'd believe anything of him.'

'You're so cruel,' she said, holding back tears. 'He was mortified when Mother went missing. You should read the letter he sent me about it. He said that it was the worst thing that ever happened to him. He was paralysed with fear.'

'Yes, he was afraid that the truth would come out.'

'I won't let you sneer at him like this.'

'I'm not sneering, Eve. I simply don't see the

point of being a hypocrite. He and I never saw eye to eye. Why pretend to mourn his passing when I'm glad that he's gone?'

She was stunned. 'You're actually *glad* that he died in such a dreadful way? How can you be so callous? If that's how you feel, why did you bother to come here today?'

'I came for Mother's sake,' he replied. 'I want to find out exactly what happened to her. Since we must accept that, after all this time, she's dead, I'll admit that something else brought me here as well.'

'What was that?'

'I came to seek my inheritance. You married a wealthy merchant and live in a fine mansion. I've had more modest accommodation. Well, not any-more,' he added with a sweeping gesture. 'This house will have been left to me. If I put it on the market, it will bring in the sort of money that I deserve. At long last, I'll be rich!'

CHAPTER SIX

'Was the stationmaster right about that room at the Swan?' asked Colbeck. 'Did you have to contend with cobwebs and beetles?'

'They were the least of my worries,' complained Leeming. 'The place was draughty, the mattress like a board and I saw two mice scurrying about. There was also an empty keg in the room so I had to put up with the smell of stale beer. Then, of course, there was the noise from above. Every time someone moved about, the floorboards creaked.'

'We'll have to find you better accommodation, Victor.'

'It was the superintendent's decision to put me there.'

'If we can persuade him to return to London,' said Colbeck, 'then you can have his room at the Black Bull. They looked after us very well there.'

The two men were travelling by rail to Northallerton. It gave Colbeck the chance to describe the frosty confrontation with Frederick Skelton, the obdurate rector, and it allowed Leeming time to moan about his unhappiness.

'I miss my wife dreadfully,' he confessed. 'It's not the same when Estelle is not there. When can I go back to her?'

'Not until this mystery is solved.'

'Well, I think that it already has been. I didn't take to that self-important railway policeman but

I fancy that he may be right. The colonel's wife ran away from him.'

'Then whom did she run *to*, Victor?' asked Colbeck. 'That's what puzzles me. The obvious person to go to would be her daughter yet that's not what happened. Mrs Tarleton would hardly just take to her heels without any idea of a destination.'

'She could be in hiding somewhere.'

'I doubt that. The suicide has had widespread publicity. It will even be in the London newspapers. Were she still alive, the colonel's wife would surely have seen the news by now. With her husband dead, there'd be no need for her to conceal herself. No,' he went on, 'I incline to the view that she was murdered and that her body is still in the vicinity. We have to stay here until we can find it.'

Leeming groaned. 'That could take ages, sir.'

'Estelle will have to do without you for a little longer.'

'Wait until you're married. Then you'll understand how painful it is to be without the woman you love.'

'Oh, I've already found that out,' said Colbeck, resignedly.

Northallerton was a long-established community with a population of around five thousand. It was a thriving market town, a parliamentary borough and the administrative centre of the North Riding. Though he'd already been there, Leeming had only touched the outskirts and he was interested to see the busy streets, fine houses, churches, public buildings, suites of offices and the countless shops at the heart of the place. The bank was situated in a prominent position in the High Street and, once they'd introduced themselves, they were conducted to the manager's office.

Bertram Reader gave them an effusive welcome.

'I'm so relieved to see you, gentlemen,' he said, shaking their hands in turn. 'This whole business needs to be sorted out once and for all. Do sit down.'

'Thank you, sir,' said Colbeck.

While he and, Leeming settled into an armchair apiece, the manager returned to the high-backed chair behind his desk.

'The North Riding has everything that one could desire,' he went on, 'but in one instance, it is glaringly deficient. It has, as yet, no county constabulary.'

'Then it's one of the last places in England to be without one,' said Colbeck. 'In the wake of a Royal Commission over fifteen years ago, an Act was passed enjoining all boroughs to examine the possibility of reorganising their police forces. Most have complied.'

'I have high hopes that we will follow their example in the near future,' said Reader. 'What's held us back, I need hardly tell you, is the fear of great expense.'

'It's more expensive to let crime go unchecked,' said Leeming.

'I couldn't agree more, Sergeant. However, let's forget our shortcomings with regard to law enforcement. We're honoured to have two detectives from Scotland Yard to help us at this time of trial.' He spread his arms. 'Please feel free to ask me anything you wish.'

Reader was a trim figure in immaculate clothing. Still in his forties, he'd retained all of his hair and most of his youthful energy. The office was large and well appointed and the general impression was of an efficient man holding an important position at a high salary. They noticed how tidily he kept his desk, papers and files stacked neatly in order. Across that desk, thousands of transactions had been made over the years. Reader exuded a quiet benevolence. He was a man whom clients of the bank could trust.

'I believe that you and the colonel were friends,' Colbeck began.

'That's correct, Inspector,' replied the other.

'So you saw him and his wife a great deal.'

'At least once a week, I'd say – until recently, that is. Over the last few months, it was more like once a fortnight.'

'Why was that?'

'The colonel told us that he was very busy. He turned down some of our invitations and accepted others. The four of us liked to play whist together.'

'Did you play for money, sir?' asked Leeming.

Reader smiled. 'I'm a banker, Sergeant. I never gamble.'

'That's very wise of you. When I was still in uniform, I lost half a week's pay in a card game. I learnt a lesson from that.'

'On the day of her disappearance,' said Colbeck, 'Mrs Tarleton set out to walk to your home.'

'She and Agnes – that's my wife – intended to go shopping.'

'What did Mrs Reader think when her visitor

didn't turn up?'

'Well,' said the banker, 'she thought it very strange. It was unlike Miriam Tarleton to be late. Were she indisposed, she'd have sent someone with a message to that effect. By the time I got home that evening, my wife was very anxious. To put her mind at rest, I offered to ride over to the house but Agnes felt that unnecessary. She decided that a mistake had been made about the arrangements.'

'Was Mrs Tarleton in the habit of making mistakes?'

'Far from it – ordinarily, she was very reliable.'

'How did she get on with her husband?' asked Leeming.

'What an odd question!' said Reader. 'If you'd known them, you'd never have needed to ask it. They were happily married and always had been.'

'We were told there were tensions in the house.'

Reader was terse. 'Then you've been misinformed, Sergeant. There were some tensions when the children wcre there, I grant you, but everything was much more serene after that. Adam was the problem. He was a natural rebel. His sister was a sweet girl and I was sorry when she left to get married. In all honesty, however, I have to admit that I was glad to see the back of Adam Tarleton.'

'Adam and Eve,' noted Colbeck. 'Was Mrs Tarleton religious?'

'She came from a clerical family,' explained Reader. 'Her father was a rural dean and her brother was in holy orders. Her first husband – God rest his soul – was a parish priest. He died of cholera and left her with two small children.

When the colonel came into her life, it was a real blessing.'

Having hit his stride, Reader went on to describe the marriage in more detail and to pour scorn on the idea that Colonel Tarleton had murdered his wife. Appalled at the news of the suicide, he viewed it as an act of temporary madness and refused to condemn his friend.

'It's reassuring to hear someone speaking up for him,' said Colbeck. 'Early this morning, the super-intendent and I were cornered by the rector of St Andrew's, who told us bluntly that he wouldn't allow the deceased to be buried in the church-yard.'

'I think I know what's behind that decision,' said Reader.

'So do I – ignorance of the law.'

'There's a more personal reason. Frederick Skelton studied theology with Miriam Tarleton's first husband. They were very close. In fact, he was godfather to their children. The colonel attended church every Sunday but, clearly, he was nowhere near as devout a Christian as his predecessor.'

'Did Mr Skelton resent that?'

'Very much,' said Reader. 'And he resented the way that Adam – his godson, remember – was brought up by the colonel. There was no spiritual dimension to the boy's life. No wonder he veered off the straight and narrow. Regarding the rector's attitude to the funeral,' he continued, 'that's not just an aversion to an act of suicide. Like so many other misguided people, he believes that the colonel killed his wife and is therefore a species of devil.'

'Everyone must be presumed innocent until proved guilty.'

'The colonel has been denied that right.'

'Have you any idea who the killer is?' asked Leeming.

Reader sighed. 'I wish that I did, Sergeant. My wife and I both joined in the search for her. The colonel was distraught. Nobody who saw the state he was in could think for a moment that he committed the crime. His innocence must be attested.'

'If she's here,' said Colbeck, 'we'll find her.'

'I sincerely hope that you will.'

'Before then, however, we have to make extensive enquiries. One of the people to whom I'd like to speak is your wife. She was, after all, the person Mrs Tarleton was on her way to see.'

'Call at my home whenever you wish,' urged Reader, taking out his wallet and extracting a card. 'This is our address.'

'Thank you, sir,' said Colbeck, getting up to receive the card.

'Agnes will be as eager to help you as I am, though you'll find her in very low spirits. The Tarletons were good company. We spent so many happy times with them. We watched their children grow up and shared a number of family outings with them. Not to put too fine a point on it, they were our best friends.'

Leeming was curious. 'Did they have any enemies?'

'None at all – unless you count their son, that is.'

'Was he really such a problem?'

'His stepfather loathed him and his mother indulged him. He must have drunk and gambled his way through a small fortune. When the money dried up, Adam became angry and sent his mother the most abusive letters.'

'You say that the money dried up,' said Colbeck, seizing on the phrase. 'We had the feeling that the family had run into financial difficulties. Is that true?'

Reader was wary. 'Yes, it is, Inspector,' he replied. 'I can't go into details without breaching confidentiality. Suffice it to say that the colonel and his wife had to draw in their horns a little.'

'I'll press you no further on the subject, sir. You've been very helpful. Now that we happen to be in town, we'll avail ourselves of the opportunity to call on Mrs Reader.' He signalled to Leeming who rose to his feet. The banker also got up. 'Thank you, sir.'

'I'd be grateful if you would keep me informed of any developments.'

'We will, sir.'

'Have you picked up any clues at all since you've been here?'

'Oh, yes,' said Colbeck. 'At least, we have a starting point.'

'And what's that?' asked Reader.

'The railway.'

Clifford Everett's office was on the top floor of the building, obliging Tallis to walk up three long flights of stairs. By the time he reached the top, he was panting. He took a few moments to recover before rapping on the door with his

84

knuckles. In response to a crisp invitation, he went into the lawyer's domain.

'Good morning, Major Tallis,' said Everett.

'Actually, I'm here in a different guise today.'

'In what way, pray?'

Tallis explained that he was employed by the Metropolitan Police Force and that a letter from the colonel had brought him to Yorkshire to unravel a mystery. Everett listened stonily. Years earlier, the two men had met more than once at social gatherings when Tallis was always introduced by his former rank. Everett had assumed that he was a retired army man. Hearing that he was, in fact, a detective made the lawyer defensive.

'You misled us, Superintendent,' he said.

'I didn't wish to court any embarrassment,' Tallis told him. 'Policemen are never popular. Everyone is suspicious of us. It was easier for me to pass myself off as an old soldier when I visited the colonel. That, in effect, was exactly what I was.'

'I don't accept that. You lied to us.'

Everett was a portly man in his fifties with a round, red face and a large head decorated by tufts of white hair. He had piggy eyes that lacked any sparkle and were constantly on the move. Gesturing his visitor to a chair, he resumed his seat behind the desk and clasped his hands tightly across his stomach.

'So ... you are not here merely as a friend,' he observed.

'I'm here to investigate a terrible crime.'

'Are you referring to murder or to suicide?'

'Both are interlinked,' said Tallis. 'In finding the killer, I'll be absolving the colonel of any wrongdoing and bringing to justice the fiend who provoked a blameless man to take his own life.'

'There are some who think the colonel was far from blameless.'

'Are you one of them, Mr Everett?'

'Heavens, no!' exclaimed the other, hastily. 'I take no sides in the matter.'

'Well, you should, sir. As Colonel Tarleton's lawyer, you should be protecting him from some of the vile accusations that are flying around. He paid you well for your services. Earn your keep.'

'What am I supposed to do?'

'To begin with, you can take legal action against those who are whispering vicious lies into the ears of journalists. Libel and slander are abroad, Mr Everett. Strike them down and show no quarter.'

'Where am I to start, Superintendent? What you call slander is the general opinion. Go into any public house and you'll find dozens of people convinced that the colonel murdered his wife. It's the same elsewhere. How am I to take action against such overwhelming odds?'

'By making an example of the worst offenders,' said Tallis.

'I can do nothing until the inquest is over tomorrow.'

'Why should that delay you?'

'Because it may throw more light on what actually happened,' said Everett, raising his voice to hide the sound of subterranean gurgles from his stomach. 'Evidence of all kinds will be introduced. After his body was discovered on the railway line, certain items were taken from the colonel's house. They may not only tell us about his state of mind when he set out that day, they may also give us a fuller understanding of why his wife disappeared.'

Tallis was livid. 'What are you expecting – a signed confession?'

'It's not beyond the bounds of possibility.'

'You should be ashamed even to entertain such thoughts. Do you have no respect for the concept of loyalty to your clients?'

'Of course I do,' said Everett, indignantly.

'When did you last see the colonel?'

'It was about a week ago.'

'And what brought him here?'

'I'm not at liberty to divulge that, Superintendent. All that I can tell you is that our meeting had an elegiac feel to it.'

'Are you saying that he was ... taking his leave of you?'

'That was how it felt.'

'Given the way you've deserted him,' said Tallis, hotly, 'he should have taken his leave of you a lot earlier.'

Everett was on his feet. 'I won't have you casting aspersions on my professional competence,' he said. 'I served the colonel to the best of my ability for many years and I regret his passing. As a lawyer, I'm in an invidious position because I have his last will and testament in my safe. I promised to fulfil his wishes to the letter but I can hardly do that if the inquest rules that his goods and chattels are forfeit to the Crown. So you see, I have enough on my plate without your coming in here and insulting me.'

Tallis gave a gruff apology and Everett sat down again, only partially mollified. Prompted by Tallis, he gave an account of his dealings with the colonel in recent times and he spoke well of the dead man's character. Since he also acted for Mrs Tarleton, he was able to talk about her occasional visits to his office in the preceding months.

'Did they ever come here together?' asked Tallis.

'Once or twice,' answered Everett. 'Actually, I preferred it when it was a joint visit. The colonel could be a trifle short-tempered. You and he have that in common, Superintendent. When Mrs Tarleton was with him, he was always on his best behaviour.'

After brooding for a while, Tallis rose from his chair.

'Thank you, Mr Everett,' he said. 'I'll impose on you no longer.'

'I'm always available to an officer of the law.'

'Why do *you* think that Miriam Tarleton went missing?'

'I prefer to reserve my judgement, sir.'

'You mean that you'd rather sit on the fence.'

'Fences are too precarious. I'd rather lurk in the shadows.'

'It's the best place for you,' said Tallis, pointedly, and headed for the door.

'One moment, Superintendent,' called the other, opening a drawer in his desk and taking something out. 'You may find this interesting.'

'What is it?'

'I'm afraid that it's a fairly accurate reflection of what the people of Northallerton – and still more of South Otterington – are thinking and feeling.

It's a broadside entitled *Railway to the Grave*.'

Tallis wrinkled his nose. 'What a revolting title!'

'When I arrived this morning, this was on sale in the street.'

'I'm surprised you'd bother with anything so tasteless.'

'I wanted to see what the general mood was.' He handed it over. 'Read it for yourself. The poet will never rival Mr Tennyson but he has an earthy directness about his style.'

Gritting his teeth, Tallis read the opening stanzas.

Now here's a murd'rous tale of woe,
See a hero misbehave.
For it shows a valiant soldier go
By railway to the grave.

What drives a man to take his life
Upon the iron rails?
Is it to do with the death of a wife
And the guilt that then prevails?

Suicide is a fearful crime,
Of darkest deeds, none chiller.
When he lay crushed upon that line
Had he simply killed a killer?

Tallis had seen enough. Spluttering with fury, he screwed the paper up and hurled it to the floor with disgust.

'If I find the man who's selling this detestable slime,' he yelled, 'I'll tear him limb from limb!'

Agnes Reader's account of the fateful day was protracted because she kept breaking down to sob. Colbeck and Leeming listened without ever daring to interrupt. She was a slight woman in her early forties with an attractive face distorted by pain and awash with tears. Having relived a harrowing experience, she ended on a pleading note.

'Should I have done more?' she asked. 'After waiting and waiting for hours on end, should I have gone out to search for her there and then? Had I done so, would I perchance have saved Miriam's life? Tell me, please, that I did all that I should have done.'

'You've nothing to reproach yourself with, Mrs Reader,' said Colbeck. 'The likelihood is that Mrs Tarleton was killed shortly after she parted company with the colonel. Someone must have trailed them and – the moment he saw her unaccompanied – he struck.'

'I have nightmares when I think about it.'

'Your husband told us how fond you were of them both.'

Agnes gave a hopeless shrug. 'They were our best friends.'

It was a sizeable house on the edge of the town with views of the fields over which anyone coming from South Otterington would have walked. The detectives were in the drawing room, seated opposite the vision of sadness that was Agnes Reader. Dressed in black out of respect, she had a black-edged lace handkerchief to wipe away her tears.

'Mrs Reader,' said Colbeck, gently, 'I'm given to understand that Mrs Tarleton always took the same route here from the village.'

90

'That's true, Inspector,' she replied. 'It's a well-worn path and the one that my husband and I have often taken when we've walked over there on a summer afternoon. When it's too cold or rain is in the air, we travelled in the trap.'

'Could you please show us the precise route?'

Colbeck had brought an ordnance survey map of the area and he unfolded it on a low table, smoothing it out with the flat of his hand. Agnes leant over to peer at it.

'Here,' she said, pointing at a spot beyond South Otterington. 'This is the house. They would have left there and followed the track to the village. After that, they'd come this way.' Her finger traced the journey. 'When they reached this point here, Miriam would have parted from Aubrey – from the colonel – and kept to a path that zigzags its way before eventually straightening out.'

'It's not all open countryside,' noted Leeming, interpreting the symbols. 'There's a wood marked here and I daresay there are odd copses dotted about.'

'That's quite right, Sergeant,' she agreed.

'In addition to that,' said Colbeck, 'there'd be bushes and trees along the margins of the fields and perhaps a hollow or two. There are probably several places where someone could ambush a passer-by. Did Mrs Tarleton have no fear of walking here alone?'

'None whatsoever,' said Agnes, 'and the same goes for me. I've done that walk on my own many times and so had she. Neither of us had the slightest fear. This is a law-abiding part of the county. We can come and go in complete safety.'

'That's good to hear,' said Leeming. 'You couldn't say that about some of the districts we visit in London. You take your life in your hands when you walk down some streets.'

'The situation here is very different, Sergeant,' said Colbeck. 'The murder – if indeed that's what it was – is all the more shocking for being such an unusual event. Mrs Tarleton was caught off guard.'

'What could have been the motive, Inspector?'

'We can't hazard a guess until we find the body. Presumably, she'd have been carrying a handbag and wearing jewellery of some description. If all that is missing, then theft might be the motive.'

'I don't want to hear any other suggestions,' said Agnes, hands to her ears. 'I just pray that she was not molested in any way. I couldn't bear that thought. My husband says that I must try to put it out of my mind the way that he does when he's at work. But I find it impossible to do that. A few weeks ago we had two wonderful friends. One of them has disappeared and the other was mangled by a train. How can I put such horrors out of my mind?'

'You can't, Mrs Reader. You have too many emotional ties to the victims. It's only right and proper that you should dwell on their deaths. I know that your husband feels the loss deeply as well. His position at the bank requires him to put on a brave face,' said Colbeck, 'but we could see that he was suffering inside.'

'Bertram has been my salvation,' she confided. 'I don't know how I would have borne up without him. He's had to find the strength to keep both of us from sinking into absolute despair. And yes, he has suffered. He loved them as much as I did. He's just better at hiding his feelings than I am.'

'He told us that, on the day in question, he got back here to find you in great distress.'

'He was late home that evening because he'd been to see a client in Darlington. By that time, I was sick with worry. Bertram wanted to ride over to the house to make sure that all was well and to put my mind at rest. For some reason,' she admitted, 'I wouldn't let him. I convinced myself that, if anything unpleasant had happened to Miriam, her husband would have sent word. Oh dear!' she wailed, a hand to her mouth. 'I'll have to go through it all again at the inquest tomorrow. I'm not sure that I'll be able to manage it.'

'I'm sure that you will, Mrs Reader,' said Leeming.

'And so am I,' added Colbeck. 'You've done splendidly here with us and you'll do the same in public.' He folded up his map. 'We'll intrude on your grief no longer.'

'The pain is all the more searing because we don't know what befell Miriam that day. Until the truth comes out, I'll never be able to mourn her properly.' She turned moist eyes upon Colbeck. 'We've been everywhere but the search has so far been in vain. Is there any hope at all that you can find her, Inspector? Is there any hope that we'll finally know the truth?'

Touched by her plight and by the ravaged beauty of her face, Colbeck weighed up the evidence he had already gathered.

'I think that I can guarantee it,' he said.

CHAPTER SEVEN

It had been a full day for Madeleine Andrews. After sending her father off to work, she'd cleared away the breakfast things and checked what was in the larder before making her shopping list. She then let in the woman who came to clean the house and dressed to go out, taking a large basket with her as she walked towards the market. Buying the week's rations never seemed like a chore to Madeleine because she always met friends with whom she could chat and she invariably called in on her aunt. Afternoon was given over to her work and she spent a long time at her easel, bringing another vivid railway scene painstakingly to life on the canvas. Only when the light began to fade a little did she abandon her art, turning instead to the latest novel borrowed from Robert Colbeck.

Mrs Gaskell's *Cranford* diverted her for an hour or so with its charming portrayal of events in a quiet Cheshire village, describing, as it did, a leisurely existence that had great appeal to her. It certainly bore no relation to the more hectic metropolitan world in which she lived. Madeleine was still engrossed in the book when she heard familiar footsteps on the pavement outside. Caleb Andrews had returned from Euston after his usual stop at a public house frequented by fellow railwaymen. He was in an affable mood when she let him in, taking off his cap and coat before slipping into the kitchen to wash off some of the day's grime.

'Supper will be ready soon,' she told him.

'It can wait until you've read the article.'

'What article is that?'

'The one about Inspector Colbeck, of course,' he said, popping his head around the door. 'Well, it's not exactly about *him* but he's mentioned in it.'

'Where?' she asked, seizing the rolled-up newspaper from the pocket of his coat. 'What page is it on?'

'Where else would it be but the front one?'

She saw the headline. 'Is it this one about suicide in Yorkshire?'

His head vanished. 'That's it, Maddy.'

She recoiled with dismay when she read the article because it went into unabashed detail about the injuries sustained by Colonel Tarleton. While she was pleased to see a word of praise for Colbeck's record of solving crimes relating to railways, she was sorry that he was involved with such a grisly event. It was a long article and she read it through twice. Face and hands now scrubbed, Andrews came out of the kitchen.

'It's something we all fear, Maddy,' he said. 'We're all afraid that some fool will step out in front of us one day when we're driving along at top speed. It could happen to any of us.'

'The colonel was no fool, Father. He was an educated man and, according to this, he had a distinguished military career. It seems that he took his life because his wife was missing, presumed dead.'

Andrews nodded. 'He has my sympathy. I know what losing a wife can do to you.' He put a grateful arm around her. 'This fellow didn't have a daughter like you to help him through it.'

'He has a daughter and a son. They must be horrified.'

'Don't forget the driver. He's probably suffering badly as well.'

'What made the colonel choose that way to die?'

'Madness – it's the only explanation. Why didn't he shoot himself if he couldn't carry on? Or why didn't he drown himself in a river? That's what I thought of doing.'

'Father!' she scolded.

'It was only on the day of the funeral, Maddy,' he said, holding up an apologetic palm. 'It was when I realised that I'd never see your mother again that I had a moment of weakness. Luckily,' he went on, brightening, 'I had you to make me see sense and I've found a new life – for a while, anyway.'

'What do you mean?'

'Well, it's not going to last, is it? Sooner or later, you're going to marry Inspector Colbeck and live in his house.'

'You'll be very welcome to visit us any time you wish,' she said, putting the newspaper aside. 'Robert has told you that himself.'

'Newly married couples like their privacy.'

She gave a dry laugh. 'I'm not sure that we'll have much of a private life. Robert works long and irregular hours. He's ever likely to charge off to a different part of the country at a moment's notice.'

'I don't mind that – as long as he has the sense to travel on one of *our* trains.'

'Don't be silly!'

He gave her an affectionate squeeze. 'Are you pining?'

'I always miss him.'

'And I daresay that he misses you. He'd better. I want my daughter missed good and proper. I don't want a son-in-law who forgets you the moment you're out of his sight.'

'He'd never do that, Father.'

'Good,' he said. 'No matter what I was doing, your mother was never far from my mind when she was alive. You and her were what kept me going through hard winters and long shifts. As for the inspector, he should be on his way back to London soon. The inquest is tomorrow. Once that's over, he can catch the next train.'

'You didn't read the article properly, Father.'

'Yes, I did.'

'Then you should have realised that Robert would never leave a place where there was unfinished business. A woman is missing and feared dead. He'll want to find her and arrest someone for the murder. It could keep him in Yorkshire for some time.'

Andrews frowned. 'I don't like the sound of that.'

'It's something we have to accept.'

'I don't mean him staying there,' he explained. 'It's the danger he might be in. Now that he's going to be one of the family, I've started to

97

worry about him. Investigating a suicide is harmless enough but he's also looking for a missing person.'

'Robert has a way of finding people he's after.'

'Someone may decide to stop him doing that.'

'I don't understand,' she said.

'I'm talking about the killer, Maddy.'

She swallowed hard. 'Oh, I see.'

'He's not going to give himself up without a fight,' said Andrews. 'When a man has already committed one murder, he won't be slow to commit another. Can you hear what I'm saying to you? If he finds that missing woman, Inspector Colbeck could put himself in jeopardy.'

He was there. Colbeck sensed it. Somewhere in the crowded room was the man who'd taken the life of Miriam Tarleton. He scanned the faces of those who'd come to give testimony, those who sat on the jury and those who'd packed the coroner's court out of sadness or curiosity. There was no sign of an obvious killer and no hint of a troubled conscience. Whoever had done the deed was unaffected by feelings of guilt. It made Colbeck even more determined to catch him.

Seated near the front with Leeming, he was able to see at close quarters the main participants in the inquest. The coroner controlled the proceedings, a tall, stooping man of advanced years who peered over the top of his pince-nez with mild alarm at the way even more people were trying to get in. Colbeck had a first sighting of the colonel's children. Eve was a study in bereavement, mourning the death of her stepfather and still poleaxed by the disappearance of her mother. Adam had the courtesy to keep his head bowed but Colbeck thought he detected the ghost of a smile on his lips. Others were patently consumed by grief but it had not yet touched Adam Tarleton. He was detached from the whole event.

While he felt sorry for Eve Doel, Colbeck was more concerned about Edward Tallis. Since his visit the previous day to the solicitor, the superintendent had been preoccupied and uncommunicative. Saying nothing about what passed between him and Clifford Everett, he showed scant interest in what his colleagues had learnt from their respective conversations with Bertram and Agnes Reader. Tallis looked ill, visibly bracing himself for the ordeal of being called as a witness.

'The strain is too much for him,' decided Leeming.

'He'll rally when it's his turn,' said Colbeck.

'What if he collapses?'

'That won't happen, Victor. If anyone is going to feel faint, it will be one of the ladies.'

"Then it will be the colonel's daughter. She seems to be such a delicate creature.'

'What do you make of her brother?'

'He looks as if he'd rather be playing billiards somewhere.'

'That was my impression. He's a denizen of gentlemen's clubs and drinking establishments, I fancy.' He glanced around. 'Keep your eyes peeled, Victor.'

'What am I looking for, Inspector?'

'A murder suspect – he's here.'

Though he looked senile and doddery, the

coroner turned out to be brisk and efficient. When he rose from behind the table to declare that the court was in session, the hubbub died immediately. In clear and concise detail, the coroner explained the procedure and reminded everyone that they were simply there to reach a verdict about the death by his own hand of Colonel Aubrey Redvers Martin Tarleton. The first witness was sworn in and the searching questions began.

Margery Withers came first, telling them how the colonel had behaved in the wake of his wife's disappearance and insisting that he appeared to be his usual self on the day of his suicide. Her testimony was interspersed with tears. Lottie Pearl was too recent an employee to have built up any emotional ties with the colonel and his wife so her comments – though delivered in a quaking voice – were more objective. She agreed that there had been no sign at all of what the colonel had in mind when he left the house for the last time.

The same story was repeated time and again by those whom he'd passed in the village on his way to commit suicide. Dorcas Skelton, the rector's wife, a plain, pallid, roly-poly woman with a tendency to sniff at the end of each sentence, took her turn.

'Did you encounter the colonel that day?' asked the coroner.

'I did, sir,' she answered.

'At what time would that be, Mrs Skelton?'

'It was nearly eleven o'clock in the morning.'

'Did any words pass between you?'

'None at all,' she said. 'The colonel simply tipped his hat to me and smiled. In view of my feelings about the fate of his wife, I was unable to acknowledge his smile.'

'The fate of Mrs Tarleton is immaterial,' said the coroner, quelling the heavy murmur that arose. 'We are here simply to make a judgement in respect of her husband. Did you notice anything at all unusual about him that morning?'

'I did not, sir.'

'You'd consider him to be of sound mind, then?'

'Yes, I would – indubitably.'

'Thank you, Mrs Skelton.'

Peeved that her testimony had been so short, she returned to a seat beside her husband who patted her hand in approval of her performance. Others came forward in succession until Tallis's name was eventually called. Leeming's fears were groundless. As Colbeck had predicted, the superintendent straightened his shoulders and set his jaw as he stood before the coroner. The fact that he had a faint resemblance to the deceased caused a ripple of interest. Nobody was surprised when they heard that he served many years in the army.

'When did you last see your friend?' asked the coroner.

'I'm ashamed to say that it was some time ago,' replied Tallis. 'My work precludes any travelling for pleasure.'

'Could you be more precise, Superintendent?'

'It was five and a half years ago – just before the rector came to the village. The last service I attended at the church was taken by his predecessor, Canon Jermyn. However,' he went on, 'the colonel and I remained in constant touch by letter. I was his confidant.'

'May we hear what he said to you in his farewell missive?'

Tallis was uneasy at having to read a private message in such a public place but he spoke the words aloud. Mrs Withers was moved to tears and had to be consoled by Eve Doel. Others, too, were affected by the poignancy of the letter. Some, however, were immune to its implications. Frederick Skelton pursed his lips in disdain, Sergeant Hepworth, standing at the back of the room, gave a wry grin and Adam Tarleton had to put a hand over his mouth to suppress a snigger. As the witnesses continued to have their fleeting moment under oath, Colbeck was concerned that the verdict had already been reached. It seemed like a foregone conclusion. Everyone had testified that the deceased had been in full possession of his faculties during the period before he committed suicide.

Suddenly, it all changed. Eve Doel, who spoke of her stepfather with affection, recalled the visit she and her husband had made to the house immediately after her mother had been reported missing. During a long conversation that went on into the night, the colonel had made some strange remarks which, in retrospect, had been indications that he was considering suicide. At the time, she hadn't recognised them as such. She blamed herself for not staying with him at the house to offer support but she'd been so overwrought at her mother's disappearance that her husband insisted on taking her home and seeking medical help for her. When Eve finished her testimony, she returned unsteadily to her seat.

Bertram Reader told of the intense pressures under which the colonel had been and he remembered a time when his friend had been so distracted that he'd driven to Northallerton in the middle of the night to bang on their door and to ask if his wife was still there. Agnes Reader later endorsed the statement and, between sobs, told of other occasions when the strain had taken its toll on the colonel. But it was the evidence of the family doctor that was really crucial. Slowly and with some reluctance, he described the colonel's inability to sleep and of his wild request for a venomous poison that he could take to end his agony. There were several instances of worrying conduct by the colonel, culminating in a frightening incident when he accused the doctor of murdering his wife and tried to attack him.

While the whole room was roused by these revelations, the coroner treated them dispassionately. Adjusting his pince-nez, he sought to get a definitive medical opinion.

'Did you see signs of mental instability?' he asked.

'I did, sir,' said the doctor, 'and they were unmistakable.'

'Was there any deterioration in his condition?'

'After the disappearance of his wife, the colonel consulted me four times in a row. Each time, there was a slight deterioration in his state of mind. He could keep it from less discerning eyes but not from mine.'

'Do you believe he was unbalanced when he took his own life?'

The doctor was unequivocal. 'I'd stake my reputation on it.'

There was a mild uproar and it had to be subdued before the coroner could make his voice heard. The court was adjourned while the jury retired to consider their verdict. Most people dispersed in search of fresh air, ready to return in due course when they were called to hear the verdict.

Colbeck's only concern was for the health of the superintendent. Tallis was still reeling from the doctor's opinion, refusing to accept that his friend's mind had finally crumbled. Colbeck was firm.

'This has taxed you too much, sir,' he said. 'I think that you should return to the village on the next train and try to get some rest. I'll stay here to await the verdict.'

Tallis shook his head. 'I'm not running away now.'

'It could take hours before they reach a decision. There's no point in lingering here for that long. The sergeant will see that you get back safely to the Black Bull.'

'My place is here,' said Tallis.

Colbeck was frank. 'Your place is behind your desk in London, sir,' he argued, 'organising the fight against crime in the capital. That's where you belong, sir, and that's where you'll be most effective. Time and again, you've preached a sermon on the importance of remaining impartial in our work. You're unable to follow your own precepts here. Since you and the colonel were such close friends, your response to events is bound to be subjective. Simply *being* here is hurting you, superintendent. It's better for all concerned if you spare yourself any further agony.'

Fists clenched and eyes ablaze, Tallis seemed to be on the point of eruption. Leeming could not believe that Colbeck had dared to speak to the superintendent so bluntly and he expected devastating retaliation. Miraculously, it never came. Instead, Tallis reached out to shake Colbeck's hand.

'Thank you, Inspector,' he said. 'Not for the first time, you are quite right. I can't see beyond the respect and affection I have for a cherished friend. Even the slightest criticism of him makes me wince. When I read a scurrilous broadside about him yesterday, my stomach heaved. The longer I stay here, the more torture I'll suffer. So, yes,' he decided, 'for my own sake, I will return to London.'

'Does that mean I can have your room at the Black Bull, sir?' asked Leeming, hopefully.

'It means that I trust you and Colbeck to do what I came here to do myself. Find out what happened to Mrs Tarleton. Pursue her killer with all the vigour you can muster. Most of all,' he went on, looking at each of them in turn, 'clear the colonel's name. His reputation has been unjustly fractured. I count on you to restore it.'

'We'll do our utmost, sir,' said Colbeck.

'One last thing,' added Tallis, taking a letter

from his pocket and handing it over. 'This is the malicious letter sent to Colonel Tarleton on his last day alive. Fortunately, he never had to read it but he received many others like it. Seek out this fellow with a poisoned pen and put him under arrest. I want the vindictive fiend behind bars.'

Eve Doel could not bear to remain in the coroner's court. Hearing evidence about her stepfather had been a continuous torment for her. She'd found the strength to bear up in public but, the moment she returned to the carriage which had brought them to the inquest, she dissolved into tears. Mrs Withers, sharing her grief, put a comforting arm around her. It was twenty minutes before they'd recovered enough to wipe their eyes and to be able to review what they'd heard. The housekeeper was adamant.

'I don't care what the doctor said,' she said. 'There was nothing amiss with the colonel's mind. He was perfectly sane.'

'You saw more of him than anybody, Mrs Withers.'

'He was a private man. He kept his thoughts to himself.'

'He must have suffered so much. Had I been there to help him, it might not have ended so tragically.'

'You had your own anxieties to cope with, Mrs Doel.'

'I should have done more.'

'You came,' the housekeeper reminded her. 'When your mother went missing, you came to the house at once. That was not the case with your brother. The colonel had no idea how to reach him. He had no address to which he could write.' She tried to keep disgust out of her voice. 'You'd have thought he'd let his mother and stepfather know where he was living.'

'Adam was always on the move,' said Eve, sadly. 'He'd lost touch with Mother and with our stepfather. I deeply regret that but there was nothing I could do about it.'

The conversation was interrupted by sounds of commotion. They looked out of the carriage to see people hurrying back toward the court. Evidently, the jury had reached its verdict.

'Have they made up their minds so soon?' asked Mrs Withers.

'It appears so.

'Do you wish to go back in there, Mrs Doel?'

'I don't think that I could manage that,' said Eve. 'Adam is still inside. He'll tell us what they've decided.'

Before she could speculate on what the verdict would be, Eve saw Frederick Skelton and his wife approaching the carriage. The sight of her god-father made her sit up and she made an effort to regain her composure. The newcomers offered their condolences and congratulated Eve on bearing up so well at the inquest. The rector then felt the need to broach a sensitive topic.

'Much as it grieves me to say this,' he began, 'I owe it to my conscience – and to God – to do so. Whatever verdict is reached today is irrelevant to me. Suicide is suicide. It's a deplorable act. It's against the law and expressly against Christian teaching. "Thou shalt not kill" is one of the Ten

Commandments and it must be obeyed. Those who disobey it,' he said, 'must suffer the consequences.'

Eve was flustered. 'What consequences do you mean?'

'I hate to say this – especially to a god-daughter whom I love and respect – but there is no place for the colonel's remains in my churchyard. My refusal is absolute. I simply can't stand by and see him buried in consecrated ground.'

'But that's his right.'

'Not in my opinion.'

'It would be cruel to deny him that right.'

'Suicide is self-murder. By taking his life, your stepfather surrendered all rights. St Andrew's church, I must insist, is closed to him. The funeral must take place elsewhere.'

Eve was so overwhelmed with emotion that she was unable to speak. Having issued his command, the rector raised his hat in farewell then he walked away with his wife on his arm. Mrs Withers was as shocked as Eve. At a time when they most needed the succour of the Church, it was being withheld from them. They were still trying to absorb the shock when Adam came out of the court and ran across to the carriage.

'The jury returned its verdict,' he declared. 'Suicide while the balance of mind was disturbed. I always said that the old man was insane.

'Mr Tarleton!' cried the housekeeper, reproachfully.

'And what are you doing in our carriage, Mrs Withers?' he demanded. 'Get out of there at once and make your way back by train. And take that pathetic waif of a maid with you. There'll be plenty of work for the pair of you when you get back to the house.'

The departure of the superintendent on a train to London allowed Victor Leeming to take over his room at the Black Bull. Though he was still unhappy to be separated from his family, the sergeant was pleased by the improvement in his accommodation. He and Colbeck met for a drink in the bar.

'I never thought that he'd go so meekly,' said Leeming.

'It was in his best interests, Victor, and he was sensible enough to realise that. He needed to put distance between himself and events in South Otterington. The field has now been left clear for us.'

'Where do we start, sir?'

'The first thing I'd like to do is to take the same journey that Mrs Tarleton took on the day of her disappearance. We'll walk back in the direction of Northallerton.'

'That stretch of ground has already been covered by the search parties. What can we expect to find that they didn't?'

'A likely place of ambush,' said Colbeck. 'Supposing she was dead, they were looking for her body and I don't believe it's there. Working on the same supposition, we'll be trying to locate the spot at which she was intercepted. There may be signs of a struggle, small clues that others may have missed. If she was such a keen walker, Mrs Tarleton must have been a robust woman. She'd have had the strength to resist any attack.'

'Yet you say that the body will not be there.'

'No, Victor, it could be miles away. The killer would know in advance where the search would take place. To cover his tracks, I suspect that he took the body well away from the area.'

'Then it could be anywhere in the North Riding,' said Leeming in despair. 'It would take us years to search an area of this size.'

'I'm hoping that we may not have to do it entirely on our own,' said Colbeck. 'This is walking country. People are out and about all the time. It was broad daylight on the day she went missing. If she is indeed dead, whoever murdered her wouldn't have taken the chance of digging a proper grave. He'd have concealed the body as quickly as he could then got away from there fast. My guess is that Miriam Tarleton probably was killed and that she's waiting to be found,' he concluded. 'Sooner or later, someone is going to stumble on her remains.'

When they left the farm, their hearts were beating fast. They couldn't believe their boldness in sneaking out in the middle of the night. Hand in hand, they ran through the darkness until they felt it was safe enough to laugh aloud. The girl was a milkmaid and her swain was a labourer. All that they'd done so far was to exchange warm smiles and meaningful glances. Yet a bond had gradually developed. When the friendship evolved gently into a form of romance, they both yearned to be together and this was their moment.

As their eyes eventually became accustomed to

the gloom, he stopped to kiss her for the first time. Stirred by passion, they laughed gleefully and ran on until they skirted the woods. He led the way, looking for a grassy spot where they could lie beside each other. They went into the trees until they came to a suitable place. When they sank down on the soft grass, it was too dark for them to notice the low mound of earth beside them. The time alone together for which they'd both longed had at last come and they relished it. He rolled her onto her back and began to caress her body but she suddenly stiffened in fear. Something protruding from the mound had just brushed against her face. It was a human hand.

Her scream was heard a mile away.

CHAPTER EIGHT

Word of mouth travelled swiftly. Almost everyone in the North Riding seemed to know that detectives from Scotland Yard had arrived. Wilf Moxey, the young farm labourer, had caught wind of the news in the local pub. There was a dead body in the wood. The detectives had to be told. His first task, however, was to comfort his sweetheart, Lorna Begg, who was close to hysterics after the discovery. As he walked her back to the farm with his arm around her shoulders, he could feel her shivering with fear. They agreed that they'd say nothing about their nocturnal tryst. It would not only preserve the secrecy of their love, it would save Lorna from having to recount the heart-stopping moment when she was touched by a corpse.

They parted near the farm with a kiss. Lorna crept back to her loft above the stables, musing that she would have to be up in a couple of hours to milk the cows. Moxey, meanwhile, was running at a steady pace in the direction of South Ottering-ton, downcast that his rendezvous with Lorna had been such a disaster and hoping that it was not a bad omen. When he finally reached the Black Bull, he was lathered with sweat and panting for breath.

'Where exactly did you find it?' asked Colbeck.

'In the wood, sir,' said Moxey, 'just beyond Thornton.'

'Would that be Thornton-le-Moor?'

'No, sir – Thornton-le-Beans. I work on a farm nearby.'

'And did you see if the corpse was that of a female?'

'I daren't look that close, sir. It gave me such a shock.'

Colbeck didn't mind in the least being roused from his slumbers and he thanked Moxey for coming to alert him. Leeming was less happy about being dragged away from dreams of his wife and family. By the time he clambered onto the cart hired from the blacksmith, the sergeant was still not fully awake. Colbeck drove with Moxey beside him. Leeming sat disconsolately behind them on some sacks. Colbeck questioned the labourer gently.

'What were you doing out at that time of night?' he wondered.

'I went for a walk, sir.'

'And were you alone?'

'Oh, yes,' replied Moxey, hurriedly. 'I was looking for rabbits. I'd set a few snares some nights ago. That's the only time I get to slip away from the farm, sir.'

Colbeck knew that he was lying but that didn't concern him. He had no wish to pry into the other's private life. All that mattered was that a body had been found and that it was possibly that of Miriam Tarleton. Moxey was nervous, intimidated by someone as important as a detective inspector from London and terrified that he might somehow be under suspicion. He was already regretting his decision to run to the Black

113

Bull. Sensing his unease, Colbeck spent the journey trying to make him relax.

'What do you do at the farm?'

'Just about everything, sir,' said Moxey.

'This must be a busy time of the year for you.'

'It's always busy.'

'What – even in winter?'

'We've sheep and dairy cows to look after. Then there are fences to mend, walls to rebuild, timber to cut and a hundred other chores. Farm work never ends.'

'All the more surprising, then,' observed Colbeck, 'that you can find time to go out after rabbits at night. I'd have thought you'd be exhausted at the end of the day.' Moxey said nothing. 'How many of you are employed at the farm?'

'Five of us, sir,' said the other, 'though that's not counting Mr Higginbottom's sons – he's the farmer. They look after the stock. There's three of us work the land and we've got two milkmaids.'

There was something about the way his voice lingered on the word 'milkmaids' that gave Colbeck a clue as to who had been his companion in the wood. He didn't express the thought. The further they went in the jolting cart, the less tense Moxey became. Colbeck had no wish to unsettle him.

'Have you always worked there?' he asked.

'No, sir, I started out with my father.'

'Does he have a farm?'

'It's only a smallholding and there's not enough work there for me and my brother. So I moved away.'

'And where is this smallholding?'

'Leeming,' said Moxey.

The sergeant's ears pricked up. 'Did I hear my name?'

'It's a place, Victor,' said Colbeck.

'Yes,' explained Moxey. 'It's a village further west, sir, over towards Bedale. I was born and brought up there.'

'Is that so?' said Leeming with a chuckle. 'I didn't know they'd named a village after me. I must go over there some time.'

Dawn was making its first gesture when they reached the wood and they could see the trees silhouetted against the sky. Not wanting the cartwheels to destroy any potential evidence, Colbeck brought the horse to a halt well short of the place indicated by Moxey. The three of them dismounted and moved forward in a line. Colbeck was carrying the oil lamp that he'd just lit. Approaching with great trepidation, Moxey took them to the place he'd visited earlier with Lorna Begg. When they got near to the mound of earth, the labourer came to a halt and let them go on together.

The lamp illumined both the protruding hand and parts of the body. After carefully scooping back the earth with his hands, Colbeck exposed the face of a woman, her hair matted with filth, her features hideously distorted by the work of insects. He then examined the area around the shallow grave. Leeming had brought a spade with him.

'Shall I dig her up, sir?' he asked.

'By the look of it,' said Colbeck, 'animals have already started to do that. Hold on a minute,

Victor. I want to see if he's left us anything by mistake.' He moved the lamp so that the pool of light shifted to some ruts in the earth. 'Now that's interesting.'

'What have you found, Inspector?'

'A cart of some description was here.'

'What's so unusual about that?'

'It's well off the beaten track. The cart – or trap, most likely – would have had to pick its way through the trees. It would be completely hidden in here. Think back to yesterday evening,' said Colbeck. 'Do you remember that walk we had along the road to Northallerton as we traced Mrs Tarleton's footsteps?'

'I do,' sighed Leeming. 'My legs are still aching.'

'Near one of the places we thought suitable for an ambush, we found ruts very similar to these. They were concealed in a place where nobody would have thought of driving a trap.'

'I see what you mean, Inspector. Someone may have killed her there, put the body in the trap and brought it here to bury it. No,' he went on, thinking it through. 'That can't be right. Shots were heard. If Mrs Tarleton had been shot at close quarters, there'd have been blood near the place we're talking about yet there was none. And those search parties found no blood anywhere along that route.'

'That was only because the killer made sure that none was left behind.'

'How could he do that, Inspector?'

'Why don't we find out?' said Colbeck, putting the lamp down.

116

Removing his hat and coat, he hung them on a bush then took out a handkerchief to hold over his mouth. He held the spade while Leeming took off his hat and coat. The sergeant also produced a handkerchief. Both of them had unearthed decomposing remains before and they knew that the reek could be powerful. A handkerchief over the nose and mouth helped to ward off some of the stench. Moxey looked on in amazement as Leeming used the spade to dig up the makeshift grave with almost reverential care. In the course of his work, the labourer had had to slaughter animals and he had no qualms about handling their carcases. A human body was a different matter altogether and he made sure that he didn't get too close.

When the body came fully into view, so did an item that Colbeck picked up and brushed off before holding it close to the lamp. It was a bloodstained sack.

'There's the answer,' he said, using a hand to tilt the corpse's head to the left and seeing the gaping wound. 'Mrs Tarleton was shot in the back of the head. My guess is that this sack was put over her first so that it would absorb any blood. Look,' he went on, 'there are holes in the sack.'

'So she was shot *through* it,' said Leeming.

'It's a strong possibility. Come on, Victor. We must bring the cart as close as we can. We'll put her onto the sack and lift her up that way. She deserves to be handled very gently.'

It took time. The cart was too big to go all the way up to the grave, though there would have been just enough room for a trap to get through the trees. Moxey held the horse and tried to make it back up. The animal protested and had to be coaxed. Eventually, the cart got within a dozen yards of the remains of Miriam Tarleton. He then watched as the detectives lifted her onto the sack then used it like a stretcher to transfer her to the cart. Once there, she was covered by the sacks they'd brought with them. While the detectives retrieved their hats and coats, Moxey eyed the corpse, not relishing the idea of travelling on a cart with such a cargo aboard.

'Thank you, my friend,' said Colbeck, coming to his rescue. 'You did us a great service in finding the body. We've no need to detain you any longer. Get back to the farm and tell Mr Higginbottom that I have nothing but praise for you.'

'Will you need to speak to me again, Inspector?'

'No – but you'll be called upon to give evidence at the inquest.' Moxey's face fell. 'All you have to do is to say how you discovered the body,' Colbeck told him. 'In doing so, you've taken the first vital step in a murder investigation. You should be proud of yourself.'

Moxey smiled inanely. 'Should I?'

'You're a hero,' said Leeming. 'You've saved us weeks of looking for the lady. We can now start to search for the villain who brought her here. The family will be very grateful to you.'

'Oh, well, that's all right, then.' He shuffled his feet. 'In that case, Sergeant, I'll be off.'

'Before you go, I've got a question for you.'

'What's that, sir?'

'Where exactly *is* this village called Leeming?'

Colbeck didn't hear the exchange between the two men. He'd already returned to the grave and was using the spade to sift through the earth, aided by the fact that more light was now beginning to poke its way through the fretwork of branches. His search was thorough and it eventually bore fruit. Something clinked against the end of the spade. Kneeling on the ground, he felt with his hands until his fingers closed around something. He brushed off the dirt and examined what he'd found. In his palm were two spent cartridges.

The letter was addressed to Adam Tarleton and delivered by a messenger sent from Northallerton. His sister was with him when Colbeck's missive was opened.

'They've found the body,' said Tarleton.

Eve brought both hands up to her face. 'Oh, my God!' she exclaimed. 'Mother was killed, after all. I dreaded this moment. I knew in my heart that she must be dead.' Using a handkerchief to dab at moist eyes, she made an effort to control herself. 'Where was she found?'

'Over towards Thornton-le-Beans.'

'What on earth was the body doing there?'

'I've no idea.' He handed the letter to her. 'Mother's been taken to Northallerton. They want a member of the family to make a positive identification.'

'I'll go,' said Eve, impetuously.

'No, this is no job for a woman. It would be too distressing. After all this time, it won't be a pretty sight.'

'She's my mother. I've a right to be there.'

'You'd get too upset, Eve,' he argued. 'Look how harrowing the inquest was for you. Leave this to me. Mother would never have wanted you to see her in that state.'

She read the letter. 'Who is Inspector Colbeck?'

'He's one of the detectives Mrs Withers told us about.'

'How did he manage to find the body?'

'We'll have to ask him that.'

'In one sense, I'm pleased,' she said, biting her lip, 'because we now know the truth of what happened to her. But in another sense, of course, I'm terribly upset. This news is devastating. I'd hoped against hope that Mother might still somehow be alive. Yet she isn't. Someone murdered her.'

As she spoke the words, she felt their full impact and it was like a blow from a sledgehammer. Eve shuddered, dropped the letter then slumped to the carpet in a heap. Her brother bent over her in concern.

'Mrs Withers!' he shouted. 'Mrs Withers!'

'I'm coming, sir,' said the housekeeper, hurrying along the passageway and into the drawing room. She saw Eve. 'Goodness! What's happened?'

'Fetch some water.'

'Is Mrs Doel ill?'

'She fainted when she heard that the body's been found.'

Mrs Withers was curious. 'It has? Where was it, sir?'

'Fetch the water, woman. And tell the gardener to saddle the horse for me. I have to ride over to Northallerton. Well, go on,' he ordered as the housekeeper continued to stare at Eve, 'my sister is not dead. She'll be as right as rain in a minute.'

The body of Miriam Tarleton had been taken to the undertaker in Northallerton and was in the same dank room as that of her husband. While the colonel's coffin had now been nailed down in readiness for his funeral, the remains of his wife were under a shroud on a table. Colbeck had been there during the doctor's examination and he passed on the findings to Leeming in a pub nearby. After the horror of the exhumation, they both felt the need for a restorative drink.

'When the body had been washed,' said Colbeck, 'the doctor found bruising on the neck consistent with her being strangled. Mrs Tarleton was first overpowered so that the sack could be slipped over her head. Then she was shot twice.'

'God rest her soul!' said Leeming before sipping his beer.

'I've sent word to the house so it's only a question of time before her son comes to identify the body. I'll wait for him.'

'Superintendent Tallis needs to be informed as well.'

'That's your job, Victor.'

'Do you want me to write to him, sir?'

'No,' said Colbeck. 'He'll want the full details. You must catch the next train to London and present a full report.'

Leeming was delighted. 'I can go *home?*'

'Only for one day. That's all the time I can spare. You can deliver your report then reacquaint yourself with your wife and children for a night.

However,' he added, 'please don't discuss the case with Estelle. She wants to enjoy her husband's company, not to hear any unpleasant details about two corpses.'

'Thank you, Inspector,' said Leeming. 'This is a treat for me.'

'Let's call it compassionate leave, shall we?'

'Call it what you will – it's an unexpected blessing.'

'There is one other duty for you, Victor.'

'Just tell me what it is.'

'I want you to deliver this,' said Colbeck, slipping a hand into his pocket to take out a letter. 'I think you know how to find a certain house in Camden.'

'It's for Miss Andrews, I presume.'

Colbeck grinned. 'Your detective skills are improving.'

'I'll deliver this first,' said Leeming, taking the letter from him, 'then I'll go straight to Scotland Yard. When am I to return, sir?'

'On the earliest possible train,' replied Colbeck. 'And remember that I have my copy of *Bradshaw* with me so I'll know the precise time when you're due to arrive.'

Clifford Everett was a valued customer at the bank. Whenever he came to make a deposit or to seek financial advice, he was shown straight into the manager's office. On this occasion, he was there to pass on the tidings to Bertram Reader.

'They've found the body at last,' he said.

'Where?' asked Reader with keen interest.

'It was over towards Thornton-le-Beans. Someone from a nearby farm stumbled on it in a wood. He ran miles to South Otterington to raise the alarm. It was Inspector Colbeck and his sergeant who brought the corpse here.'

'And it's definitely Miriam Tarleton?'

'There's no doubt about that, Bertram. Besides, who else's could it be? I'm pleased to say that murder is not exactly an everyday event in the North Riding. I have it on good authority that it's her.'

'How did you get the news?'

'The undertaker is a client of mine. Since I'm the family solicitor for the Tarletons, he felt that I should know at once. By the same token, I thought that you'd appreciate being told.'

'Oh, I do,' said Reader. 'Thank you, Clifford. Most of the work that needs to be done falls within your remit, but there are some financial matters that will need my attention.' He pursed his lips. 'I do hope the children are not expecting vast sums to be on deposit here because, as you well know, that's not the case at all.'

'I did warn the colonel,' said the lawyer, virtuously.

'So did I but there was no holding him back.'

'He lived to regret his bad decisions.'

'I was deeply saddened when he took his own life,' said Reader, 'and I still quake when I recall the manner of his suicide. But at least he's been spared the ordeal of having to identify Miriam's corpse. He loved her to distraction. It would have broken him.'

'Grief had already done that.'

'That's true, Clifford, horribly true.' He

123

reached for some stationery on his desk. 'I must send a note to my wife. Agnes will want to go over to the house to offer her support to Eve – to Mrs Doel, as she now is. There's nobody else who could do that.'

'What about the rector? He's her godfather.'

Reader grimaced. 'Well, he's not acting like one. There's a rumour that he's forbidden the family to bury the colonel in the churchyard. Legally, I don't believe he can do that.'

'He can't,' agreed Everett. 'A Burial Act was passed over thirty years ago, permitting suicides to be interred in consecrated ground.'

'Then he may be forced to back down. Notwithstanding that, it will be very upsetting for Eve and – to a lesser extent – for Adam if the rector digs in his heels and causes trouble. We both know what Mr Skelton can be like when he gets his teeth into something.'

'Hell hath no fury like the rector on a mission.' They traded a laugh. Everett moved away. 'I'll leave you alone to write to your wife. Do please give her my best wishes. Oh,' he went on, pausing at the door, 'there's something I ought to ask you. What am I to expect from the children? I saw very little of them when they lived here. You and Agnes were the people who knew them best.'

'Eve is a delightful woman,' said Reader, fondly. 'Any man would have been proud to have her as a daughter and that's the way that Aubrey looked at her. You'll have no problems with her, Clifford.'

'What about Adam Tarleton?'

Reader rolled his eyes. 'He's a different proposition altogether. I don't think he's done a decent

124

day's work in his entire life. In a word, he's a parasite. He sponged off his mother for years and treated Aubrey appallingly. I don't know why he was christened Adam,' he said, bitterly. 'If they wanted a biblical name for him, a far more appropriate one would have been Cain.'

When the undertaker conducted them into the room, Colbeck stood in a corner and watched. Adam Tarleton spared his stepfather's coffin no more than a cursory glance and his mother claimed little more of his time. As the undertaker drew back the shroud to reveal the ravaged face, Tarleton gazed at it for a brief moment before turning away.

'It's her,' he said.

'Take a proper look, sir,' suggested Colbeck.

'I don't need to, Inspector. I know it's my mother. Apart from anything else, the circumstantial evidence points to her. As far as I'm aware, no other woman of her age has gone missing.'

'Circumstantial evidence can sometimes be misleading, Mr Tarleton. I've seen juries reach unsafe verdicts as a result. I'd advise you to take another look. It's vital that identity is established beyond all doubt by next of kin.'

'It's my mother,' insisted Tarleton, 'and I've no wish to look at her again. This place stinks. I want to get out of here.'

Colbeck followed him out, leaving the undertaker to pull the shroud over the cadaver. When he stepped into the street, Tarleton inhaled deeply. He was in mourning attire but Colbeck didn't feel that he was actually mourning anyone.

'What happens next, Inspector?' asked Tarleton.

'An inquest will be held to establish cause of death.'

'Isn't that obvious? She was murdered.'

'Yes,' said Colbeck, 'but we need to know when, where and how. Those details will help us in our investigation.'

'But you already know them, surely. You found the body.'

'All that we did was to exhume it. The actual discovery was made by a farm labourer. He deserves our gratitude.'

'Well, if he's expecting any money from me,' said Tarleton, harshly, 'he can go whistle for it. And how do you know he really found it? Couldn't it be that he took you to the place where he'd buried the body himself?'

'That never even crossed my mind.'

'It should have, Inspector. Do I have to do your work for you?'

'It never crossed my mind because it would be a ludicrous supposition,' explained Colbeck. 'Mrs Tarleton was killed by a shotgun fired at close range. Where would a farm labourer get such a weapon from? He'd have to steal it. More to the point, where would he acquire the trap that brought the dead body miles from the location of the actual murder? Then there's the farmer who employs him. I think that Mr Higginbottom would surely notice the absence of one of his men for a length of time, especially if he'd been last seen walking towards a trap he didn't own with a stolen shotgun under his arm.'

Tarleton was surly. 'Very well, I was wrong about the fellow.'

'Do you have any other theories to offer, sir?'

'I just want the killer caught and the case cleared up.'

'I'll endeavour to do just that,' said Colbeck, 'and, as part of my investigation, I'd like to question you and your sister. Would you have any objection to my accompanying you back to the house?'

'Is it really necessary, Inspector?'

'I'm afraid that it is, sir.'

'What can we possibly tell you?'

'You might have some idea who could have done this. I know that you moved away some time ago but you must have kept in touch with your mother. Did she hint at any tensions with neighbours?'

'Mother and I had no contact whatsoever for the last two years,' said Tarleton, 'so I can't help you on that score. Everyone liked her, I can tell you that. Those who visited us were mostly her friends. My stepfather was a prickly character. He was better at making enemies than friends.'

'Can you think of any particular enemies?'

'Why should I? He wasn't the murder victim – Mother was.'

'Of course,' said Colbeck, 'but it's not beyond the bounds of possibility that she was killed in order to get back at the colonel. All reports confirm that he doted on your mother.'

'Then why did he control her life so closely?' snapped the other. 'Why did he treat her – and

127

me, I should add – as if we were lowly members of his regiment? He couldn't seem to remember that he was no longer in the army and was always issuing orders of one kind or another. It's the reason I left home.'

'What about your sister?'

'Eve was the exception to the rule,' recalled Tarleton. 'If he doted on anyone, it was her. She was his favourite.'

'I look forward to meeting her. I was impressed by the way she bore up under questioning at the inquest yesterday.'

'She's still quite frail, Inspector. Can't you delay your visit?'

'I'm afraid not, sir. I'm not merely coming in order to talk to you and to Mrs Doel. My visit to the house has another purpose.'

'Oh ... what's that?'

'I want to establish something once and for all,' said Colbeck. 'I need to find out if your step-father should be our prime suspect.'

CHAPTER NINE

Madeleine Andrews was thrilled to receive the letter from Colbeck but her delight was tempered by disappointment when she heard that he might be away from London for a considerable time.

'It could take us an eternity,' admitted Leeming.

'Do you have no clues at all, Sergeant?'

'Well, *I* certainly don't – but I think that the inspector does. That's not unusual, mind you. No matter how puzzling a case, he always manages to find a way to solve it in the end.'

'What sort of a place is South Otterington?'

'It's a pretty little village with countryside all round it. That's why I couldn't wait to get back here. I didn't take to it at all.'

'Why ever not?' she asked. 'It sounds rather attractive.'

'It's a bit too quiet for my liking, Miss Andrews. It's too isolated and nothing ever happens there.'

Madeleine smiled. 'You've had a murder and a suicide in just over a fortnight. What else do you want?'

'I'd like more action,' said Leeming, 'and we get that every day here in London. Yes, there've been two violent deaths, I grant you, but that's exceptional in a backwater like South Otterington. It might never happen again for years. When I was walking my beat in uniform, we'd have a

129

murder at least once a week, not to mention a string of other serious crimes.'

They were in the house in Camden and Leeming had a cab waiting for him outside. Madeleine was very fond of him. Though they'd met infrequently, she liked the way he'd accepted her and was touched by his habit of talking so affectionately about his wife and two children. Leeming was also very discreet. If it became known that Madeleine had actually taken part in some criminal investigations, Superintendent Tallis would have gone berserk. He believed that women had no place at all in law enforcement. Colbeck thought otherwise and Leeming had been grateful for the contribution Madeleine had made in some of the cases they'd handled.

For his part, the sergeant felt honoured to have been the first person to know of their engagement. It had pleased him beyond measure. Over the years he'd worked very closely with Colbeck and had noticed the subtle changes brought about in the inspector by his friendship with Madeleine Andrews. Now that the friendship would blossom into marriage, Leeming knew that, in Madeleine, he'd be acquiring a new colleague, albeit one whose work behind the scenes had to be kept secret. The thought contented him.

'I have to go,' he said. 'I must report to the superintendent.'

'I don't suppose...'

Madeleine's voice tailed off but he read the question in her eyes.

'No, Miss Andrews – the superintendent still hasn't been told of your betrothal. So far Inspector Colbeck hasn't managed to find him in a receptive mood.'

'I know that Mr Tallis has a jaundiced view of marriage.'

'That's because he's never experienced its joys,' said Leeming. 'I only started to live properly when Estelle and I wed. Until then, my life had been narrow and selfish. It had no real purpose. Suddenly, everything changed. I knew where I was going and what I wanted to do. And when the children came along, that made it perfect.'

Madeleine said nothing. She harboured dreams of becoming a mother one day but that time, she'd realised, might be distant. She envied Leeming and his wife. They'd married within months of meeting each other and were parents within a year. She and Colbeck were destined to have a longer engagement. Madeleine understood why Tallis had not yet been told.

'The superintendent will never approve of me,' she said.

'Any normal man would approve of you, Miss Andrews,' said Leeming with clumsy gallantry. 'It's just that Mr Tallis takes a strange view of these things. It's not personal. If the inspector announced that he was about to marry a royal princess, Mr Tallis would still try to talk him out of it. And in my view,' he went on, emboldened to pay a second compliment, 'you are the equal of any princess.'

She almost blushed. 'Thank you, Sergeant.'

'In any case, now is not the time to raise the topic.'

'No.'

131

'Look at what's happened,' he told her. 'The one marriage that the superintendent held up as a success was that between Colonel Tarleton and his wife. Yet both of them died in the most frightful ways. Now, that's hardly likely to endear Mr Tallis to the institution of holy matrimony, is it?'

Colbeck arrived at the house to find that Eve Doel was being consoled by Agnes Reader. Introduced to the bereaved daughter, he hoped that she'd be more forthcoming than her brother. On the journey there in the trap, Adam Tarleton had been less than helpful. All that interested him were the details of his inheritance. After giving his sister a brief description of his visit to Northallerton, he went off upstairs and left the two women alone with Colbeck. All three were comfortably ensconced in the drawing room.

'How did you come to hear of the latest development, Mrs Reader?' asked Colbeck.

'My husband sent me a note from the bank,' she replied. 'He'd been informed by Mr Everett, the lawyer, who, in turn, had been told by Mr Froggatt, the undertaker. In a town like North-allerton, news will spread like wildfire.'

'So I see.'

'You actually unearthed the body, I gather?'

Giving them an attenuated account of what had occurred, Colbeck kept one eye on Eve to make sure that the details were not disturbing her. In fact, she remained calm and unruffled through-out. When he finished, it was she who pressed for information.

'Would she have suffered in any way, Inspector?'

'No, Mrs Doel – death would have been fairly quick.'

'What about her handbag and her jewellery?'

'They'd been buried with her. This wasn't the work of a thief.'

'Then who could it have been?'

'Was it some random act of violence?' asked Agnes.

'There's no suggestion of that, Mrs Reader,' said Colbeck. 'The one thing I can say with certainty is that calculation was involved. The murder was carefully planned. That points to someone local.'

Eve trembled. 'What a dreadful thought!' she cried. 'I shan't be able to sleep properly, knowing that the villain is still out there.'

'I'm hoping that you may be able to help me find him. You, too, Mrs Reader,' he continued, turning to Agnes. 'You know the people and the area. I'm a complete stranger.'

'I left years ago, Inspector,' said Eve.

'But you corresponded regularly with your mother.'

'Yes, I did, and her letters were full of news.'

'Did she ever mention falling out with someone?'

'Mother would never have fallen out with anybody.'

'I can endorse that,' said Agnes. 'Miriam was far too nice a woman to have enemies. It was impossible not to like her. In all the years we knew her, I don't believe I once heard her raise her voice.'

'Oh, she did,' countered Eve. 'Mother raised her voice to me when I broke a mirror by accident and she had to reprove Adam all the time when he was young. But Agnes is right. By and large, she went out of her way to get on with people.'

'What about your stepfather?' asked Colbeck. 'According to your brother, he could cause offence without realising it.'

'He did have a gruff manner, Inspector, I concede that. And he did try to order people about.'

'Can you think of anyone in particular he might have upset?'

'No, I can't.'

'I think I can,' volunteered Agnes. 'I know that he had a fierce row with Eric Hepworth, the railway policeman. Hepworth's daughter had worked here and been dismissed. He felt that the girl should be reinstated and told the colonel so to his face. I remember Miriam recounting the story to me. Hepworth was very angry, it seems.'

'I've met Sergeant Hepworth,' said Colbeck. 'He told us that his daughter, Ginny, had worked here but there was no mention of an argument with the colonel.'

'It certainly took place,' confirmed Eve. 'Mother wrote to me about it. She felt that Hepworth should've shown more respect.'

'Is there anyone else who crossed swords with your father?'

'I can't think of anybody, Inspector.'

'What about the stationmaster?' suggested Agnes.

'What about him?'

'He and your stepfather had words about something or other. I remember it well. When Bertram and I came to play cards here that same evening, Aubrey was still seething. Apparently, he threatened to have the man dismissed for insolence.'

'Are we talking about Mr Ellerby?' asked Colbeck.

'That's the man, Inspector – Silas Ellerby.'

'He didn't strike me as the argumentative type.'

'Men can change when drink is taken. I've seen it happen.'

'So have I, Mrs Reader,' said Colbeck, ruefully. 'Alcohol causes more crime than almost anything else. It removes inhibitions. When a man has too much beer inside him, he surrenders to his demons.'

'And he forgets the need for deference,' complained Agnes. 'My husband has encountered that at the bank. He had to dismiss one of his clerks last year for being drunk and unruly.'

'Coming back to the colonel, you've given me two names so far.'

'I can't add to them,' said Eve with a shrug.

Colbeck looked at Agnes. 'Mrs Reader?'

There was a long pause as Agnes wondered if she should offer another name. Consideration for Eve told her to say nothing but she felt that the incident ought to be out in the open. At length, she reached her decision, prefacing her words with a warning.

'I don't want you to imagine for a second that this person is even remotely connected with the crime,' she began, 'because that is frankly impossible. But there is someone with whom

Aubrey was at loggerheads for a time.'

'And who was that?' pressed Colbeck.

'It was the rector, Mr Skelton.'

'I never heard about any dissension between them,' said Eve.

'Your mother was too embarrassed to tell you. After all, the rector is your godfather. You looked up to him. Miriam didn't want to alarm you with tales of a rift.'

'What caused the rift, Agnes?'

'It was some trifling matter over a donation to the church. It blew up out of all proportions. Bertram tried to intercede and pour oil on troubled waters but his efforts were in vain.'

Eve was shaken. 'I knew none of this,' she said. 'It might explain why the rector told me at the inquest that my stepfather was not welcome in his churchyard. He refuses to have him buried there.'

'He said the same to me,' explained Colbeck, 'but I shouldn't let it upset you, Mrs Doel. The church is in the diocese of York so there's a court of appeal in the person of the archbishop. I fancy that he'll rap the rector over the knuckles about this.'

'All the same, it's very unnerving.'

'Mr Skelton can be very unchristian at times,' observed Agnes.

'It was certainly a shock when he confronted me yesterday.'

'You have my sympathy, Mrs Doel,' said Colbeck. 'It was both wrong and inconsiderate of him to accost you at a time like that. A man whose profession involves comforting the bereaved should

136

know better. I hadn't realised that personal animus came into it.'

'No more did I,' said Eve.

Casting the conversational net wider, Colbeck got them to talk about friends and acquaintances of the Tarletons in other parts of the county. It emerged that they had a relatively wide social circle but that, as time passed, several of their friends had fallen away. Neither Eve nor Agnes could offer any explanation for this beyond the fact that the colonel might inadvertently have upset them by being too brusque. When he felt that he'd drawn all he could out of them, Colbeck had a request to put forward.

'When we first called here,' he said, 'the housekeeper showed us the colonel's arsenal. It's a fearsome assembly of weapons. I wonder if I might have a look at them again?'

'Of course, you may,' said Eve. 'Mrs Withers will take you there. Are you looking for anything in particular, Inspector?'

'Yes,' replied Colbeck. 'I'm searching for inspiration.'

Leeming had long ago learnt an important lesson about Edward Tallis. The worst time to enter his room was when you were the bearer of bad tidings. Knowing that he was about to cause distress to the superintendent, Leeming hovered outside the door for minutes before finally plucking up the courage to knock.

'Come in!' roared an unwelcoming voice.

Leeming opened the door. 'Good day to you, sir.'

'What on earth are *you* doing here, Sergeant?'

'I was told to deliver a report in person. The body of Mrs Tarleton was found during the night.'

Tallis sat up with interest. 'How and where?' he demanded. 'Close the door, man, and sit down. I want to hear all the details. What state was the body in?'

'I'll come to that, sir,' said Leeming, shutting the door and perching on the edge of a chair. 'What happened was this.'

On the train journey back, he'd spent a considerable time rehearsing what he was going to say and, on Colbeck's advice, had made some notes so that he had the sequence of events in order. Faced with Tallis, however, and hit by a steady stream of questions from the hectoring superintendent, he faltered. Forgetting certain details, he repeated others unnecessarily and beads of sweat began to break out on his forehead. He expected a reprimand for being so confused but Tallis had no criticism to offer. Grateful that the news had been delivered to him, he rose to his feet.

'I'll return to the village this very evening,' he declared.

'That's the last thing you must do, sir.'

'Now that we have a body, the investigation has moved on.'

'And it will move on even further if Inspector Colbeck and I are allowed to continue on our own. We are impartial observers. You are not, sir. You suffered the agonies of one inquest,' said Leeming. 'Do you really wish to endure a second one?'

Tallis pondered. 'Probably not, if I'm honest,' he conceded.

'Then spare yourself, sir. Put your trust in us.'

'I just feel that I should be *there*.'

'That means you'd want your room at the Black Bull,' thought Leeming, moaning inwardly. 'I'm not going back to the Swan. I'd rather sleep in a tent than put up with that place again. It was unhealthy.' He saw the pile of papers on the desk. And spoke aloud. 'You look as if you're busy, sir.'

'I am,' said Tallis. 'We've had assaults, robberies, damage to property and a case of arson to investigate. Then there's an alleged rape in Hyde Park.' His voice became a whisper. 'When Miriam — Mrs Tarleton, that is – was examined, was there any evidence of sexual interference?'

'There was none whatsoever, sir.'

'Thank heaven for that!'

'And nothing was stolen from her.'

'Apart from her life, of course – that's the most monstrous theft of all.' Tallis stared at the mound of papers. 'By rights, I should stay here to supervise the investigation of these crimes. But I feel that I have an obligation to some dear friends.'

'The only obligation you have is to see the colonel's name cleared and to make sure that his wife's killer is caught. The best way you can do that,' Leeming went on, amazed at the confidence now surging through him, 'is to leave everything to us. As long as you're there, you'll be holding us up without meaning to do so.'

'There may be some truth in that, Leeming.'

'Does that mean I can go back there alone?'

'Yes, it does. Here, I'm desperately needed;

139

there, I'll be nothing but a handicap.' He sat down again. 'I'll stay. But I'll want regular reports,' he warned, 'even if you have to send them by telegraph.'

Leeming got up. 'We'll keep you fully informed, sir.'

'Thank you. I appreciate your coming here like this.'

'It was no trouble at all,' said the sergeant as something jogged his memory. 'By the way, did you know that there's a village in the North Riding that's named after me? It's called Leeming.'

Tallis scowled. 'Does this have anything to do with the case in hand?' Leeming shook his head. 'Then get out of here and don't introduce irrelevant material into a police report again. I don't care if there's a herd of sheep named after you. It's beside the point.' He banged the table. 'Well, don't just stand there, man. Clear off.'

As he fled through the door, Leeming gave a smile of relief. The superintendent was back to something like his old self. His anger was reassuring. Tallis might not be interested in a village called Leeming but the sergeant knew someone at home who would be. When he left Scotland Yard, he was brimming with joy.

Margery Withers led him to the room for the second time and took the opportunity to gather information from Colbeck.

'Is it true that nothing will now be confiscated?' she asked.

'That's right,' said Colbeck. 'When a verdict of suicide while the victim is *non compos mentis* is

140

reached, no seizure is exercised on his property. Everything will pass to his heirs.'

'Oh, I'm so pleased to hear that.'

'The evidence given was honest and compelling. On the basis of that, the correct verdict was unavoidable. Unhappily, that's not always been the case at inquests.'

'What are you talking about, Inspector?'

'Fraud, Mrs Withers, the impulse in some people to tell the most outrageous lies in order to get every penny left behind by a deceased relative. No family wants to admit that any member of it was so unhappy with his or her life that suicide was the only option left to them. It would be a terrible stigma,' said Colbeck. 'So they'll go out of their way to convince a jury that someone who's perfectly sane was, in fact, completely mad. That way, they gain sympathy and lose nothing of the inheritance.'

'That's criminal, Inspector.'

'It's the way of the world, I fear.' He looked around. 'This really is a fine collection. Some of it should be in a museum.'

'Young Mr Tarleton has talked of selling some items.'

'What's that you're saying about me, Mrs Withers?' asked Adam Tarleton, coming into the room. 'And why are you in here?'

'It was at my request, sir,' explained Colbeck.

'And what could possibly interest you in this place?'

'I wanted to see the firearms again.'

'I have the keys if you wish to open any of the cabinets,' said Mrs Withers. 'The colonel entrusted them to me.'

Tarleton laughed. 'What she means,' he said, 'is that he told her where they were hidden. I wasn't supposed to know, you see. The shotguns were out of bounds to me. My stepfather thought that I was too irresponsible to be given a loaded weapon.'

'Did you mind that?' asked Colbeck.

'I minded very much, Inspector. It was one of the many ways in which he sought to keep me down. Will you require the keys?'

'No, I don't think so.'

'There you are, Mrs Withers,' said Tarleton, rounding on her. 'You can leave them in their hiding place – but only until I ask for them.' He waved a hand. 'Off you go.'

'Yes, sir,' she said, withdrawing quickly.

'So, Inspector, what did you wish to see?'

'Those boxes behind you, sir,' said Colbeck, pointing to the shelf. 'It looks to me as if your stepfather was very methodical. Everything seems to have been clearly marked.'

'He was obsessed with order. Even little things annoyed him. If any of the knives and forks were not perfectly aligned on the dining table, for instance, he'd castigate one of the servants for hours.'

'Yes, you had more of them in the old days.'

'In the old days,' echoed Tarleton, 'we had money.'

'Where did it all go?'

'I'm hoping to find that out myself, Inspector.' He moved aside. 'But don't let me come between you and your interest in those boxes of ammunition.'

'It's only one box that I want to examine, sir.'

'Is there any special reason?'

'There are two of them,' said Colbeck, opening a hand to show him the spent cartridges he was holding, 'and here they both are. I recovered these from the shallow grave in which your mother was buried.'

Tarleton was startled. 'Oh,' he said, 'I didn't realise that you were here as part of your investigation. What are you trying to prove?'

'I just want to satisfy my curiosity, sir. On the day that your mother went missing, your step-father was carrying a shotgun.' He indicated one of the cabinets. 'In all likelihood, it was that Purdey with his initials carved on it. I gather that it was his favourite. Major Tallis, as he was known here, told me that he'd seen the colonel take this particular weapon out regularly so it's logical to assume that he had it with him on the day in question. Thanks to the way he's marked these boxes,' he went on, reaching to take one off the shelf, 'we know that this is the correct ammunition. Would you care to open the box for me, sir?'

'I will if you insist, Inspector.' Taking the box, Tarleton opened it. 'What am I supposed to do now?'

'Put one of the cartridges into my hand.'

Colbeck extended an empty palm and Tarleton placed a shotgun cartridge into it. For the first time since he'd arrived back at his old home, he'd lost some of his arrogance. He watched as the inspector put the two spent cartridges beside the other one.

'Well?' said Colbeck.

Tarleton blanched. 'It's a perfect match.'

'And what do you deduce from that?'

'The old rogue killed my mother!'

'That's not what I see, sir.'

'Open your eyes, man. It's so obvious.'

'It's rather *too* obvious for my liking. What you see is proof of your stepfather's guilt. What I see, however,' said Colbeck, looking at the cartridges, 'is clear evidence that he was completely innocent of the crime. Colonel Tarleton did not commit murder.'

When he got back from work that evening, Caleb Andrews found his daughter hunched over the table with a pen in her hand. Taking off his cap and his coat, he hung them on a peg.

'Who are you writing to, Maddy?' he asked.

'Who else would I write to but Robert?'

'Do you know his address?'

'I know more than that,' she said, looking up. 'I even know which room he's staying in at the Black Bull. I had a letter from him, delivered in person by Sergeant Leeming.'

'Is he the ugly one with a face like death?'

'I think he has a rather kind face.'

'You wouldn't think that if it jumped out of an alleyway at you on a dark night. Anyway, what did the inspector say?'

'That he's going to be away for some time.'

'Well, you can tell him that your father wants to know when the wedding is going to be.'

'I'll tell him nothing of the kind.'

'There are times when a man needs prodding along.'

144

'Living with you has taught me that,' said Madeleine, signing the letter before folding it to put it in an envelope. 'You need to be prodded more or less every day.' She sealed the envelope. 'There – it's all done.'

'Aren't you going to address it, Maddy?'

'I don't need to. I have a courier.'

'Oh ... and who's that?'

'It's Sergeant Leeming, of course.'

'I'd never trust a man with a face like that.'

'He's the most trustworthy man you could find, Father.'

'Is he going back to Yorkshire, then?'

'Yes,' said Madeleine, 'he's leaving tomorrow on the early train. That brings me to your breakfast. You'll have to eat it on your own when you get up. It will be set out for you.'

'Where will you be?'

'I'll be walking to King's Cross, of course.'

'Won't the sergeant pick up the letter from here?'

'He doesn't even know that I've written it. But since he told me which train he'd be on, I'll be able to intercept him and use him as my courier. My letter will go speeding to Robert.'

'Does it mention that *I* was thinking of looking for a bride?'

Madeleine blinked. 'Are you really serious about that, Father?'

'Of course,' said Andrews, chortling, 'and you should use that fact to give the inspector a good, hard prod. Otherwise, you could be getting yourself a stepmother before you have a husband.'

Eve Doel and Agnes Reader were stunned by the information that the cartridges found in the shallow grave matched those used by the colonel in his favourite shotgun. They reached the same devastating conclusion as Adam Tarleton. Holding her stomach as if she were about to be sick, Eve shook her head in disbelief.

'He simply *couldn't* have done it,' she said.

'Oh, yes, he could,' asserted her brother. 'The more I think about it, the more certain of it I am. Our stepfather was a killer.'

Agnes was dazed. 'I find it hard to accept that, Adam.'

'The only shotgun that uses those particular cartridges is the one with his initials on it. He used to boast how it'd been made specifically for him with features that no other gun possessed. That's why he committed suicide,' he argued. 'He felt so guilty over Mother's death that he took his own life.'

'No, no!' cried Eve, 'I simply don't believe it.'

'You don't *have* to believe it, Mrs Doel,' said Colbeck, 'because it just isn't true.'

The four of them were in the drawing room. Tarleton had burst in and told the women that the name of the killer had been revealed at last. It was none other than that of his stepfather.

'Don't listen to the inspector,' advised Tarleton. 'He didn't know him the way that I did. I saw the swirling anger that was just below the surface. I was the victim of that black rage of his many times. It was scary. When he lost his temper, he was capable of anything. After all, he was a soldier – he used to kill for a living.'

'Stop and think for a moment, sir,' counselled Colbeck. 'The first thing apparent about this case was that the killer was not acting on impulse. This crime wasn't perpetrated in a fit of temper. He looked ahead. Knowing that the route taken by your mother that day would be searched with a fine-toothed comb, he moved the body miles away. It was only by sheer chance that it was actually found. The killer even allowed for that eventuality.'

'In what way, Inspector?' asked Agnes.

'He left these by the body.' He opened his palm to show off the two spent cartridges. 'Now ask yourselves this. Why would a man shoot his victim in one place then take these some distance away so that he could bury them with the corpse? As far as I can see, there's only one explanation.'

'I fail to see it,' confessed Eve.

'So do I,' said Agnes.

'Permit me to explain,' said Colbeck. 'The killer deliberately wanted to incriminate someone else. Cartridges are important clues. He knew that. By planting them with the body, he could point the finger of suspicion at the colonel and thereby avoid culpability himself. How convenient it would be for the real killer if we all believed that the man who murdered Mrs Tarleton was already dead.'

'I still think it was him,' maintained Tarleton.

'Then you have to provide a motive, sir.'

'He and Mother fell out.'

'That's not true, Adam,' said Eve, passionately. 'If it had been, I'd have heard about it.'

'Would you consider the colonel to have been

an intelligent man?' asked Colbeck.

'Yes, Inspector, he was very intelligent.'

'He was intelligent but pig-headed,' said her brother.

'Then picture this situation,' suggested Colbeck. 'If an intelligent man wishes to dispose of his wife, would he be stupid enough to be seen walking alone with her and carrying his shotgun? In short, would he advertise the murder in advance?'

'No,' said Eve, firmly, 'of course not. Even you must agree with that, Adam.'

'I suppose so,' said her brother, sourly.

'And look at the colonel's behaviour afterwards,' Colbeck went on. 'Had he been the killer and tormented by guilt, he wouldn't have committed suicide. He's much more likely to have confessed the crime and faced execution. Do you know one of the things that drove him to do what he did?'

'He received poison-pen letters,' replied Agnes.

'That's quite right, Mrs Reader.'

'Aubrey told my husband about them. He said they were so vile that he asked Mrs Withers to burn them.'

'Not all of them, as it happens,' said Colbeck. 'We still have the last letter sent to him. It not only accuses the colonel of murder, but of other unspeakable crimes as well.' He produced the letter from his coat. 'I wouldn't dare let any of you read it but I'd like you to examine the handwriting on the envelope to see if you recognise it.' He gave it to Tarleton. 'It was written by somebody from the area. Have you ever seen that

148

hand before, sir?'

'Never,' said Tarleton, passing it to his sister.

'I don't recognise it either,' said Eve scrutinising it. 'What about you, Agnes? Does it look familiar to you?'

Agnes looked at the calligraphy and shook her head. 'No, I'm sorry. I can't tell you who wrote that, Inspector.' She gave it back to him. 'But it was someone with a warped mind.'

'He's not the only one. Other people sent poison-pen letters. Who knows? The killer may have been one of them, trying to put the colonel under intolerable strain that would lead him to take his own life.' He glanced at Tarleton. 'Even now, I fear, there are still people making the cruel assumption that the colonel was a killer.'

'The real murderer must be very cunning,' decided Agnes. 'He seems to have worked out everything in advance.'

'That's because he underestimated us, Mrs Reader. He thought that, if the body were to be discovered, the presence of the cartridges would be proof positive to everyone that Colonel Tarleton was the villain of the piece. In my humble opinion,' said Colbeck, 'he most assuredly was not. The killer's ruse has therefore failed. In setting it up, he gave himself away.'

Eve was astounded. 'You *know* who he is, Inspector?'

'I know where to start looking for him, Mrs Doel.'

'And where's that?'

'Among the small group of people who ever joined a shooting party with the colonel. That's

149

how they'd be able to pick up his spent cartridges. You see,' he added, displaying the ammunition again, 'I don't believe that these were used in the murder at all. Your mother was shot by a different weapon altogether.'

CHAPTER TEN

Eric Hepworth would never be welcome at the Black Bull in South Otterington. The landlord resented his lordly manner, the landlord's wife disliked the way he ogled her and other customers were unsettled by the presence of a policeman. Even on the few occasions when Hepworth had changed out of his uniform, he could still discourage people from entering the bar. He loomed large and tended to force his way into private conversations. As long as he was in the Black Bull, its patrons felt that they were under surveillance. Still in uniform that evening, and with his top hat resting on the counter, he nursed a pint of beer and engaged in desultory chat with the landlord while keeping a beady eye on the door. The moment that Colbeck eventually came through it, Hepworth took a step towards him and manufactured an ingratiating smile.

'What can I get you, Inspector?' he invited.

'I want nothing for the moment, thank you,' said Colbeck, 'but I would appreciate a word with you, Sergeant Hepworth.'

'You can have as many as you wish, sir.'

'Shall we sit over here?'

Colbeck indicated a table in the corner and they sat down either side of it. Stroking his beard, Hepworth cocked an ear, hoping to hear privileged information about the investigation.

151

'Have you made any headway?' he asked.

'I think so.'

'What have you found out?'

'Lots of things,' said Colbeck. 'One of them concerns you.'

Hepworth was wary. 'Don't believe all the gossip you hear around here, Inspector. You know what it's like when you wear a police uniform. You get all kinds of nasty comments.'

'This was not gossip. It came from an impeccable source.'

'And what has someone been saying about me?'

'That you and the colonel once exchanged harsh words.'

'Most of his words were harsh,' said Hepworth, curling a lip. 'I was one of the few people in the village with the courage to stand up to him. He treated my daughter bad. Nobody does that without hearing from me.'

'The argument was about her dismissal, I understand.'

'He had the gall to say that Ginny was lazy. You've never met a more hard-working girl. She cried for days when he threw her out of there. Well,' he continued, nodding towards the window, 'you've seen the size of the village. If someone loses her job like that, everyone knows about it and there's not much else a girl like Ginny can do but go into domestic service. Who'll take her on now? Ginny's got a reputation for idleness that she just doesn't deserve. I felt I had to point that out to the colonel.'

'How did he respond?'

'He told me it was none of my business.'

'As the girl's father, you had a legitimate interest.'

'That's what I said. I didn't expect him to take her on again, of course. All that I wanted from him was a letter to say that she'd given good service. She needed a reference, Inspector.'

'Clearly,' said Colbeck, 'he refused to give it.'

'He did more than that, sir. He flew off the handle and started calling me names. He threatened to report me for insubordination, as if I was a soldier in his regiment. I wasn't standing for that,' growled Hepworth, eyes kindling at an unpleasant memory, 'so I told him what I really thought about him.'

'What happened then?'

'He said that I should be horsewhipped for my insolence but he wasn't stupid enough to raise a hand against me. In the end, he just stalked off. I came in here to cool down with a couple of pints.'

'Weren't you afraid there'd be some retaliation?'

Hepworth stuck out his chest. 'I wasn't afraid of anything.'

'Did he try to get you dismissed?'

'If he did, he failed. I've got an excellent record of service. They'd be idiots to part with someone of my experience.'

'I'm sure they realised that,' said Colbeck, with gentle sarcasm. 'But why was there an allegation of laziness against your daughter if it wasn't true?'

'I think it came from that old harpy, Mrs Withers. She made my daughter work every hour that God sends. Ginny was expected to fetch, carry, wash, clean, fill this, empty that and do a dozen other chores. The girl was exhausted.' Hepworth lowered his voice. 'Then, of course, there was the other business.'

'What other business, Sergeant?'

'I told you. Ginny knew about the colonel and his housekeeper. When she realised their secret might come out, Mrs Withers invented an excuse to have Ginny dismissed.'

Colbeck was sceptical. 'That interpretation of facts,' he said, 'only holds water if there really *was* some intimacy between the colonel and Mrs Withers. Having met the housekeeper, I find it hard to believe that she'd engage in any kind of impropriety and events have shown that theory to be wildly eccentric.'

'Ginny saw what she saw, Inspector.'

'But she saw it through rather bleary eyes if she was close to exhaustion most of the time. According to you, Mrs Tarleton learnt of this clandestine romance and fled the house.' He leant forward. 'How do you explain the fact that we exhumed her body early this morning and confirmed that she was a murder victim?'

'The colonel must have killed her,' argued Hepworth, wagging a finger. 'He had to silence his wife before she told everyone what was going on in the house.'

'Colonel Tarleton did *not* commit murder,' said Colbeck with rasping authority. 'I'm absolutely certain of that. Nor did he develop an inappropriate interest in his housekeeper. Your daughter only imagined that. What drove him to take his life was grief over the loss of a beloved wife. It's reprehensible of you to blacken his name with hints of scandal at the house.'

'I haven't blackened his name,' denied Hepworth, squirming under the reproach. 'I merely reported what Ginny sensed. You and Sergeant Leeming are the only people I told, I swear it. And even though the colonel and I had that argument, I was more than ready to help when his wife first went missing.'

'Yes,' recalled Colbeck, 'I believe you were paid for that.'

'It wasn't just me. He offered money to everyone who'd take part. But that wasn't what made me give up my free time to join the search. I felt sorry for the man.'

'Weren't you still angry that he'd dismissed your daughter?'

'It was a crisis, Inspector,' said Hepworth, righteously. 'In those circumstances, you forget petty differences. I forgot about Ginny and I even overlooked what he did to Sam.'

'Who is Sam?'

'He's my lad. Though he's a bit slow between the ears, he's very willing and does all sorts of jobs around here to earn an honest penny. One of the things Sam liked most was going on a shooting party.'

Colbeck's interest was sparked. 'Why was that?'

'He always used to carry the colonel's gun for him. Until I had the argument over Ginny, that is,' Hepworth went on. 'Next time he tried to go out with a shooting party, Sam was sent packing by that vindictive old curmudgeon. So you see,' he said as if he'd just been exonerated, 'I was ready to forgive and forget. That's the kind of man Eric Hepworth is.' He patted his chest. 'I have a big heart, Inspector.'

Refreshed and restored by a night in his wife's arms, Victor Leeming arrived at a railway station for once with a modicum of enthusiasm. When he entered the maelstrom that was King's Cross, he was still beaming. Built only a few years earlier as a terminus for the Great Northern Railway, the station was on a cramped site with tunnels close to the platform ends. What caught the eye of any newcomer, however, were the two vast glazed arches that spanned the whole structure and gave it a sense of space and wonder. Having gone there reluctantly on the previous occasion, Leeming now found a moment to look upwards and gape. He was still marvelling at the construction when someone tugged at the sleeve of his frock coat.

'Good morning,' said Madeleine Andrews, voice raised above the general hubbub.

He was astonished. 'I never thought I'd see you here.'

'I came in the hope of catching you. I was lucky. In a crowd like this, I could easily have missed you.'

'And you came on your *own?*'

'Yes, I walked along the towpath from Camden.'

'That's a very dangerous thing for a young woman to do,' he said, worriedly. 'You should really have had someone with you.'

'There were plenty of people about and lots of

barges on the canal. I sensed no danger. Besides,' she went on, 'I was anxious to give you this.' She handed over her letter. 'Could you deliver it for me, please?'

He glanced at the name on the envelope. 'The inspector will be delighted to receive this. Though he never talks about it, I know that he misses you as much as I miss Estelle.'

'Was your wife pleased to see you last night?'

'She was overjoyed, Miss Andrews, and so were the children. It was a lovely surprise for them.'

'My lovely surprise came in the form of a letter. That's why I felt I had to reply to it.' They moved aside to get away from the crush of bodies. 'I do hope this case won't take as long as you fear.'

'So do I,' he said. 'Inspector Colbeck is very tenacious. He'll not rest until the murder is solved. Even in the time I've been away, he'll have made progress.'

'The people I feel sorry for are the children. To lose their mother must have been an awful shock. Before they recovered from that, their stepfather committed suicide in the most horrible way. It seems such a strange thing to do, walking along a railway track.'

'It certainly left nothing to chance.'

'Why did he do it?'

'The Inspector believes that he was sending a message.'

'What sort of message?'

'We haven't found that out yet, Miss Andrews.'

'Did the colonel have some connection with railways?'

'None that I know of,' said Leeming, looking

down a platform at a waiting train. 'Anyway, I'm afraid that I can't stop now. My train leaves in a few minutes. I'll have to go.'

'Of course, Sergeant – I'm sorry to hold you up.'

'I don't want to miss it. After all, I have an important letter to deliver.' He held up the envelope. 'The inspector will want to see it at the earliest possible opportunity. In fact, if I know him, he'll be waiting at the station to meet me.'

Colbeck sat on a bench at South Otterington station and watched the passengers climbing on board a train to York. Railways had always held a fascination for him. He never ceased to be amazed at the way steam had conquered distance, putting the entire country within the grasp of every traveller. He loved the constant bustle, the earsplitting clamour and the distinctive smell of stations like Euston, Paddington and Waterloo. Here, in this corner of the North Riding, he'd found the perfect antidote to the large, enclosed London termini with their daily pandemonium. This station was tiny by comparison, open to the skies and intensely personal. As the village's link with the outside world, it performed a valuable function without detracting from the sense of a tightly knit and self-supporting community.

Once the stationmaster had despatched the train, Colbeck felt able to stroll across to him. Silas Ellerby gave him a warm greeting.

'Good morning to you, Inspector!'

'Good morning to *you*, Mr Ellerby,' said Colbeck, noticing that his cheeks looked more rubicund than ever. 'I envy you.'

Ellerby laughed. 'You're the first person who's ever done that.'

'You work in such pleasant surroundings, you see fresh faces every day and you exert such power over those hissing monsters we call locomotives. Once they're here, they're under your control.'

'You've only been watching me on a fine summer's day, sir. This is not such a pleasant place to work in the winter when the rain pours down and the wind sweeps through. As for the so-called fresh faces, they're usually the same ones every day. You and the sergeant are the only strangers to come here in the last month. I'm the one who envies *you*, Inspector,' said Ellerby. 'Making trains leave on time is important but it's not as exciting as the work that you do.'

'Being a detective has its drawbacks as well.'

'What sort of drawbacks?'

'Well, you have to ask searching questions that people don't want to answer. You have to delve into their private lives and they resent that.'

'That's only if they have something to hide, Inspector. When you have a clear conscience like me, you don't mind any questions.'

'In that case, I'll put one to you, if I may.'

'Then you can count on a straight answer, sir.'

'Is it true that you and the colonel once locked horns?'

Ellerby chuckled. 'Yes, it is, as a matter of fact,' he admitted. 'Luckily, I had some beer inside me and that always fires me up.'

'What was the argument about?'

'I can't remember all the details. I was too drunk at the time. But it was something to do with getting him home when his horse went lame. What did he expect me to do?' asked the stationmaster. 'Get between the shafts and pull the bloody trap for him? In any case, I was off duty that night so nobody was going to order me about. All he had to do was bang on the black-mith's door but that was beneath him. He ordered me to fetch another horse. When I refused, he was furious and told me he'd get the company to sack me. I forget what I said exactly,' said Ellerby, grinning broadly, 'but it did the trick. He went storming off in a rage.'

Colbeck warmed to the stationmaster. His red cheeks, bloodshot eyes and purple-veined nose hinted that he was a heavy drinker but it didn't seem to impair him in the exercise of his duties. When at work, he was polite, affable and efficient. From the cheerful way passengers had greeted him, Colbeck had seen how popular the little man was. What was not visible was the truculent streak that allowed Ellerby to take on a man who was effectively the local squire.

'I've been talking to the colonel's housekeeper,' said Colbeck. 'On the day he committed suicide, he told her that he was catching a train to Doncaster.'

'Oh, he often did that at one time, Inspector.'

'It seems an odd thing to do. Doncaster is pre-eminently a railway town. When the Great Northern Railway built their works there, they increased the population by thousands. They took over completely. I wouldn't have thought the town held any interest for the colonel.'

'Nor me,' said Ellerby, 'but he went there fairly regular. Well, until a year or so ago, he did. All of a sudden, he stopped. I always assumed he must have a friend there – a retired army man like him.'

Colbeck was not persuaded. 'Who would choose to spend his retirement in Doncaster? Think of the noise and the clouds of smoke coming from the Plant. Then there's the stink of industry. It's hardly a restful place to live.'

'The colonel must have had his reasons for going there.'

'What about his wife? Did she ever accompany him?'

'No,' said Ellerby. 'They rarely travelled together. While her husband went south, Mrs Tarleton used to go north from time to time. She had a cousin in Edinburgh. She won't be catching the train to Scotland again.'

'By now, I daresay, all of her relations will have been informed of the tragedies that occurred here. You'll soon have a lot of fresh faces coming to the village.'

'When will the funerals be held?'

'Not until after the inquest into Mrs Tarleton's death.'

'They'll be buried side by side in the churchyard, no doubt.'

'Actually,' said Colbeck, 'there is a doubt.'

'They're husband and wife. They must be together.'

'There's no problem with regard to Mrs Tarleton. She'll be buried with full Christian rites

161

in consecrated ground. The colonel's case is somewhat different, alas. He committed suicide and that is anathema to certain people. They feel that it's wrong for him to be buried in the churchyard.'

'They can't stop it happening, though, can they?'

'Only for a short while, Mr Ellerby,' Colbeck assured him. 'Once resistance is overcome, husband and wife will lie side by side.'

Husband and wife knelt side by side at the altar rail in St Andrew's church. Hands clasped in prayer and heads bent in humility, Frederick and Dorcas Skelton sent their pleas up to heaven in unison. Less than a decade earlier, the church had been rebuilt in its original Norman style. The result was striking. Its nave was divided from its north aisle by three moulded arches rising from slender, round pillars. The church boasted a chancel, a square tower and a porch, all finished in decorated stone. Both the pulpit and the lectern were extravagantly ornamented with deeply recessed arches and zigzag or dog-tooth moulding. It was an archetypal House of God and its two occupants were statues of Christian virtue.

It was the rector who got up first, rising to his full height before genuflecting to the cross. His wife soon followed, making light of the twinges in her knees. Having entered in silence, they also left without a word being spoken. Only when they reached the privacy of the rectory did Skelton finally initiate a conversation.

'We must be steadfast,' he insisted.

'I agree, Frederick,' she said.

'And we must move to persuade others of the rightness of our cause. The churchwardens will support me, naturally. I can always rely on their loyalty. But there must be many like-minded people hereabouts. Bringing them together will put us in a stronger position.'

'My only concern is for the children.'

'They must accept my decision, Dorcas.'

'They'll find it hard to do so, especially as it comes from their godfather. They'll feel let down. It would be much easier if only one funeral were involved,' she pointed out with her telltale sniff. 'Unfortunately, there are two. What you are telling them is that one of their parents is welcome to be buried here, but not the other.'

'The colonel was not their father.'

'He was to all intents and purposes, Frederick.'

'Not in my eyes,' he said, using both hands to brush back his mane. 'When her first husband died, I believe that Miriam should never have remarried, least of all to someone as worldly as the colonel. She should have embraced widow-hood, as I'm sure you would have done in the same circumstances.'

'Yes, of course,' she said, dutifully.

'It would have shown respect for her deceased spouse. After all, their union had been blessed. They had two children. Miriam had everything that a woman needs. Why did she even think of taking another husband?'

'She told me that it was a question of security.'

'Yet she had money of her own and was well provided for.'

'I didn't mean it in that way,' she explained. 'She wanted the security of a father for the children, someone who'd offer love and support.'

Skelton was critical. 'Well, he certainly offered support,' he said, 'I'll give him that. As for love, I remain unconvinced. I don't think the colonel loved anything except shooting game and sending people to prison for their crimes.'

'I'm sure that Miriam loved him – in her own way.'

'But did he love *her*, Dorcas? That's what I ask. I saw no sign of true devotion to his wife. What little affection he could muster was lavished on Eve.' An eyebrow arched. 'I fancy that we both know why he didn't waste any of it on Adam.'

'Adam doesn't deserve affection,' she said, sharply.

'Now, now, my dear, show some Christian forbearance.'

'He's so exasperating, Frederick.'

'That was largely because he was in rebellion against the colonel. His character may have improved with the passage of time. Adam is more mature now. All of a sudden, he has responsibilities. It could be the making of him.'

'I hardly think so. I watched him at the inquest. He still had that same sullen look about him.' She put a hand on his arm. 'He could make trouble for you.'

'I'm not afraid of Adam Tarleton.'

'Eve might accept your judgement but her brother certainly will not. He'll fight you tooth and nail, Frederick.'

'Please, Dorcas,' he said, reprovingly, 'that's a

very ugly image. We're not wild animals, competing for a bone. The whole business can, I remain hopeful, be conducted with rational argument. Even someone as defiant as Adam Tarleton will come to see that I have moral authority on my side.'

She was anxious. 'What about the law?'

'I obey the law of the Almighty.'

'What if you are overruled?'

'I have faith that I won't be, Dorcas.'

'But if you are,' she went on, searching for guidance. 'If you are overruled and forced to let the colonel lie beside his wife in the churchyard, what will we do then?'

'I know exactly what *I'll* do.'

And what's that?'

'If the colonel is buried against my will in the churchyard,' he said with unexpected savagery, 'I'll come back in the middle of the night and dig him up again. That's how strongly I feel on this issue, Dorcas. I simply won't have him here.'

Leeming was amazed how much information Colbeck had gathered while the sergeant had been away in London. The visit to the house had eliminated the colonel as a possible suspect and the encounter with Eric Hepworth had yielded some valuable intelligence. Leeming was interested to learn that Hepworth's son had been the colonel's gun-bearer during shooting parties. For his part, Colbeck was pleased to see his friend again and touched to receive Madeleine's letter. When he heard that she'd walked all the way to King's Cross station in order to hand it over, he was impressed by her enterprise.

'How did you get on with the superintendent?' he asked.

'Quite well, I suppose,' replied Leeming. 'At least I stopped him coming back here to lead the investigation.'

'Thank you. Victor. That would have been fatal.'

'He was quite restrained for once – until I made the mistake of telling him that there was a village called Leeming, that is. He nearly burst my ear-drums then.'

Colbeck laughed. 'I can imagine.'

'So what do we do next, sir?'

'We continue to gather intelligence. Now that we have a body and a string of clues, the killer will start to get worried.'

'How do we flush him out of cover?'

'I don't know yet.'

They were in Colbeck's room at the Black Bull. Though small, dark and with a sagging oak floor, it was spotlessly clean and had a homely feel to it. On the little table was the notebook in which Colbeck had listed all the salient details of their investigation. Picking it up, he flicked to the appropriate page.

'The problem is that we have conflicting evidence. Listen to Hepworth and you'll believe that his daughter was a conscientious maid-of-all-work dismissed because she uncovered a secret liaison between the colonel and his housekeeper. Look at Mrs Withers and that version of events seems utterly absurd.'

'What do you think, sir?'

'I prefer to rely on my instinct,' said Colbeck, 'and that absolves the housekeeper of any misconduct. It's unthinkable that a woman so patently fond of Mrs Tarleton would betray her in that way. I fancy that the girl was genuinely at fault. While I was waiting for you at the station, I talked to Mr Ellerby. He reckoned that Hepworth's daughter is bone idle and that his son - in Ellerby's evocative phrase – is as daft as a deaf hedgehog.'

'He obviously won't follow Hepworth into the railway police.'

'I feel sorry for the pair of them, having such an oppressive father. Living under the same roof as that pontificating oaf must be a real trial. However,' he continued, 'let's turn our minds elsewhere. We have much to do, Victor. I'd like to find out why the colonel visited Doncaster so often in the past and why he stopped doing so. I also want to know who usually accompanied him when he went out shooting. Then there's another avenue for us to explore.'

'Yes, we must find out who sent those poison-pen letters.'

'That will come later – along with another confrontation with the rector. We may need to remind him that laws can be enforced. Before that, however, I want to look at potential suspects.'

'But we don't have any yet, sir.'

'Nobody has been able to suggest any, perhaps,' said Colbeck, 'but they've overlooked the most likely people.'

'And who are they?'

'Disgruntled prisoners put behind bars by the colonel. He had a reputation for being ruthless on the bench, always handing out the longest possible sentences.'

'Prisoners bear grudges,' said Leeming. 'We both know that. If they feel they've got rough justice, they'll seek revenge. But how can we find out details of the cases that came before the colonel?'

'I've written to Mr Everett and asked him to help. As a lawyer, he'll have the necessary contacts. He'll be able to tell us who was released from prison recently and what sentence the colonel meted out to them. I'll go over to Northallerton this afternoon to see him.'

'What about me, Inspector?'

'You'll have more amenable company, Victor. While I'm talking to a lawyer, you'll be having another chat with Mrs Reader. She's our best source of information about Mrs Tarleton.'

'I'd have put the children ahead of her.'

'They've been away too long,' argued Colbeck. 'They don't really know what's been going on here. Besides, I don't want to intrude into their grief any more than we have to. Mrs Doel deserves time alone to mourn.'

'I don't think her brother will do much mourning, sir.'

'That's his affair. Having spoken to them, I don't feel that they have anything more to tell us. Agnes Reader, however, does. She's been deeply hurt by everything that's happened but her mind is less clouded by sorrow. She's eager to help us, Victor, and so is her husband, for that matter.

They are our most reliable guides.'

'We certainly need someone to guide us,' admitted Leeming, pulling a face. 'I still feel as if I'm completely in the dark.'

'Don't be so downhearted,' said Colbeck with a confident smile. 'We've made more progress than you imagine. I can see a few candles starting to flicker in the gloom. Before you know it, we'll have enough light to see exactly where we're going.'

CHAPTER ELEVEN

Bertram Reader's office was much more than just the inner sanctum from which he controlled the running of the bank. It was the place where he met important clients, a confessional box where he heard tales of financial woe, a strong room where the cash was kept in a massive safe and, when the bank was closed at the end of each day, a haven of rest from the pressures of administration. That afternoon, however, it was something entirely different – the setting for a tender marital scene. Agnes Reader was locked in her husband's embrace as she sobbed on his shoulder. Staying there for several minutes, she fought to overcome her emotions. Reader waited until his wife finally began to emerge from her grief then he offered her his handkerchief. She thanked him with a wan smile. After dabbing at her moist cheeks, she crossed to the mirror to look at herself.

'I can't go out like this,' she said, clicking her tongue. 'What on earth will your staff think?'

'They'll be too busy to think anything, my dear.'

'Anyone can see that I've been crying.'

'That's not unusual,' he said with a wry smile. 'This room has seen rather a lot of tears in its time. You'd be surprised how many apparently strong-willed people fail to cope with bad news about the state of their finances. I had one client

170

who collapsed on the carpet.'

'I spared you that embarrassment, Bertram.' She applied the handkerchief to her face again. 'How do I look now?'

'You look fine.'

'Oh, dear,' she said, gritting her teeth to ward off another attack of weeping. 'I didn't realise that it would have this effect on me.'

'I did warn you, Agnes.'

'I know.'

'There was no need for you to go there,' he said, softly. 'You should have remembered Miriam as she was, not as she is now. At the very least, you should have let me come with you.'

'It was something I had to do on my own.'

'Why?'

'I had to take my leave of her.'

'Well, I still think you suffered unnecessary pain. The time to pay your respects is at the funeral. Miriam had already been formally identified by her son. That was enough. She wouldn't have wanted you to see her in that condition.'

'No,' she conceded, 'that's probably true.'

He put his arms around her. 'How do you feel now?'

'I feel a lot better. When I left the undertaker's, I was in a complete daze. I almost got run over by a cart when I crossed the High Street. All I could think about was getting here to you.'

'You did the right thing,' he soothed. 'You're always the first to comfort others, but there are times when you need consolation as well.'

'I discovered that.'

Releasing her, he stood back. 'There'll be a big

hole in our lives from now on, Agnes.'

'I'm well aware of that.'

'We'll have to find someone else with whom to play cards.'

'Aubrey and Miriam were much more than mere card players,' she said, stung by the remark. 'They were our closest friends. We were practically aunt and uncle to the children.'

'To Eve, maybe – she was more approachable. I don't feel that we were ever wholly accepted by Adam. We were too respectable for him. He had the fire of youth in his veins and wanted to run wild. Some might say that that was only natural.'

'Did you ever feel like that, Bertram?'

He grinned. 'It's such a long time ago that I can't remember. I like to think that I wasn't as obnoxious as Adam Tarleton but, then, that would be a tall order. No,' he said after consideration, 'I never did try to kick over the traces. As a young man, I fear, I was ridiculously well behaved.'

'There's nothing ridiculous in good breeding.'

'I suppose not.'

'Your good character has been the foundation of your career.'

'Yes, one must never forget that.'

She glanced at the clock on the wall. 'I've taken up far too much of your time.'

'You could never do that, Agnes.'

'I'll let you get on with your work.'

'Are you sure that you feel well enough to go?'

'I think so.'

'I could always finish early for once and get Ferris to close the bank for me. What's the point of having a deputy manager if I don't make use of him?'

'No,' she said, 'you stay here. I'd appreciate a little time on my own. I've a lot to think about. By the time you get home, I'll be in a better frame of mind. But thank you, Bertram,' she said, planting a token kiss on his cheek. 'When I most needed support, you were here to help me.'

'That's what husbands are for, my dear.' He took her by the shoulders. 'I mourn them as well, you know. I loved them both dearly. Aubrey and Miriam were such an important part of our life.' He stifled a sigh. 'I'd give *anything* to have them back here again.'

Colbeck read the broadside with a mingled sadness and revulsion. Its crude verses both mocked and accused an innocent man who was in no position to defend himself. Unlike Tallis before him, Colbeck read *Railway to the Grave* through to the end.

'I'm sorry its so crumpled, Inspector,' said Clifford Everett. 'When I showed it to the superintendent, he screwed it up into a ball.'

Colbeck handed the paper back to him. 'I'm not surprised, sir. Mr. Tallis knew that his friend had nothing whatsoever to do with the murder of his wife.'

'That's not what people around here think.'

'How can they when they're being fed that kind of defamatory nonsense? That broadside tells them what they *want* to believe. There'll be a lot of red faces when their ignorance is finally dispelled. People will feel thoroughly ashamed at thinking such abominable things of a decent man.'

'I hope that the fiend who wrote those malign verses will be among them.'

'Then you hope in vain, Mr Everett. He'll be too busy counting the money he made out of selling his wares. It was ever thus,' said Colbeck with asperity. 'When a murder is committed, there are always self-appointed poets who descend out of the sky like vultures. They'll pick the bones of anyone's reputation as long at it serves their purpose. Once there's no more profit to be made, they'll sneak off with their blood money.'

'Do you really believe you *can* clear the colonel's name?'

'I haven't the slightest doubt, sir. All that I have to do is to catch the man who really did murder Mrs Tarleton and that person is already starting to take shape in my mind.'

'I'm heartened to hear it.'

It was a warm day and, even though the window of his office was open, Everett was perspiring. A wet line decorated the top of his collar and his tufts of hair looked as if they'd been recently irrigated. The lawyer fidgeted with some papers on his desk, rearranging them needlessly. His piggy eyes were dull.

'Have you ever been to Doncaster?' asked Colbeck.

'I've got too much sense,' replied Everett with disdain. 'Who in his right mind would go there? It's a railway town and that means smoke and noise and general filth. I've seen all I need to see of Doncaster through the window of a train. Why do you ask?'

'The colonel used to go there.'

'Really? I didn't know that.'

'That's a pity. I was hoping you could explain why he went there on a regular basis at one time. It does seem an unlikely destination for a fastidious man such as the colonel.'

'He might have had relations there, of course, or friends.'

'Then why did he suddenly stop going? I'm told that his visits came to an abrupt end well over a year ago. Yet the odd thing is that, when he left the house for the last time, he told Mrs Withers that he was catching a train to Doncaster.'

'Given what happened, that was a grotesque euphemism.'

'Perhaps the housekeeper can enlighten me.'

'Perhaps she can,' said Everett, shuffling some papers again. 'As to your request, Inspector, you didn't really give me a great deal of time to gather the relevant data.'

'I apologise for that, sir.'

'Nevertheless, I was able to rustle something up at short notice.'

'That sounds promising.'

'It helps that the prison is right here in Northallerton. I sent one of my clerks over there. He came back with the names of three people who've been released in the past couple of months.'

'Were they all sentenced by the colonel?'

'They were indeed,' said Everett, glancing at a sheet of paper before him. 'The first man was Douglas McCaw but you can rule him out of your calculations. He's already back in prison for another offence altogether.'

'Who were the others?'

'One was Harry Keedy. He served a short sentence for poaching. He's an old man now and suffered a mild stroke while in prison. I don't think he'd pose much of a threat to anyone. That leaves us,' he went on, tapping the paper with a chubby finger, 'with a much more interesting individual – Michael Bruntcliffe.'

'That name sounds familiar.'

'It should do. If you came here by train, you'll have passed Bruntcliffe's Flour Mills. It's a moneyed family so Michael wants for nothing. Yet he's been a thorn in his father's side for years. Fraud, petty theft, drunkenness, criminal damage – he has quite a long record. When he was last hauled up before the magistrates,' said Everett, 'the colonel gave him the maximum sentence for defacing some of the signs at the railway station with paint. It was only horseplay but Bruntcliffe paid dearly for it.'

'So he had good reason to resent the colonel.'

'No question about it. He was bound to feel that he was the victim of personal prejudice, Inspector.'

'Why should he feel that?'

'Years ago,' said the lawyer, 'Bruntcliffe used to be friendly with Adam Tarleton. When they were together, their high spirits often got the better of them and there was trouble. The colonel always believed that it was Bruntcliffe who led Adam astray – though, in my opinion, it might well have been the other way round.'

'In other words,' deduced Colbeck, 'there might have been an element of revenge in the sentence.'

'That's how it would have been perceived by Michael Bruntcliffe, anyway. He'd feel he was being punished for past indiscretions with the colonel's stepson. That sort of thing rankles,' Everett went on. 'While he was in prison, I daresay Bruntcliffe had very little else to think about.'

'Where are you going?' asked Eve Doel. 'I need you here with me.'

'I'm bored simply doing nothing,' said her brother.

'We're in mourning, Adam. You can't just go gallivanting around the countryside. It's improper.'

'I can do what I wish.'

'You're not even dressed properly.'

'I can't ride a horse in mourning attire, Eve. I'd look absurd.'

'I want you to stay here. I need company.'

'You've got Mrs Withers to provide that. It's about time she did something useful. I feel cooped up in the house. It's like a morgue in there. I want a breath of fresh air.'

They were standing outside the stables which were detached from the house. The horse had been saddled and Adam Tarleton was about to mount it. Distressed at being left alone, his sister had followed him out there to tug at his sleeve.

'Please don't go.'

'It will only be for an hour or two.'

'We have so much to discuss,' she said, plaintively.

'I don't think so. Let's be honest,' he said, airily. 'It's only a question of dividing the spoils. The real decision is what to do with the house. You don't need it and it's far too big for me on my own. Besides,' he went on, 'I'm not cut out for the life of a country squire. Having to be on my best behaviour all the time would drive me to distraction. I need the freedom to enjoy myself in my own way.'

She was wounded. 'How can you say such things at a time like this?' she pleaded. 'Our parents both died in the most indescribable ways and all you can talk about is enjoyment. Don't you *care*, Adam?'

'Of course I do.'

'Weren't you upset when you viewed Mother's body?'

'Yes.'

'You didn't seem anguished when you got back here.'

'Well, I was,' he said, feigning solemnity, 'I was shocked. When I identified the body, I could hardly bear to look.'

'Then how can you go off cheerfully for a ride? It's not just the inheritance we have to discuss. That, quite frankly,' she said, 'can wait. I find it rather tasteless even to raise the subject when we have more immediate problems to confront.'

'Such as?'

'There's the inquest into Mother's death, for a start.'

'That should be quite straightforward, Eve.'

'I'll be in agony from start to finish.'

'Then you don't need to attend. I'll go on your behalf.'

'I *have* to be there,' she said. 'Don't you understand? However upsetting the details, I have to know them. And once the inquest is out of the way, there's the problem of the funeral arrangements.'

'They'll both be buried at St Andrew's.'

'That's not what the rector says.'

'I don't give two hoots for his opinion.'

'He seemed so determined, Adam. He won't entertain the notion of letting someone who committed suicide lie in the churchyard.'

'He has no choice. When I was in Northallerton, I called in on Mr Everett and asked him where we stood on the matter. He told me that the law is quite clear. It's in our favour.'

'That will mean nothing to the rector.'

'Then it's high time someone knocked some sense into that thick skull of his,' said Tarleton, putting his foot in the stirrup. 'I'll ride over there this afternoon.' He hauled himself up into the saddle. 'I don't care if he is our godfather,' he continued, 'we'll make the funeral arrangements that we choose and nobody will be allowed to obstruct us. The rector can go hang!'

Digging in his heels, he rode off at a canter. Eve quailed.

Victor Leeming got to the house to learn that Agnes Reader was not there. Since she was expected back soon, however, he was invited in and asked to wait in the drawing room. It gave him time to take a detailed inventory of the place and to realise that bank managers were paid a lot more than detective sergeants. The room was sizeable. In fact, the whole ground floor of his house would have fitted into it and still left additional space. The furniture and fittings were of high quality, the carpet exquisite and the paintings indicative of excellent taste. Leeming was mesmerised by the contents of a china cabinet, marvelling at the intricate porcelain and realising how impractical it would be for use by his own family. With two lively children to accommodate, he made sure that all the crockery was solid and durable. The idea of putting it on show behind glass was a concept wholly foreign to him. The only thing on display in the Leeming household was the cup he'd helped to win as part of a police tug-of-war team and that would soon be relinquished to another member of the team so that he could have his allotted time with it.

Working as a detective was an education. It allowed him to have access to social circles that he'd never otherwise enter. Whenever he'd had to visit one of the grander houses in London, he was used to calling at the servants' entrance. It was Colbeck who'd taught him to knock on the front door and be more authoritative. Leeming's confidence had increased but he still lacked the inspector's ability to be at ease in any social situation. Low taverns and hazardous rookeries were the sergeant's natural habitat. Even in a home like the present one, the whiff of middle-class luxury unsettled him.

'I'm sorry to keep you waiting,' said Agnes Reader when she eventually arrived. 'Have you been here long?'

'Not really,' he told her, glancing towards the

fireplace. 'I was admiring your ornaments. You obviously don't have children if you can put so many fragile objects on your mantelpiece.'

'No, we don't have children, Sergeant.'

'Yet this would make a wonderful family house.'

Her voice was subdued. 'I daresay that it would but ... it was not to be. Have you been offered refreshment?'

'Yes, Mrs Reader,' he said, 'but I wanted nothing.'

'Do sit down,' she said, waving him to a seat and taking an armchair opposite him. 'Is it too much to ask that you've brought some good news?'

'You've already had that. Inspector Colbeck is in charge of the investigation. That's the best news possible.'

'He seems to be a very astute man.'

'He has a sixth sense when it comes to solving crimes.'

'I was at the house with Mrs Doel when he called yesterday.'

'So I hear,' said Leeming. 'The inspector felt that you were more helpful than Mrs Doel because she hasn't recovered from the shock of what happened yet.'

'I'm not sure that I have either,' she admitted. 'But, if there's anything else I can tell you, I'll be pleased to do so.'

'Did the colonel ever talk about cases that came before him when he sat on the bench?'

'Yes, he often did that. It was rather unnerving.'

'Why was that?'

'Well, I'd always thought of Northallerton as a

very safe place so I was alarmed to hear that it had its share of thieves, drunkards and other undesirables. In the countryside, one feels very secure but the town is definitely not a place to be late at night.'

'It's the same wherever you go, Mrs Reader. Crime is universal.'

'Colonel Tarleton taught us that. Some of the people who came before him were dreadful thugs. They made the most blood-curdling threats against him but he just shrugged them off. After all those years of facing real danger in battle, he always told us, he wasn't going to be scared by local villains.'

'Can you recall any of the names of those villains?'

'I'm afraid not, Sergeant.'

'Did anyone try to carry out the threats?'

'Not to my knowledge.'

'Let me ask you something else,' he said, changing his tack. 'Were you aware that the colonel was in the habit of going to Doncaster at one time?'

'No,' she said. 'I knew that he spent occasional days away but Miriam – Mrs Tarleton – never told me that he went to Doncaster. What could have taken him there, I wonder?'

'That's what we're trying to find out.'

'Then you'll have to look elsewhere.'

'What about Mrs Tarleton – did she do much travelling?'

'She visited a cousin in Edinburgh now and then. As a rule, she stayed the night there. I'm told that it's a beautiful city.'

'I wouldn't know,' said Leeming. 'I'm a Londoner, born and bred. I'm only happy when I'm there. If I go too far north, I start to get giddy. One last question,' he added, noting the sadness in her face and not wishing to prolong his stay. 'It seems as if the colonel and his wife had some financial problems. They had to make economies.'

'That's true. Apart from reducing the number of servants, they even had to sell off some land.'

'Do you happen to know why, Mrs Reader?'

'I don't,' she said, crisply.

'Presumably, your husband would know.'

'My husband is the soul of discretion, Sergeant. That's what makes him such a reliable banker. He never discloses details of any client's accounts to me or to anyone else.'

'I know. He refused to go into details for us. I just thought that Mrs Tarleton might have given you a hint.'

'All that she told me was that they had to make a few changes.'

'They were quite big changes, by the sound of it.'

'They happened so gradually, one hardly noticed.'

Behind her politeness, Leeming could sense a deep sorrow. To lose two close friends in such a short period of time had rocked her. It made him feel like an interloper, barging in when she really wanted to be left alone. As he rose to his feet and made to leave, something popped into his mind.

'Did the colonel and Mrs Tarleton ever go on holiday?'

'Only infrequently,' she replied.

'Was there any reason for that, Mrs Reader?'

'They were contented where they were. What they did do was to visit Eve and the grand-children in Sussex. At other times, Eve and her family would visit them.'

'What about young Mr Tarleton?'

'Oh, they saw very little of him,' said Agnes with a slight edge. 'He more or less cut himself off from them. His mother told me that she didn't even know where he was living.'

'His sister must have known.'

'I don't think so, Sergeant.'

'Then how did he become aware that his mother was missing?'

'I'm not sure that he did at first. He certainly didn't turn up to assist in the search. Eve and her husband came but not Adam. I assumed that he had no idea what was going on.'

'Yet he came when the colonel committed suicide.'

'That caused more of a stir,' she explained. 'When someone goes astray here, it will be reported in the local newspapers. But when a man of the colonel's standing takes his own life in the most ghastly manner, even the London press will take notice. That's how Adam must have picked up the news. He made contact with his sister and they came together.' She got up from her chair. 'It's the only possible way that it could have happened. Don't you agree?'

'No, Mrs Reader,' said Leeming, pensively. 'I don't.'

Adam Tarleton liked to make heads turn. As he

184

galloped through the village, his horse's hooves clacked on the hard surface and people stared in annoyance at his recklessness in riding so fast along the narrow street. When he reached the rectory, he reined the animal in and dismounted. After tethering it to a post, he rang the bell. It tinkled somewhere deep inside the house. A pretty maidservant eventually opened the door. A recent addition to the domestic staff, she didn't recognise him.

'Can I help you, sir?' she asked.

'Yes,' he said, brushing her uncaringly aside. 'You can get out of my way so that I can see the rector.'

'You can't disturb him, sir,' she wailed. 'He's in his study.'

'Then that's where I'll talk to him.'

Striding down the passageway, he came to a door and banged on it before flinging it open. Frederick Skelton was horrified at the interruption. He jumped up from the chair behind his desk.

'What's the meaning of this?' he demanded.

'I have something to discuss with you.'

'You can't just charge in here like this, Adam.'

'I'm sorry, sir,' said the maidservant, appearing at the door and anticipating a rebuke. 'I couldn't stop him.'

'That's all right, Ruth. This is my godson, Mr Tarleton.'

'Oh, I see.'

'You can leave us alone.'

'Very well, sir,' she said, bobbing once before leaving.

'I've come to talk about the funerals,' said Tarleton.

'This is not a convenient moment.'

'It's convenient enough for me.'

'You should have made an appointment like anyone else,' said Skelton, peevishly. 'I'm busy writing to the Dean of York Minster.'

'I don't care if you're writing to the Archangel Gabriel.'

Skelton flushed. 'That's a blasphemous remark!'

Tarleton was resolute. 'I'm not moving from here until we've had this out,' he warned, standing in the open doorway, arms akimbo. 'As our godfather, you're supposed to offer spiritual guidance. Instead of that, you've reduced my sister to despair by your intransigence and you've lost all respect from me.'

'I never knew that you were capable of respect,' said Skelton, acidly. 'As for Eve, I merely wanted to acquaint her with my decision.'

'And where did you choose to do it? Of all places, it was at the inquest. Her nerves were frayed enough without you upsetting her even more. Have you no tact at all?'

'I have both tact and sensitivity – two laudable qualities, I feel I must point out, entirely lacking in you. I could add several others to the list, Adam.'

'You can insult me all you like. I expect it of sanctimonious old fools like you.' Skelton was outraged. 'What I will not let you do is to insult our stepfather in this way. He will be buried at the church where he worshipped for so many years.'

'Not as long as I have breath in my body,' said Skelton, adopting the posture of an avenging angel. 'As for insulting the colonel, I bow to your superior skill in doing that. You insulted and disobeyed him for years. You were a disgrace to his name.'

'This is one way of making amends for that.'

Skelton was sardonic. 'Oh, you've discovered the concept of redemption at last, have you? I suppose that we should be grateful for that unlooked-for sign of hope.'

'Sneer all you wish. We'll have our stepfather buried here.'

'Suicide is a subversive act,' said Skelton. 'It breaks the law of the land and the divine law of the Ten Commandments. Murder of any kind is abhorrent but at least we can have the satisfaction of hanging the perpetrator. An eye for an eye is a comforting doctrine. No such comfort exists in the case of suicide,' he said, tossing back his hair. 'And in this particular instance, there is something else to consider. The colonel took his life in a manner designed to shock and disgust. It was a deliberate attempt to make us *suffer*. So don't you try to browbeat me on this issue,' he continued, as if admonishing his flock from a pulpit. 'Such a man should never lie in consecrated ground.'

Tarleton pretended to yawn. 'Your sermons always did make me go to sleep.'

'Get out of here, Adam.'

'You never liked my stepfather and this is your means of taking a spiteful revenge against him. It would be deplorable in any man. In an ordained

187

priest, it's nothing short of malevolence.'

'God is my mentor. I merely follow his direction.'

Tarleton did not stay long enough to reply. Swivelling on his heel, he went out and slammed the door behind him with such force that the sound reverberated throughout the whole house. Stunned by the violence of his godson's departure, Skelton took refuge in prayer.

By prior agreement, they met early that evening at the Waggon and Horses, a large establishment in Northallerton with a convivial atmosphere. It gave them the opportunity to review their findings over a quiet drink. Colbeck had been the more assiduous. After his visit to the lawyer's office, he'd done his best to find out as much as he could about Michael Bruntcliffe. It had been a journey of discovery and it began with the parents. They were deeply embarrassed by the antics of their younger son and almost relieved that he'd disappeared on his release from custody. Their other three children had been a credit to them but Michael was the archetypal black sheep of the family. His father couldn't understand why he felt compelled to cause so much mischief and he believed that the person to blame was Adam Tarleton. It was when the two young men became close friends that Michael Bruntcliffe's life took a decisive turn in the wrong direction. What grieved the parents most was that their son was always the one to be put behind bars while Tarleton invariably escaped with a fine.

Since he couldn't pick up Bruntcliffe's trail,

Colbeck had taken the trouble to call at the prison to ask the governor how he'd fared while serving his time.

'What did he tell you?' asked Leeming.

'That he was sullen and withdrawn,' replied Colbeck. 'He seemed to be brooding on what he saw as the injustice of his sentence. Bruntcliffe couldn't wait to get out. His father offered to collect him on his release but the son refused even to see him. He preferred to go his own way.'

Leeming was puzzled. 'How can someone from such a good family end up like that? It's perverse. Bruntcliffe had *everything*.'

'So did Adam Tarleton – until the money ran out.'

'Yes, sir, I'd like to know exactly what happened to it but Mrs Reader was as discreet as her husband. The truth is bound to come out in the end when the estate is valued.'

'We can't wait until then, Victor. The information being kept from us could be useful in the investigation. That's why I went back to the bank earlier on. Mr Reader was too busy to see me but suggested that we meet him here. Over a pleasant drink,' said Colbeck, sipping his whisky, 'he may be a little forthcoming.'

Leeming rhapsodised about the china cabinet and the delicate ornaments in the Reader household, wishing that his wife had been able to see something so fine and so beautifully displayed. Colbeck had noticed the items on their previous visit.

'Which would you rather have?' he asked. 'Your home in London with a loving family to share it with you or that rambling edifice you saw again today?'

'Oh, I'd choose my home every time, sir. The other house is much bigger but it feels empty without children. They make all the difference. But then,' he added with a knowing smile, 'you'll find that out in due course when you have children of your own.'

'Hold on,' said Colbeck, stopping him with a gesture. 'Let's not rush things. I'm not even married yet. Confiding that to the superintendent is going to be challenging enough. What sort of a response would I get if I told him that I was about to become a father?'

'I hope I'm not in the building when you do so.'

Bertram Reader noted their laughter as he entered the bar.

'Is there a cause for celebration?' he asked, coming over.

'It's a private matter, sir,' said Colbeck, 'and unconnected with the case. Thank you for joining us. May I get you a drink?'

Reader sat down, the drink was ordered and the three of them were soon talking about the investigation. The banker was able to supply some more detail about Michael Bruntcliffe.

'He came into some money on his twenty-first birthday,' he said. 'Any hopes that it might make him more responsible were soon dashed. He started to fritter it away on gambling. In that respect, he and Adam were partners in crime. When they weren't gambling or seeking female company of a dubious kind, they went out shooting together.'

'Oh?' Colbeck was surprised. 'Young Mr Tarleton told me that his stepfather didn't allow him access to any firearms. The colonel didn't trust him.'

'That's why Adam borrowed a shotgun from Bruntcliffe. It was another way of defying the colonel. The pair of them went off shooting game birds. When they'd had too much to drink, they sometimes shot out people's windows for the sheer fun of it.'

'Weren't they ever prosecuted?'

'No, Inspector – nothing could ever be proved.'

'Where could I find Bruntcliffe? He seems to have vanished.'

'Oh, I don't think he'll be too far away,' said Reader. 'He's probably living in sin with a loose woman, if I know him. He always did have a certain raffish charm.'

'Should he be considered as a murder suspect?'

'He's not an obvious one, I must confess, because he's never been guilty of real violence. But he did make dire threats when he was sentenced. I remember the colonel telling me about them.'

'Wait a minute,' said Leeming. 'Surely, the threats were against the colonel and not Mrs Tarleton.'

'I suppose that the way to hurt him most would be to kill his wife,' said Reader. 'The colonel would then be left behind in torment until he could bear it no longer.'

'You seem to have known him better than anyone, Mr Reader,' said Colbeck. 'Perhaps you can tell us why he used to make regular visits to Doncaster?'

Reader shrugged. 'I wasn't aware that he did so.'

'Didn't he confide in you?'

'Well, yes, but there were certain areas of his life that he never talked about. His army service was a case in point. Evidently, he enjoyed that period yet it remained a closed book to me. I could give you other examples of his secretiveness.'

'This could be another example,' said Leeming. 'Your wife had no idea why he might choose to go to Doncaster, sir. Do you?'

'No, I don't,' replied Reader. 'I'm as intrigued as you are.'

'What really intrigues us,' said Colbeck, 'is the abrupt change in the family's fortunes. How did they come to lose so much money?'

Reader was brisk. 'That will be revealed in the fullness of time. Even the children are unaware of the full details so I'm not able to divulge them to you. After all, they have no bearing on the murder.'

'They might have a bearing on the suicide,' argued Colbeck.

'I'm sorry. My lips are sealed, Inspector. I have a professional duty here. The colonel and his wife were clients of mine for many years. I don't feel able to discuss their affairs with you.'

'So be it.'

'I daresay that you've tried to wheedle the information out of Mr Everett as well. I can see that you failed.'

'He was as reticent as you, sir,' said Colbeck, 'so we'll bide our time. The priority now is to find and question Michael Bruntcliffe. I'm surprised that his name hasn't come into consideration before.'

'It didn't need to,' suggested Leeming. 'When Mrs Tarleton went missing, everyone here seemed to think her husband had killed her.'

'*We* didn't think so,' stressed Reader, 'but you're quite right, Sergeant. The colonel was the prime suspect and, to most people, he still is. There have even been broadsides published to that effect.'

'Yes,' said Colbeck. 'I read one of them. It was almost as vicious as this.' He took an envelope from his pocket. 'This is a poison-pen letter sent to taunt the colonel. Do you recognise the hand, sir?'

Reader studied it. 'I can't say that I do.'

'Take the letter out, if you wish.'

'There's no need, Inspector. Looking at the name and address is enough. It's a distinctive calligraphy. I'd remember it.' As Colbeck put the envelope away, Reader tasted his drink then ran his tongue over his lips. 'A malt whisky at the end of a working day is an excellent tonic. So,' he went on, becoming serious, 'have you made any progress in the investigation?'

'We believe so, Mr Reader.'

'The person we're after is used to handling a shotgun,' said Leeming, 'and you've just told us that Bruntcliffe comes into that category. We need to track him down quickly. But what about the people with whom the colonel went out shooting? You were one of them, I presume.'

'Oh, I was hopeless with a weapon in my hands,' said Reader, modestly, 'so I rarely joined a shoot-

193

ing party. I love eating game but take no pleasure from killing it. I could name several people who often made up a shooting party but there was only one person who went out alone with the colonel.'

'Oh?' said Colbeck. 'Who was that?'

'A rather unexpected marksman,' replied Reader with a smile. 'To look at him, you'd never believe that he knew one end of a shotgun from the other, but I have it on good authority that he is a dead shot.'

'What's his name, sir?'

'Clifford Everett.'

CHAPTER TWELVE

Lottie Pearl couldn't believe the transformation that had taken place during her short time at the house. Having lost both her employers to frightening deaths, she was now forced to minister to the needs of two guests. Worst of all, she had to do so in a badly dyed black dress that hung in folds off her body, gathered dust on its hem and gave off a musty smell. With a thick apron over the dress, she felt as if she were about to suffocate in the heat of the kitchen. After her long service to the family, Mrs Withers might be truly bereaved, but it soon dawned on Lottie that she herself was mourning the imminent loss of her job. Her days there were numbered. Eve Doel had no need of the house and the girl knew that, even if he stayed, she could never work for the brother. Since he'd been there, Adam Tarleton had either glowered at her or, when he'd drunk half a bottle of brandy, appraised her in a way that made her skin crawl. When she complained about it to the house-keeper, she was told to get on with her job and stop letting her fevered imagination run away with her.

In fact, there was little time for her imagination to become fevered. She was expected to get up early, draw water from the well and help in the preparation of breakfast. Whenever she had a respite, it was swiftly curtailed by Mrs Withers who had a genius for inventing new jobs that had to be done instantly. Lottie had been ready for hard work when she took on the post but the intensity of it exceeded all her fears. That evening, however, she was given a small measure of relief. Instead of scrubbing the kitchen floor as usual, she was sent off to a farm to fetch two dozen eggs. She was undeterred by the long walk there and back. Her concern was that she had to do it in her mother's dress and face certain mockery from the children when she got to the farm. Because she wore black, one of them had called her a witch and asked her why she hadn't arrived on a broomstick.

In the event, Lottie was spared any ridicule. The children were playing in the field and the dog that had harassed her on her last visit was nowhere to be seen. Although the girl had money to pay for the eggs, the farmer's wife refused to take it, saying that it was her small contribution to a house in mourning. After a brief chat with her, Lottie took her leave with the basket over her arm. The walk there had been without incident but hazards lurked on her return journey. The first was a half-hidden rabbit hole into which she put an unsuspecting foot, causing her to trip up and fall. While she wasn't injured, her basket was jolted and a few of the eggs cracked open, emptying their sticky contents. Climbing over a stile also proved perilous. She caught her dress on it and heard an ominous tearing sound.

But it was the third hazard that really upset her because it came in human form. An old pedlar rolled towards her on his cart and eyed her with interest. Tugging his horse to a halt, he leered at the girl and offered her a trinket in exchange for a kiss. When she declined, he hopped off the cart and tried to molest her. Even though she eluded him with ease and ran away at speed, she felt hurt and vulnerable. When she reached a stand of trees, she slipped behind them and sat down to rest, examining the tear in her dress then trying to remove the broken eggs from the basket. Lottie was still trying to wipe her hands clean in the grass when she heard the approach of horses. Fearing that the pedlar had come after her, she leapt to her feet and peered around the trunk of a tree.

There were two riders and, from their carefree laughter, she could tell that they'd been drinking. They reined their horses in only twenty yards from her hiding place. Lottie recognised Adam Tarleton but she'd never seen his young companion before. They were patently happy in each other's company and loath to part. Lottie watched as Tarleton took something from his pocket and handed it over to the other man. His friend thanked him and made a jocular remark that she couldn't quite hear. Then they waved farewell and went their separate ways.

The girl was both mystified and excited, bewildered by what had occurred yet feeling that she'd somehow witnessed a moment of real significance. She spent the rest of the journey trying to work out what it could possibly be.

After their ill-starred rendezvous in the dark, Wilf Moxey and Lorna Begg had seen very little of each other. Both had chores that kept them working apart and neither deliberately sought out the other. Because he'd raised the alarm about a dead body, Moxey had acquired a spurious celebrity in the eyes of his workmates on the farm. His name had appeared in the newspaper and he'd been praised in print by a detective inspector for what he'd done. Unaccustomed to such fleeting fame, Moxey found it a burden. He was compelled to repeat the lie about going out in search of rabbits and his mouth went dry every time he did so. That evening, therefore, he snatched a moment to speak alone with Lorna. They met behind the cowshed and, though she gave off the unmistakable odour of stale milk, he found her as entrancing as ever.

'I've been thinking,' he began.

'So have I. It was a mistake.'

'No, that's not true. What we did was right. We were unlucky.'

Lorna trembled. 'I keep feeling the touch of that hand.'

'Forget it.'

'I can't, Will I've tried.'

'What I've been thinking is this. There's an inquest.'

'It's nothing to do with us,' she said, anxiously.

'I have to go, Lorna.'

'Why?'

'I told them what ... what we found.'

'You said you'd pretend you were on your own.'

'I did. The detectives believed me. This is different. When I go to the inquest, Mr Higginbottom says I'll be under oath.' His face was contorted with apology. 'I can't tell a lie. That'd be perjury.'

She was terrified. 'But everyone will *know*.'

'Is that such a bad thing?'

'You swore it'd be a secret, Will. You promised me.'

'That was before.'

'I trusted you. I don't want people to know about us.'

He was hurt. 'Are you ashamed?'

'You promised me,' she insisted. 'It was our secret.'

Moxey was in a quandary. Infatuation with Lorna Begg made him eager to tell any amount of lies on her behalf but he had a conscience. It had reminded him that a lie under oath was a sin as well as a criminal offence. He would be questioned in public by the coroner, a man seasoned in the art of ferreting out the truth from witnesses. Even if he'd wanted to, Moxey wasn't sure that he could lie convincingly enough. Yet he had to do so if he wanted to retain the milkmaid's affections.

He reached out for her hand but she pulled it away.

'What are you going to do?' she asked, nervously.

It was the kind of journey that Victor Leeming preferred. Seated in the trap with Robert Colbeck, he felt perfectly secure and able to enjoy the sight of rolling countryside on a summer evening. There was none of the deafening noise and continual juddering of a train. This was by far the more civilised way to travel. When the house was finally conjured into view, his jaw dropped in astonishment.

'You didn't tell me it was *that* big, sir,' he protested.

'It's the old manor house, Victor.'

'I begin to see the sort of position the colonel held.'

'People looked up to him,' said Colbeck. 'Wealth is always an easy way to impress. It buys respect. He had status in the county.'

'But it wasn't only based on money.'

'No, he earned it in other ways as well. He also earned a good reputation. Our task is to rescue it from oblivion.'

After driving the vehicle to the stables, Colbeck alighted and took the sergeant across to the front door. The housekeeper had seen them through the window so they had no need to ring the bell. The door was opened wide. Colbeck exchanged greetings with Mrs Withers then introduced Leeming.

'I hope you haven't come to speak to Mrs Doel,' she said. 'She's asleep at the moment. I'd rather she wasn't awakened.'

'It's her brother we came to see, Mrs Withers, but I'd also like to ask you a few questions as well.'

She stood back so that they could step inside, closing the door after them. Leeming's unbecoming features troubled her slightly so she kept her eyes fixed on Colbeck.

'How can I help you, sir?' she asked.

'Before he left this house for the last time,' Colbeck said, 'the colonel told you he was taking a train to Doncaster.'

'That's correct.'

'Had he ever done that before?'

'I can't remember him doing so, Inspector.'

200

'Did he say *why* he was travelling to Doncaster?'

'But he wasn't,' she pointed out. 'That was only an excuse. As we know, he didn't catch the train at all.'

'Not on that occasion, I agree. Think of others. When he went somewhere by rail, did he always tell you what his destination was?'

'No, sir, the colonel didn't. All I knew was the time when he was likely to return so that everything was ready for him. He only told me what I needed to know.'

'So the mention of Doncaster was unusual?'

'It was very unusual. I'd have been less surprised if he'd said he was going to York or somewhere like that. But, then, it wasn't my place to question his movements.'

'I suppose not,' said Colbeck. 'Does the name Michael Bruntcliffe mean anything to you?'

Her face clouded. 'Yes, it does.'

'Well?'

'The colonel spoke harshly about him.'

'Did you ever see Bruntcliffe here?'

'Only the once, Inspector,' she replied. 'It was years ago when the colonel and Mrs Tarleton were in Sussex. Young Mr Tarleton was still here then. I kept out of their way.'

'How would you describe Bruntcliffe?' asked Leeming.

'He seemed a personable young man,' she said, trying to recall an image in her mind. 'Some might call him handsome. He was tall and well dressed. Oh, and he had long, black hair that curled at the ends. That's all I can say, really.'

'Thank you, Mrs Withers,' said Colbeck. 'We're really here to see young Mr Tarleton. I assume that he's at home.'

'He is now, Inspector. He was out riding all afternoon and came back a short while ago. I'll take you to him now.' She looked sheepish. 'I had to give him the key, sir. He's the master now.'

Expecting to be conducted to the drawing room or the library, the visitors were instead taken to the room where the firearms were kept. The housekeeper knocked, entered, then explained to Tarleton that the detectives wished to speak to him. She retreated before she was told to leave. Colbeck introduced Leeming, who was agog at the weaponry that had been amassed. Tarleton was holding the Purdey shotgun with his step-father's initials carved into the stock. He replaced it in the cabinet.

'That was the colonel's favourite,' observed Colbeck. 'Did you intend to go out shooting?'

'No,' said Tarleton. 'I was just wondering how much money it would fetch. A tidy amount, I hope.'

'Are you thinking of selling it, sir?'

'Well, I can hardly keep everything here, can I? What use is it to me when I go back to London? I'll have to get it valued.'

'I think you should wait before you do that, sir,' said Leeming, surprised that Tarleton was not in mourning apparel. 'The will has to be read first. You have to be sure that these items are yours to sell.'

'Well, they'd hardly be left to my sister, would they?'

'The sergeant makes a valid point,' said Colbeck. 'Since your stepfather wouldn't even let you handle the firearms, he might have left them to one of the friends who joined him on shooting parties.'

Tarleton scowled. 'He might have done just that,' he said, stung by the notion, 'if only out of spite. If that's the case, I'll contest the will. All this is *mine*.'

'Be that as it may, sir. Now, would you rather we had this conversation in the drawing room or are you happy to talk to us here?'

'This is as good a place as any, Inspector.'

'I don't know about that,' said Leeming under his breath, gazing at a pike and imagining the fearful wounds it could inflict. Aloud, he said, 'You saw very little of your parents in recent times, I believe, sir.'

'My mother was my only living parent,' corrected Tarleton. 'I could never accept the colonel as my father. As it was, I drifted apart from both of them in the end.'

'So you loved your mother and resented your stepfather?'

'It was rather more complicated than that, Sergeant, and I've no intention of explaining why.'

'That's your privilege, Mr Tarleton.'

'If you loved your mother,' said Colbeck, 'why didn't you join the search for her when she went missing?'

'I had no idea that she'd gone astray,' said Tarleton. 'I told you. We'd lost touch. I was trying to make my own way in life.'

'Had you lost touch with your sister as well?'

'Not to the same extent.'

'Didn't she contact you about your mother's disappearance?'

'Eve wrote to my last known address but I'd moved twice since then. The first time I heard about Mother vanishing was when I read a newspaper report about my stepfather's suicide.'

'What did you do then, sir?'

'I got in touch with my sister, of course. When I heard that Eve's husband was abroad,' said Tarleton, donning the mantle of a caring brother, 'I went to her house to comfort her then brought her here.' He became protective. 'If you're hoping to speak to her, you're out of luck. I'm afraid that I can't allow it. She needs time to mourn.'

'You don't seem to share that need, sir,' said Leeming.

'Each of us is dealing with the catastrophe in our own way.'

'Yours involved going for a ride, we're told.'

Tarleton was angry. 'Is there any law against that, Sergeant?' he asked. 'If you must know, I went to the rectory to make our views known with regard to the two funerals. The rector is trying to stop my stepfather from being buried in the churchyard.'

'Yes,' said Colbeck. 'I had an argument with him over that.'

'I wasn't prepared to argue. I simply stated our demand.'

'There may be wrangling ahead, sir. The rector has an obsession about death by suicide. My advice is to go over his head and appeal to the archbishop. You'll surely get his support.'

'I want the bodies buried as soon as the second inquest is over. It's frustrating to have an obstacle like this thrown in our way by Mr Skelton. Where's his Christian forgiveness? He knows the verdict reached at the inquest. Our stepfather's mind was unbalanced. Why can't the rector accept that and show some compassion?'

'Because he has another reservation,' said Colbeck. 'In the short time that I spent with the reverend gentleman, one thing became crystal clear. He's convinced that the colonel killed your mother. It's a secondary reason for denying him a place in the churchyard. When we catch the real killer, of course, that excuse will disappear.'

'Do you have any suspects?'

'We do, as a matter of fact. One of them is an old friend of yours, as it happens – Michael Bruntcliffe.'

'Michael is no killer,' snapped Tarleton.

'He was furious when your stepfather sent him to prison.'

'That doesn't mean he'd commit murder. He does have a vengeful streak, I grant you, but it would express itself in very different ways.'

'Can you give us an example, sir?'

'Well, there was the business with that farmer years ago. When he prosecuted Michael for trespass, there was a hefty fine to pay. That irked Michael. He got his revenge by opening a gate at night and letting the farmer's sheep wander off.'

'Was he ever taken to court for that?' asked Leeming.

'No – they had no proof. But you take my

205

point. If Michael wanted to get back at someone, there was always a touch of humour in what he did.'

'I don't find letting sheep out very amusing, sir.'

'Neither do I,' said Colbeck. 'Some of them could have been attacked by dogs or even rustled. Mr Bruntcliffe could have cost the farmer a lot of money.'

'Michael had the last laugh,' said Tarleton. 'It's all that mattered to him. The farmer kept out of his way after that.'

'When did you last see your friend, sir?'

'Oh, it was years ago.'

'So you didn't keep in touch at all?'

'Not really, Inspector.'

'But you seem to have been good friends.'

'We were for a time.

'Why did the friendship fall off?'

'I left here and forged a new life for myself in London.'

'Do you have any idea where Mr Bruntcliffe is?'

'No,' said Tarleton, 'and I don't care. Michael is part of my past. With the inquest pending and the funerals to organise, I've got enough to keep me fully occupied. I just don't have time for old friends. To be absolutely candid, I want to forget all about the North Riding. I can't wait to get away from here for good.'

While she was waiting for her father to come home, Madeleine was not idle. After preparing his supper, she read another chapter of *Cranford* then took out Colbeck's letter once more and pored over it. Simply holding it in her hand gave her a thrill and its sentiments warmed her to the core. The village of South Otterington was clearly very different from the one in Cheshire evoked in such detail by Mrs Gaskell. Violent death did not disturb the even rhythm of life in Cranford. Colbeck had said little about the events in Yorkshire but she'd gathered something of what had been happening there from the newspaper reports. The description of the suicide had been horrific and she'd felt sick at the thought of Colbeck having to exhume a rotting body in the wood. He took such events in his stride and Madeleine wondered if the time would ever come when she could cultivate the same indifference to morbid tasks. When they were married, she felt sure, she'd learn a great deal from him and, in turn, teach Colbeck certain things.

Caleb Andrews returned slightly earlier than usual, having trotted much of the way to escape the rain that started to fall. He let himself into the house, kissed his daughter then took off his coat and hat. Before he could stop her, Madeleine had taken the newspaper from his pocket.

'It's on the back page,' he told her. 'Everybody up there thinks that the colonel shot his wife.'

'Robert doesn't think that. Sergeant Leeming told me.'

'The local people *knew* the colonel, Maddy. They could turn out to be right. For once in his career, the inspector may have made a big mistake – apart from travelling on the Great Northern Railway.'

Madeleine laughed. 'How else could he get

there?' she said. 'In any case, he didn't go all the way on the GNR. The stretch between York and Darlington is operated by the Great North of England Railway. Robert mentioned that in his letter.'

'What about your letter to him?' asked Andrews. 'Did you manage to deliver it to Sergeant Leeming?'

'Yes, I met him at King's Cross.'

'Does that mean you'll be here for breakfast tomorrow?'

'I'll be here,' she said, still reading the newspaper. 'According to this article, the investigation is faltering. That's not true.'

Andrews went into the kitchen to wash his hands. Madeleine followed him in so that they could eat their supper together.

He was in a teasing mood. 'Did you do what I suggested?'

'And what was that, Father?'

'When you wrote your letter, I wanted you to tell him to get a move on with the wedding arrangements. I may be making some arrangements of my own in the near future.' He wiped his hands dry. 'I hope that you mentioned that to the inspector.'

'You know quite well that I didn't.'

'Then you can put it in your next letter, Maddy, and there's something you can add about that book he loaned you.'

'*Cranford?*'

'That's the one.'

'I didn't know that you'd read it.'

'I've been reading a chapter a night after you've

gone to bed.'

'It's so interesting, isn't it?'

'I thought it was boring.'

'But it shows you the pleasures of life in a country village.'

'If that's all the pleasure you get, I'll stay here in Camden.'

'Well, I love the book,' she said, levelly.

'That's because you're a woman, Maddy,' he told her, sitting at the table. 'There's nothing in it for a man. Tell the inspector you'd like something by Dickens next time, something with murder in it to add a little spice. That's what I like to read late at night.'

It was dark by the time they reached South Otterington. After returning the horse and trap to the place from which they'd hired it, the detectives strolled towards the Black Bull. Colbeck savoured the sense of tranquillity. He inhaled deeply.

'The air is so much cleaner here than in London,' he noted.

'That makes no difference, sir,' said Leeming. 'I could never settle here. There are too many things I couldn't stand.'

'Give me an instance.'

'Take the way they speak. They all sound funny to me.'

Colbeck smiled. 'We probably sound funny to them, Victor. What you hear is the genuine Yorkshire accent. I find it very pleasant.'

'Well, I don't, Inspector. It grates on my ears. Some of them are not too bad – Mr and Mrs Reader, say, or young Mr Tarleton – but the rest talk in a sort of foreign language. Sergeant Hepworth is the worst. I couldn't listen to that voice, day in and day out.'

'His wife has no choice. My guess is that his is the only voice you can hear when he's at home. He loves to hold forth.'

'I hope we don't find him in the bar again this evening.'

'So does the landlord. Hepworth is bad for business.'

As they approached the pub, Colbeck noticed someone lurking in the shadows nearby. At first, he thought it was someone waiting to ambush them and he got ready to repel any attack. In fact, when they got closer, the figure withdrew completely. Saying nothing to Leeming, the inspector followed him into the bar, handed him his top hat then walked straight through the rooms at the rear of the building and let himself out into the yard. He unlocked the door in the high stone wall and let himself out as quietly as he could. Creeping along, he reached the corner and peeped carefully around it. Colbeck could just make out the shape of someone, crouched furtively against the wall as if waiting to pounce on a passer-by.

The inspector sensed trouble and sought to nip it in the bud. Easing his way around the corner, he moved on tiptoe until he got within reach of the man, then he dived forward, gripped him tightly and pinioned him to the wall.

'What are you doing here?' asked Colbeck.

The man struggled to get away. 'Nothing, sir – let me go.'

'You're up to no good.'

'Is that you, Inspector?' said the other, respectfully.

Colbeck recognised the voice. 'Moxey?' He let his prisoner go. 'I didn't realise it was you.'

'That's all right, sir.' The labourer turned to look at him with obvious unease. 'I'm sorry to cause you any bother, sir. I'll have to get back to the farm.'

'No, no, stay here. You came to see me, didn't you?'

'It was a mistake,' said Moxey. 'I changed my mind.'

'Well, I'm not letting you go now that you're here,' said Colbeck. 'The first thing I insist on doing is to buy you a drink. You brought us vital information and that deserves a reward.'

The labourer smiled. 'Oh, I see.'

'Come on, let's go inside.'

Before Moxey could resist, Colbeck put an arm around his shoulders and shepherded him into the bar. Leeming was already seated at a table with drinks for himself and Colbeck. The inspector ordered a pint of beer for their visitor then took him across to the table. He knew that Moxey had come to see him and lost his nerve at the last moment. The first task, therefore, was to make the labourer relax. It wasn't easy. Moxey was overawed. He'd never shared a drink with two gentlemen from London before and couldn't believe they were so friendly to him. His awkwardness slowly faded. Colbeck let him get halfway through the pint before questioning him.

'You came about the inquest, didn't you?' he asked.

Moxey looked hunted. 'How did you know?'

'I couldn't think of any other reason for you to be here.'

'It's nothing to worry about,' said Leeming. 'You'll only be questioned for a few minutes then you'll be free to go. The inspector and I will then have to take our turn.'

'Do I *have* to be there?' asked Moxey.

'Yes – you found the body.'

'What will I be asked?'

'How you came to be there and how you stumbled on it.'

'Can't you write that down and show it to the coroner? That would save me going. Mr Higginbottom's not happy about me taking time off. Write it down,' said Moxey with enthusiasm as the idea took hold on him. 'I'd do it myself but I never learnt writing and such.'

'I think I see the problem here,' said Colbeck. 'When you went out after rabbits that night, you might not have been on your own.'

'But I was, I *was* alone, Inspector.'

'I'm sure that you were, Wilf, but let's assume – for the sake of argument – that you did have a friend with you. And let's assume that you have a very good reason for keeping that friend's name out of it altogether.' He gave an understanding smile. 'Do you follow me?'

'I do, sir.'

'In that case, there's a simple solution.'

Moxey went blank. 'Is there?'

'Yes,' said Colbeck. 'The coroner isn't really interested in what you were doing in that wood in the middle of the night. The point is that you discovered the body. Until you did that, Sergeant Leeming and I had been floundering.'

'We didn't know if the lady was alive or dead,' said Leeming. 'All we knew was that she was missing.'

'You solved the mystery for us, Will.'

'Yes,' said Moxey with a slow smile, 'I did, didn't I?'

'The coroner will realise that and take it into account.'

'Will he, sir?'

'He will, if I speak to him beforehand,' explained Colbeck. 'Even on a short acquaintance, I can see that you're an honest man. It would upset you to lie on oath, wouldn't it? You're afraid you'd be committing perjury.' Moxey lowered his head to his chest. 'Then the coroner will simply say that he believes you were out walking that night and found the grave by accident. He won't try to interrogate you about why you went to that particular place.' Moxey's head was raised hopefully. 'How does that sound?'

'Would you do that for me, Inspector?'

'We need your evidence and I'll make sure that you don't have any embarrassment while giving it.'

'Then you can go back to the farm and boast about appearing at a coroner's court,' said Leeming.

'It's nothing to boast about, sir. I'm just sad about the lady.'

'So are we,' said Colbeck. 'But the best way to get rid of that sadness is to catch the man who murdered her. Now then, have I put your mind at rest?'

'Oh, you have, sir. Thank you. It's been preying on me.'

'Have you had a hard day at work, Wilf?'

'Yes, Inspector, we started to get the harvest in.'

'Then you'll have built up a good thirst,' said Colbeck, patting him on the back. 'Drink up and the sergeant will get you another.'

Moxey thought about Lorna Begg and laughed inwardly. He'd have so much to tell her when he got back to the farm.

Dorcas Skelton was an obedient wife who readily took instruction from a husband she regarded as a kind of saint. She never questioned his decisions nor tried to take the initiative in their marriage. The fact that it was childless was something she'd long ceased to feel slight qualms about. Life with Frederick Skelton was a blessing. Maternal instincts were smothered beneath a blanket of wifely devotion. Yet she was not the sedate creature that she appeared. Adversity could bring out the essential steel in her character. Whenever she felt that the rector was unfairly criticised or undervalued, she leapt to his defence like a guard dog straining at the leash. The visit of Adam Tarleton had her barking wildly.

'His behaviour was atrocious,' she cried. 'He had no right to force his way in here and abuse you in your own study.'

'It was rather alarming,' he confessed. 'He must have been drinking.'

'That's no excuse, Frederick. You told me that he might have matured in the time he's been away. I saw no maturity in the account you gave of him. He sounded like the same wilful young rascal that he always was. Someone should thrash him soundly.'

'I never resort to violence, Dorcas.'

'It's what the colonel should have done.'

'I'm sure it's what he would have wanted to do, my dear, but Miriam always interceded. She was far too soft on the lad.'

'And look at the result,' she said. 'Adam has turned into an uncontrollable ruffian with no respect for a man of the cloth. I think that he should be reported.'

'He already has been,' he said, casting a pious glance upward.

'God may punish him for his sins in time but he needs more immediate chastisement. Adam should be reported and flogged.'

'By whom? There's no agency to which we can turn.'

They were in his study and she was standing in the precise spot occupied by Adam Tarleton when he unloosed his tirade against the rector. On the wall behind Skelton's head was the crucifix before which he prayed every morning before beginning work at his desk. Its very presence had buoyed him up at times of crisis and it seemed to fill the room with a precious sanctity. Glancing at the crucifix now, he made the sign of the cross with a grace for which he was renowned. The gesture helped to calm his wife down a little.

'What are you going to do, Frederick?' she asked.

'You know my mind. The colonel will not be buried here.'

215

'I wasn't talking about that. I was thinking about Sunday when you have to take a service in the church. Members of the family might turn up. Eve will want to come and she might even persuade that lout of a brother to accompany her – though I think he should be refused entry to any place of worship.'

He spread his arms. 'All are welcome in my congregation.'

'Will you let him abuse you like that again?'

'I'll be firmly in control in my church, Dorcas,' he said. 'It's my spiritual fortress. Nobody can attack me there. Besides, I doubt very much if Adam will turn up on Sunday. His sister may come with Mrs Withers and there'll be friends of the family here as well.'

'That's what worries me,' she admitted. 'They'll be here for solace. They'll want your sermon to give them moral guidance to cope with their loss. They'll expect eulogies of the deceased.'

He clenched his teeth. 'I will not offer praise of the colonel.'

'You could talk about his charitable work, perhaps.'

'Dorcas,' he said, stroking his hair with offhand vanity, 'I'm not a man to compromise. Colonel Tarleton doesn't deserve even to be mentioned in my church, let alone given a tribute. He flouted the teaching of the Bible. He committed suicide and we both know why he took that desperate and irrevocable step.' His voice soared like a chord on the church organ. 'He murdered his wife. I'll not let his bones corrupt my church-yard. Miriam is the only person for whom we'll pray on Sunday. My sermon will explain why and it will be fearless.'

Having eaten their supper, the detectives remained at their table to discuss the evidence they'd so far gathered and to decide what they needed to do on the following day. Neither of them was pleased when Eric Hepworth hove into view, his bald head gleaming in the light of the oil lamps, the sight of his uniform causing some of the other customers to sidle out of the bar. Without invitation, Hepworth took an empty seat at the table and gave them a conspiratorial smirk.

'Have you made an arrest yet, gentlemen?' he asked.

'No,' replied Colbeck, 'but it's only a matter of time.'

'That means you have someone in view.'

'We have a number of suspects, Sergeant, but we prefer to be certain of our facts before we make a move. Had we listened to you, for instance, we'd have believed that Mrs Tarleton had simply fled from a domineering husband.'

Hepworth bridled. 'That was only a theory.'

'A foolish one, as it turned out,' said Leeming.

'Ginny heard the colonel arguing with his wife. Others may tell you that they were happily married but I know the truth.' His tone became placatory. 'Anyway, the body was found. We know the truth now. All we need to do is to find the killer.'

'That's our task.'

'But I'm the one with local knowledge, Sergeant.'

'With respect,' said Leeming, 'it's not entirely reliable. Your view of the colonel is coloured by the fact that he dismissed your daughter and treated your son badly.'

'I saw him for the petty tyrant he really was,' argued Hepworth.

'That opinion is not yours alone,' said Colbeck, thinking of the stationmaster. 'And we do respect your local knowledge. In fact, I'd like to draw on it now.'

Hepworth beamed. 'Feel free to do so, Inspector.'

'We're trying to find a man named Michael Bruntcliffe.'

'Why – is he a suspect?'

'We just wish to speak to him, that's all, and eliminate him from our enquiries. Do you know who he is?'

'I should do,' said Hepworth, proudly. 'I was the one who arrested him for defacing railway property. That's a serious offence in my book. Signs and notices are there to guide the travelling public. If someone paints out certain words, the information can be very misleading. What annoyed me was that Bruntcliffe treated the whole thing as a joke.'

'Did you catch him in the act?'

'Yes, Inspector, he was painting vulgar messages on the side of a goods wagon.' He grinned at the memory. 'Fortunately for me, he resisted arrest. I had to overpower him.'

'The colonel sent him to prison,' said Leeming.

'That's where he belonged. If it was left to me, he'd still be there. Bruntcliffe likes to make mischief. His family have disowned him. Or, to be more exact, Bruntcliffe has disowned them.'

'Yes,' said Colbeck, 'I spoke to the prison governor. He said that Bruntcliffe refused to see his family on release. He just disappeared. Nobody seems to know if he's in the area or not.'

'There's one person who should be able to tell you.'

'Oh? And who's that?'

'Young Mr Tarleton. He and Michael Bruntcliffe were friends. They were also birds of a feather.'

'We spoke to Mr Tarleton earlier,' said Colbeck, 'and he claimed that he hadn't seen Bruntcliffe for years.'

'Then he was lying to you, Inspector.'

'How do you know?'

'My brother is a warder at the prison. He tells me what happens there. When you spoke to the governor, did you ask him if Bruntcliffe had had any visitors while he was serving his sentence?'

'No, I didn't,' said Colbeck.

'Then you should have done,' said Hepworth, relishing a minor triumph, 'because you might have learnt what I did. So young Mr Tarleton hasn't seen Bruntcliffe for years, has he? Ask him to explain why he visited his friend in prison more than once. The last time was less than a month ago.' He gave a ripe chuckle. 'Do you see what I mean about the value of local knowledge?'

CHAPTER THIRTEEN

Instead of mourning the death of an old friend, Edward Tallis threw himself into his work with such commitment that there was little room left for brooding on his grief. Policing a city as large and turbulent as London was well beyond the limited resources allocated to the task. Crime flowed through the capital with the force and inevitability of the River Thames. Nothing could stop it. The most that could be achieved was to divert a small proportion of it into tributaries where it could be contained and, even then, success was only ever temporary. Puffing on his cigar, Tallis looked at the list of serious crimes perpetrated in the previous twenty-four hours. It was daunting. Many of them could be dealt with by uniformed constables but some called for the specialist assistance of the Detective Department.

Before he could begin to assign his men to deal with specific cases, however, there was a tap on the door. It opened to allow Robert Colbeck to step in, looking as suave as ever. Tallis was flabbergasted.

'How did you get here this early, Inspector?' he asked.

'It involved some personal discomfort, sir,' said Colbeck, smoothly. 'I took a milk train to York, inveigled my way into the guard's van of a goods

220

train to Peterborough then picked up an express to King's Cross. I intend to return by more direct means.'

'Have you identified the killer yet?'

'We have two main suspects in mind. It's our belief that they may have been acting together.'

'Give me the details.'

Unlike Leeming, the inspector was never intimidated by Tallis. He was able to give a clear, succinct, well-presented account of what they'd been doing since the sergeant had delivered his more garbled report. Tallis was impressed by his thoroughness but he had doubts that Adam Tarleton was involved.

'He's not the sort of man to kill anyone,' he asserted.

'He may not have done it himself, sir,' said Colbeck, 'but he could be capable of hiring someone else to commit the murder.'

'You believe that he suborned Bruntcliffe?'

'We are coming around to that view.'

'I can see that this fellow might have had a strong enough motive. If the colonel sent him to prison, Bruntcliffe could have wreaked his revenge by killing the person the colonel loved most. What I can't see is a motive for Adam.'

'Do you remember how he conducted himself at the inquest?'

'Only too clearly,' said Tallis, disapprovingly. 'He didn't look like a son who'd just lost a stepfather by suicide. There was no sense of genuine bereavement.'

'We felt the same, Superintendent,' said Colbeck. 'While his sister was suffering agonies, he behaved as if he had no connection with the deceased. All that interests him is the money he stands to inherit. When we met him at the house yesterday, he hadn't even put on appropriate mourning wear.'

'That's unforgivable.'

'He admitted quite freely that he resented the colonel and had never acknowledged him as a father. By the same token, he must have borne a grudge against his mother for foisting her second husband on him. From what I can gather, Mrs Tarleton sought to retain his affection by providing him with money. But as we're aware,' said Colbeck, 'that source of income ceased. How would a parasite like Adam Tarleton react when he could no longer sponge off his mother?'

'He'd be very angry – even vengeful.'

'There's your motive, sir.'

Tallis scratched his head. 'I wonder.'

'The only way to get the money he felt was his due was to kill his mother in such a way that suspicion fell on the colonel. The stratagem worked. Most people still believe that he killed his wife.'

'I know and it's monstrously unjust.'

'Yet it's shared by people like the rector. He's an intelligent man who wouldn't simply follow the herd. The problem,' Colbeck went on, 'is that he exerts such influence in the village and its environs. He has a hold on people's minds.'

'That's why we must trumpet the colonel's innocence,' said Tallis, tugging the cigar from his mouth, 'and there's only one way to do that.' He shot Colbeck a shrewd look. 'How convinced are you that Adam is the real killer?'

'To be frank,' admitted Colbeck, 'I'm only partially convinced, even though he lied about not seeing Bruntcliffe for years. On his own, he might baulk at the idea of murder. Given assistance, however, it might be a different matter. That's where Bruntcliffe comes in.'

'But he was locked up in Northallerton.'

'And he was visited there by Adam Tarleton.'

'That may be,' said Tallis, 'but they could hardly have hatched a murder plot together. Prison visits are closely supervised. He and this Bruntcliffe wouldn't have been alone for a second.'

'Then they could have waited until Bruntcliffe's release.'

'Is there any evidence that Adam was in Yorkshire at that time? And where did the discharged prisoner go when they let him out? How would he have known that the colonel's wife would be walking to Northallerton on that particular day? Where would Bruntcliffe have acquired those two cartridges found with the dead body? No,' decided Tallis, 'there are too many imponderables here, Inspector. All that you have at the moment is a series of coloured marbles. You need to find the thread that will link them together in a pearl necklace.'

'I'd prefer to see it as a hangman's noose, Superintendent.'

Tallis smiled grimly. He was grateful that Colbeck had taken such trouble to report to him in person but disappointed that no incontrovertible proof had been found. As he sat there in the swirling cigar smoke, he wondered if he should return to Yorkshire with the inspector. He was sorely tempted. Colbeck tried to stifle the notion.

'Sergeant Leeming and I are very grateful for the freedom you've granted us to pursue this investigation,' he said. 'Had you been there, we'd have been hampered by the need to defer to you at every stage.'

Tallis glared. 'Are you telling me that I'd be in the way?'

'We work better when you're not looking over our shoulders, sir,' said Colbeck, easily. 'It's the same for anyone. I'm sure that you work more effectively when you're not under continual scrutiny.'

'There's something in that.'

'Then stay in London and rule the roost here, Superintendent.'

'I'll give you the weekend,' warned Tallis. 'If you've made no real advance by Monday, I may well join you to lend my assistance.'

'You might be able to assist us right now, Superintendent,' said Colbeck, dismayed to hear that he'd been given only two days to solve a complex case. 'It's this business about the colonel's regular visits to Doncaster. Can you suggest why he went there? Nobody else can.'

'I'm sorry, I can't help you.'

'Did the colonel make no mention of it in his letters?'

'No, Inspector, our correspondence usually took the form of reminiscences about our time in the army. I can't recall a single reference to Doncaster.'

'Can you explain why he'd want to keep his visits so secret?'

Tallis was annoyed. 'I know what's behind that question,' he said, irritably, 'and I find it impertinent. When a married man disappears from time to time, the obvious assumption is that he's going off for an illicit assignation.'

'That's not an assumption that *I* made, sir,' said Colbeck.

'Well, it's one that other people will make and I want to tell you why it's both unkind and untrue. This, mark you,' he went on, 'must go no further than this room.'

'You have my word of honour, Superintendent.'

'Whatever else took the colonel to Doncaster, it was definitely not a woman. When we saw action together in India, I escaped with minor injuries but the colonel was less fortunate. A bullet ricocheted and wounded him in the groin. The damage was permanent. *That's* why the colonel and his wife never had children of their own,' he said, pointedly, 'and why he'd never be led astray by a female.'

Eve Doel was still crushed beneath the combined weight of grief and remorse. Back in the house where she'd been brought up, she found it curiously empty and deeply upsetting. Wherever she looked, she saw reminders of happier days. One glance into her mother's bedroom had been all that she managed before she was overwhelmed by a tidal wave of loss and regret. One of the things that made her pain so hard to bear was that it was patently not shared by her

225

brother. Over breakfast that morning, she taxed him with his lack of sympathy.

'You're not even *pretending* to mourn,' she said.

'That time will come, Eve,' he promised her. 'At the moment, I have to keep my mind clear to defend our rights.'

'Mr Everett can do that. He's a lawyer.'

'He's no match for someone like the rector. A decision needed to be reached about the funerals. The inquest into Mother's death is on Monday. As soon as that's over, we can take possession of the body and have a joint funeral at St Andrew's.'

She was dubious. 'Did the rector actually agree to that?'

'I gave him no chance to *disagree*.'

'So all you've done is to antagonise him further.'

'I simply put him in his place,' said Tarleton through a mouthful of food. 'Trust me, Eve. When we go to church tomorrow, he'll be ready to accede to our wishes.'

'I think that's highly unlikely,' she said. 'Besides, it would be very unwise of you to attend the service. It would be like red rag to a bull.'

'You can't go to church on your own.'

'I won't have to, Adam. Mrs Withers will come with me. There's even a chance that my husband will join us. Lawrence is due back in England today. When he realises what's been happening while he was abroad, he'll catch the first train here.'

'I need to be there as well,' said Tarleton, 'to discuss the details of the funerals with the rector.'

226

'There's no point. He won't budge. After the way you confronted him, he'll be even more determined to prevent our stepfather's body from being buried in the churchyard. Inspector Colbeck made the best suggestion. We must appeal to the archbishop.'

'That could take time.'

'Not if you write a letter and deliver it by hand today.'

'I'll do it my way, Eve,' he insisted. 'I showed the rector that we won't be pushed about by him. He's bound to capitulate.'

Eve was about to reply but she saw Lottie hovering at the door, waiting to clear away the breakfast things. She beckoned the servant over and the girl entered hastily, gathering up the plates with a clatter then backing out with a string of mumbled apologies.

'Where on earth did they find that useless creature?' complained Tarleton. 'Why couldn't they hire someone more efficient?'

'Lottie is cheap.'

'She's a liability. I've never seen anyone so nervous.'

'That's because of you, Adam. You scare her. She's terrified to make a mistake in case you punish her.'

'Well, she made a mistake yesterday. I heard Mrs Withers scolding her in the kitchen. The girl was sent to get two dozen eggs from Rock Farm. She managed to break three of them on her way back here. She's a ditherer and I can't tolerate that.'

'Coming back to tomorrow,' she said, 'I don't

think it would be wise for you to go to church.'

'Of course I'll go,' he asserted. 'It will be expected of me.'

'I find that ironic. When we lived here, the one thing we could expect was that you *wouldn't* go to church. You did everything you could to get out of it.'

'The services were so tedious. Once he gets into that pulpit, the rector can spout for hours. It was like purgatory sometimes,' he recalled. 'Tomorrow is different. People will want to commiserate with us. Family friends will be there.'

'That's why I don't want any unpleasantness.'

'I'll be as good as gold, Eve.'

'The rector is bound to talk about the tragedies we've had to endure. He'll ask everyone to pray for us. What if he refuses in public to accept one of the bodies for burial?'

'In that case,' said Tarleton, grinding his teeth, 'he'll get a lot more than mere unpleasantness. I can vouch for that.'

Madeleine couldn't believe her good fortune. After doing some chores in the house, she'd intended to visit a friend in Highgate. Instead of that, Colbeck had arrived out of nowhere, told her to change into her best dress, then helped her into a cab that took them to King's Cross. The two of them now had a first-class carriage to themselves in a train that was thundering north. She was still dizzied by the turn of events.

'What am I to tell Father?' she asked.

'Tell him that you were abducted by a handsome stranger.'

'He'll worry about me, Robert.'

'You'll be safely back home long before he finishes work,' said Colbeck. 'I'm only taking you as far as Peterborough. You can catch the next train back to London from there.' He indicated the book she'd brought. 'You can finish *Cranford* on the return journey.'

'Father will hate the fact that I travelled on the Great Northern Railway. You know how much he complained when you took me on the GWR. He called that an act of treason. According to him,' she said, 'the only company who should be allowed to take passengers is the London and North Western.'

'I admire his loyalty to the LNWR,' said Colbeck with a grin, 'but it's not as faultless as he thinks. Captain Huish, the general manager, has stooped to all kinds of machinations to keep rivals at bay. Take this very line, for instance. Huish had wanted to preserve the LNWR's monopoly between London and Edinburgh. He did all he could to starve this eastern route of traffic. Every company touched by the Great Northern was coerced into the so-called Euston Confederacy whose sole aim was to undermine the GNR. I'm pleased to say that his skulduggery failed,' he went on. 'Four years ago, Huish got a royal slap in the face when Her Majesty abandoned his company's route to Scotland and went to Balmoral by means of the GNR instead.'

'I wouldn't dare say that to Father. He idolises Captain Huish.'

'Then he's worshipping a false god, Madeleine.' He squeezed her arm and pulled her closer. 'But

229

why are we talking about railways when we have so many other things to discuss?'

'You haven't even mentioned the investigation yet.'

'I was enjoying this short-lived break from it.'

'How much longer will you be away, Robert?'

'Ideally, the murder will be solved by Monday.'

'That's wonderful!' she cried, nestling closer. 'Are you so near to making an arrest?'

'The truth is that I don't know, Madeleine. Ideally, everything will become clear in the next two days. If it doesn't, Superintendent Tallis will resume control and that will slow the whole process down.' He pulled a face. 'I want to avoid that at all costs.'

'Is he really the ogre that Sergeant Leeming says he is?'

'No, he's a dedicated man with a firm belief in the importance of law and order. Everything else in his life is subordinate to his work.'

'Is that why he disapproves of marriage?'

'I'd rather nor go into that now, Madeleine.'

'You haven't told him, have you?'

He took a deep breath. 'No, I haven't.'

'It's not like you to be afraid, Robert.'

'It's a question of being diplomatic. At the moment, he's so caught up in the horrors of this case that he can think about nothing else. I have to take matters slowly.'

She searched his eyes. 'Is that the real explanation?'

'What other explanation is there?'

'Some people might say that you're too ashamed of me to tell the superintendent that we're engaged to be married.'

'That's absurd!' he said, enfolding her in his arms. 'And you must never think that, Madeleine. I love you and I'm proud of you. When you accepted my proposal, I couldn't wait to put details of the engagement in the newspapers. Had it been left to me, it would have been in headlines on the front pages.' She laughed with gratitude. 'How could I be ashamed of you when you're the most wonderful thing that ever happened to me?'

'Is that what you're going to tell the superintendent?'

'Well ... maybe not in exactly the same words.'

'Why didn't you mention it to him this morning?'

'It would have been the worst possible time.'

'You mean that he's too distracted?'

'No, Madeleine,' he said, 'that's only part of the reason. The one marriage that Mr Tallis admired was that between the colonel and his wife. When he was with them, he really understood the true value of holy matrimony. Without warning, he's confronted with the fact that their marriage might not have been as happy as he'd assumed. One of them is murdered and the other commits suicide. All sorts of secrets are being unearthed and that's shaken him.'

'I can see why you'd rather wait now, Robert.'

'When this business is over, I'll tell him immediately.'

'Thank you. I'll say no more on the subject.' He kissed her then pulled her close. It was minutes before she spoke again. 'You said that secrets are being unearthed.'

'That's right, Madeleine.'

'What sort of secrets?'

'Well,' he said, 'one of them concerns Doncaster.'

'What happened there?'

'That's the trouble – we don't know. I'm hoping that Victor will be able to find out. I told him to go there today.'

He was wrong. Because it was a flourishing railway town, Leeming had assumed that it would be covered in industrial grime and that, in fact, was the aspect that first presented itself to him. Alighting at the station, he found it swarming with passengers, waiting to go on the main line north or south or on the branch line to Sheffield. A goods train carrying coal went past on the through line. Other wagons were being loaded with coal in a siding. A strong breeze whipped up the coal dust and sent it flying through the air in clouds, mingling with the dense smoke from departing locomotives. The din was continual, its volume increased by the turmoil from the railway works nearby.

Yet when he went into the town itself, Leeming realised that it was a charming place with a pleasant situation on the River Don. Many of the vestiges of its time as a coaching town still remained. Its long, wide high street was an impressive thoroughfare, lined with houses, shops, inns, eating houses, banks and business premises. As he explored the town, Leeming found much to admire. Doncaster had a mansion house, a town hall, fine churches, a theatre, schools, a hospital, almshouses and other institutions for promoting the welfare of its inhabitants. New terraced housing had been built by the railway company for its employees but the serried ranks didn't detract from the weathered graciousness of the older buildings.

Leeming's problem was that he didn't know where to begin. In a town with a population of several thousand, he could hardly knock on every door in search of anyone who'd known Colonel Tarleton. By the time he'd finished his initial stroll around the town, he could think of several reasons why the colonel had visited it. Many of the larger residences might have been the home of friends from the same social class. Leeming sought out one of the town constables for advice.

Claude Forrester knew exactly who the colonel was.

'It was him what was took mad,' he said, darkly. 'Him what threw himself in front of that train. It were in the newspaper.'

'That's right,' said Leeming. 'Are you aware that he used to come to Doncaster quite often at one time?'

'Lots of people do that, Sergeant.'

'But they're not all as distinctive as the colonel.'

'He'd be lost in the crowd. Know your trouble? You're searching for a grain of sand on Blackpool beach.'

Forrester was a lugubrious individual in his forties whose days in uniform had convinced him of the existence of criminal tendencies in most human beings. As they talked, his eyes flicked suspiciously at every passer-by.

'There's two reasons why the colonel came,' he said.

'He could have had friends here.'

'That's a third reason but I think there's two main ones.'

'What are they?' asked Leeming.

'I can see you've never been to Doncaster before,' said Forrester, mentally frisking an old woman who waddled past. 'We have one of the finest racecourses in the country on Town Moor. Come here in September when the St Leger is run and you'll find the world and his wife in this part of Yorkshire. I know,' he added, 'because I'm always on duty there. Last year, almost a quarter of a million people came to Doncaster during the week of the St Leger.'

'That's only once a year, Constable.'

'There's plenty of other race meetings as well.'

'Yes,' said Leeming, 'but there's nothing to suggest that the colonel was a betting man. Besides, if he'd simply been here for the races, he'd have brought his wife. There'd be no need to be so secretive about it.'

'Ah, now, if it's secrecy we're talking about,' said the constable, 'then I come to my second main reason.' He tapped the side of his nose. 'He was paying a visit, sir.'

Leeming was impatient. 'I said that at the very start.'

'He was paying a visit to a certain place.'

'What I need to find out is where that certain place was.'

'I could take you there, if you wish.'

'You *know* where it is?'

234

'I know everything about this town,' boasted the other. 'This particular house is where rich men go to spend their money.'

'It's a gambling den?'

'They take a gamble of sorts, I suppose. They gamble that their wives won't ever find out. I'm talking about harlotry. You should see some of our ladies of easy virtue, Sergeant. They're quite a sight.'

'No, thank you,' said Leeming. 'When I was a young constable, I raided enough brothels in London to last me a lifetime. The colonel wasn't here for the delights of the flesh. He was a faithful husband.'

'No? Then I can't help you.'

'Do you know anyone who could?'

'No,' said Forrester, rubbing his chin. 'Unless you talk to Ned Staddle – but I daresay you've already done that.'

'Who's Ned Staddle?'

'He's the stationmaster. Got a keen eye and a good memory, for all that he's long in the tooth. Talk to Ned and mention my name. He's a friend.'

Leeming was glad to part from the cheerless constable. Yet the man had a useful suggestion. On his way back to the station, Leeming rebuked himself for not thinking of questioning people there when he first arrived. Since the colonel had been such a regular visitor – and since his name had been given prominence by the suicide – a member of the staff might well recall him. The sergeant soon learnt that talking to the stationmaster required a long wait. Ned Staddle was too busy controlling the traffic in and out of the

235

different platforms to spare him a moment. Tall, skinny and with silver hair hidden beneath his hat, Staddle seemed to be in constant motion. It was only when he took his morning break that he was able to find time for Leeming.

'Aye, I know who the colonel was,' said the stationmaster. 'Used to see quite a bit of him at one time.'

'Constable Forrester said that you had a good memory.'

'You been talking to that miserable old devil?'

'He claimed to be a friend of yours.'

Staddle laughed. 'He doesn't have a friend within a hundred miles of here,' he said. 'If this was a village, Claude Forrester would be its idiot. Looking like that, he should have been a gravedigger.'

'Yes,' agreed Leeming, 'chatting to him was a bit like attending a funeral. Putting the constable aside, can you tell me why the colonel used to come to Doncaster?'

'It wasn't to see Forrester, I know that much. Let me think.' Staddle put a hand to his forehead as he ransacked his memory for details. At length, he gave a sigh of regret. 'I'm sorry, Sergeant. I did speak to the colonel whenever he came but we never really talked. The only person who might be able help you is Mr Kinchin.'

'Who's he?'

'Mr Kinchin retired a few years ago. He used to work for the Great Northern as a manager. I seem to remember that he was here to meet the colonel sometimes.'

'Does this gentleman live in Doncaster?'

'Aye,' said Staddle, 'but you won't find him at home. He caught the early train to Sheffield. He always goes to see his mother on the first Saturday of the month. She's in her eighties.'

'Will he be returning here today?'

'Oh, aye, he'll be back in Doncaster this evening.'

'I take it that you'll still be on duty, Mr Staddle.'

The stationmaster chortled. 'I'm always on duty, sir.'

'Then perhaps you'll give a message to this gentleman. I'll write it down, if you wish.'

'There's no need. Constable Forrester was right about one thing, but then even a fool says a wise thing sometimes. I do have a good memory. I'll pass on any message word for word.'

'Thank you,' said Leeming, feeling that he was at last getting close to the answer he sought. 'Impress upon him that he may have some information that will help to further a murder investigation. Tell him to catch the next train to South Otterington and to ask for me or for Inspector Colbeck at the Black Bull.' He paused to give Staddle time to absorb everything. 'Can you remember all that?'

'He's to come to the Black Bull at South Otterington.'

'We'll pay his rail fare. No matter how late it is, it's vital that he comes. If I had the time, I'd wait here until he returned but I've lots of other enquiries to make so I must go back.'

'I understand.'

'What sort of person is Mr Kinchin?'

'He was a manager – the kind you tip your hat to.'

'Do you know much about him?'

'Not really, Sergeant Leeming.'

'Had he ever been in the army?'

'You'll have to ask him at the Black Bull in South Otterington,' said Staddle with another chuckle. 'See? I did remember. He's to speak to you or to Inspector Colbeck.'

Having had the pleasure of Madeleine's company all the way to Peterborough, Colbeck spent the rest of his journey addressing his mind to the investigation. It was a paradox. Though certain that a man committed the murder, he somehow felt that they needed the help of a woman to solve the crime. Their names popped into his head in order of importance - Eve Doel, Agnes Reader, Mrs Withers, Lottie Pearl and Dorcas Skelton. He hadn't forgotten Ginny Hepworth, the daughter of the railway policeman. Then there was the anonymous female who'd been there when the body of Miriam Tarleton had been discovered. Colbeck began to wish that he'd taken Madeleine all the way with him. In the past, her instincts about other women had always been acute and reliable.

Instead of getting off the train at South Otterington, he stayed on until it reached North-allerton so that he could call on Clifford Everett. Even on a Saturday, the lawyer was at his office. Colbeck tripped up the stairs and was soon settling into a chair opposite Everett. After exchanging a few niceties with him, Colbeck came to the point.

'I understand that you're quite a marksman, sir,' he said.

'Oh, I wouldn't say that,' replied Everett with a self-deprecating smirk. 'I just seem to be lucky with a shotgun in my hands.'

'I think you're being too modest.'

'I will admit to having some success – much to the chagrin of our cook, I may say. Whenever I bring home pheasants or other game birds, she hates having to pick the shot out of them.'

'What about the colonel?'

'He was the best of us all – until his eyesight began to fade.'

'I'm told that you and he often went out together.'

'It was my one indulgence, Inspector,' said Everett. 'My wife is very tolerant because she knows that it could be far worse. Other husbands turn to drink or gambling to while away their free time.'

'How often did you and the colonel go shooting?'

'We went whenever we could. If there was a shooting party at the weekend, we always joined in. Office work is very sedentary. It's important to get some exercise.'

Colbeck gave a nod of agreement even though the lawyer didn't look like a man who got much exercise. He couldn't imagine Everett with a shotgun in his hands but knew that appearances could be deceptive. He saw the perspiration forming on the other man's upper lip and wondered if he was making him nervous.

'One of the things that puzzles me,' admitted Colbeck, 'is how the killer knew that Mrs

Tarleton would be walking here that day.'

'There's no mystery there, Inspector. It was the day of the week when she always visited Agnes Reader. Miriam Tarleton was as methodical as her husband. She had a day for this, a day for that and so on. Everyone in her circle knew her routine,' said Everett. 'On a Saturday morning, for instance, you'd always find her at St Andrew's, arranging the flowers. She had a real knack for it.'

'Did Mrs Reader visit her on a particular day?'

'Oh, yes. You could probably set your watch by it. What did fall by the wayside a little were the occasions when the four of them played cards together. If they met at the colonel's house, it would mean feeding the guests and savings had to be made. Bertram Reader was very understanding about that.'

'Yes,' said Colbeck, 'he seems a very understanding man.'

'You have to be if you're a banker. Bertram gets to see even more human misery in his office than I do. Money troubles can destroy whole families.' He sat back and regarded Colbeck for a few moments. 'If you've come to see me again, Inspector, I suspect that you've made very little progress.'

'That's not true, sir. We've already made some connections.'

'Between whom, may I ask?'

'Between Adam Tarleton and Michael Bruntcliffe, for example,' said Colbeck. 'It seems that they've been in touch quite recently.' Everett was startled. 'Young Mr Tarleton visited his friend in prison.'

'Then why didn't he tell his parents he was in the area?'

'I doubt if he wanted them to know.'

'What are those two up to, I wonder?'

'That's what I intend to find out. Even as we speak, Sergeant Leeming is conducting a search for Bruntcliffe. I'm hoping that he may have made another connection for us as well – the link between the colonel and Doncaster.'

'Yes, I'd be interested to know that.'

'The sergeant spent the morning in the town.'

'Do you have any theories about what he might have found, Inspector?'

'There's a connection with the railways somehow,' said Colbeck. 'I felt that from the start. It's worth bearing one thing in mind. When he committed suicide that day, the colonel was walking in the direction of Doncaster.'

Though the bank was closed, Bertram Reader was not off duty. He visited one client in Cowton that morning then had luncheon with another in Thirsk. It was mid afternoon when he finally returned home and was able to anticipate a period of rest. His wife gave him a sympathetic smile as he came into the drawing room.

'You shouldn't have to work on a Saturday,' she said. 'People ask too much of you. They should visit you during banking hours.

'Most of my clients do that Agnes,' he told her, 'but there are exceptions. When someone asks for a loan to extend their house or to increase the size of their herd – which is exactly what today's clients wanted to do – I like to take a close look at their premises to make sure that everything is as it should be. I always ask to see their account books as well. My predecessor lost his job because he advanced loans without due care. One of the clients absconded with two thousand pounds that was never repaid.'

'You're back home now, that's the important thing.'

'What have you been doing?'

'I've been thinking about this and that.'

'Have you been brooding again?' he asked, taking her by the shoulders. 'You mustn't keep blaming yourself.'

'But if Miriam hadn't been coming here…'

'How many times must I say it? You did nothing wrong.'

'Then why do I feel so guilty?'

'It's because you're a dear, lovely, caring woman. I have *my* share of guilt, you know. If I hadn't been with a client that day, you could have summoned me from my office to begin the search. I let you down and, indirectly, I let Miriam down.'

'You weren't to know, Bertram.'

'Exactly,' he said, taking his hands away. 'I wasn't to know any more than you were. We can't be held responsible for what happened. It was a terrible tragedy but it can't be laid at our door.'

'You're right.'

'Then remember that I'm right,' he said with mock sternness.

When they moved to the sofa and sat down, he noticed a piece of paper on the table beside her. Seeing his interest, she picked it up and passed it over to him. Reader studied the long list of names his wife had compiled.

'I didn't spend all my time brooding,' she said.

'Who are all these people?'

'They're murder suspects.'

He was offended. 'Do you mind?' he said with mild outrage. 'My name is down here.'

'And so is mine, Bertram.'

'What do we have to do – confess?'

'Don't be silly,' she scolded. 'I've tried to be useful. Every person on that list knew that Miriam would be coming to see me that day. They could have planned an ambush.'

'You've got well over twenty names here,' he said.

'That's the trouble. There were so many of us. Clifford Everett is one of them, though I ought to exclude him because he's the least likely person to have committed a murder.'

He examined the list. 'There's something you've forgotten, Agnes. Anyone on this list could inadvertently have mentioned that Miriam came to Northallerton on a particular day. Sharp ears might have picked up the information. Or there's something else we ought to consider,' he went on. 'The culprit may simply have watched Miriam for weeks beforehand and seen a pattern emerge. Inspector Colbeck said that calculation was involved.'

'Are you telling me that my list is useless?'

'No, no – simply that it's not comprehensive.'

'Oh dear!' she said, forlornly. 'I wasted my time.'

'Don't think that,' he urged. 'It was a very useful exercise and the villain may well be hidden somewhere in that list. I think that I should show it to the inspector.'

'Very well, Bertram – please do that.'

He looked at her fondly. Though she was still in mourning attire, he was glad to see that she was not as pale and distraught as she had been. There were no visible signs of another bout of sustained weeping. Agnes was composed and dignified. He was reassured. As he let his gaze drift to the mantelpiece, he noticed a card that hadn't been there before. He got up from the sofa.

'What's that?' he asked.

'It came this morning,' she replied.

'Who sent it?'

The question was answered when he saw the name at the bottom of the message inscribed inside the card. As he read it, his body tensed and his face hardened.

'Is something wrong?' she asked, noting the sudden change in his demeanour.

'It is, my dear,' he said, moving to the door. 'You'll have to excuse me. I have to find Inspector Colbeck as soon as I can.'

CHAPTER FOURTEEN

One of the first things that Victor Leeming had learnt when he joined the Detective Department was that perseverance was a virtue. No matter how intractable a murder case might seem at first, it could always be solved, he was told, by a blend of patience and tenacity. A day spent largely on his feet had made the sergeant question the dictum. While he remained as tenacious as ever, his patience was wearing thin. The visit to Doncaster had brought what he considered to be a marginal success but the search for Michael Bruntcliffe was a story of sustained failure. His starting point had been the family of the released prisoner but they'd been able to give him scant help. While the mother still yearned for him to come home and mend his ways, the father had abandoned all hope of his doing so and wished never to see his son again.

What the parents were able to give Leeming, however, were the names and addresses of some friends of Bruntcliffe. The sergeant's perambulation around Northallerton began in earnest. He went from house to house, only to be met by the same response. Bruntcliffe's former friends all claimed that they were merely acquaintances and tried to distance themselves from someone who'd ended up in prison and brought disgrace to the family name. While nobody could say where

Bruntcliffe was, the general feeling was that he wouldn't be too far away. His first move on release, they all agreed, would be to search for amenable female company. Leeming managed to elicit the names of three young ladies who'd been close to Bruntcliffe in the past.

That set him off on the next stage of his journey. Since none of the trio lived in the town, he had to hire a trap in order to drive out to the respective houses where they lived. For a man like the sergeant, questioning a young lady about an emotional attachment they once had was highly embarrassing. Leeming had married the only woman he'd ever loved and had never been tempted to stray. He was therefore shocked to learn that Bruntcliffe had dallied with three beautiful women without the slightest intention of proposing marriage to any of them. It had left all three with a deep reservoir of bitterness. The first hotly denied ever knowing Bruntcliffe, the second was horrified that what had been a clandestine relationship was now the subject of police interest and the third, daughter of a minor aristocrat, was so indignant at being asked such personal questions that she ordered the butler to show Leeming out. All that the sergeant had to show for driving many unproductive miles in unfamiliar countryside was a bill from the man who'd provided the horse and trap.

When he finally caught the train back to South Otterington, he found Colbeck waiting for him at the Black Bull. Each told the other what their day had so far yielded. Leeming seized on a threat.

'Superintendent Tallis is coming *here?*'he cried.

'I did my best to dissuade him.'

'We'll be here for ever if he takes charge. I'll never get home to Estelle and the children.'

'There is one way to head the superintendent off,' said Colbeck, 'and that's to solve the murder by Monday.'

Leeming goggled. 'We can't do that, sir. We seem to be going around in circles. I've spent all morning and most of the afternoon hard at work and I've come back empty-handed.'

'Don't be so defeatist, Victor. You brought back the name of this gentleman from Doncaster. He may unwittingly have some useful evidence for us. As for Michael Bruntcliffe,' he continued, 'you found out a great deal more about our prime suspect than we knew before.'

'He was a philanderer,' said Leeming with revulsion. 'I met three of his victims and I suspect there were many others.'

Colbeck was thoughtful. 'A successful philanderer must have two attributes – charm and money. We know that Bruntcliffe has great charm, though it might have been blunted somewhat by his time behind bars. What he no longer has is the wherewithal to fund his romantic entanglements. He'll need money,' he said. 'Where could he get it?'

'He won't get a penny from his parents, I discovered that.'

'Then he might turn to Adam Tarleton.'

'But he doesn't have any money either, does he?'

'He has prospects, Victor,' said Colbeck. 'He probably stands to inherit half of the estate. On the strength of that, he wouldn't have much difficulty in raising a loan.'

Leeming snapped his fingers. 'That makes it almost certain that Bruntcliffe is the killer. His old friend paid him to commit the murder.'

'You've overlooked something. That, on its own, wouldn't have brought in the cash that Adam Tarleton coveted. He needed both his mother and his stepfather to die. Only on the death of the colonel would he be able to claim his inheritance.'

'Ah!' Leeming was instantly deflated. 'I never thought of that, Inspector. How could Tarleton know that his stepfather would take his own life?'

'He'd know how bereft the colonel would be at the loss of his wife,' reasoned Colbeck, 'and he'd be aware that his stepfather would be under suspicion. The pressure on the colonel was intense. It may even be that his stepson added to that pressure by getting someone to write poison-pen letters on his behalf.'

'It's all beginning to make sense at last,' said Leeming.

Colbeck was cautious. 'Well, let's not get ahead of ourselves. At the moment, we're constructing a hypothesis on the basis of limited facts. We need far more information, Victor, and we only have until Monday to get it.'

'Then we're doomed, sir.'

'Have more faith, Victor. Our efforts will soon be rewarded. Remember what the superintendent always tells us.'

'Perseverance is a virtue,' groaned Leeming.

They were in the bar at the Black Bull, enjoying

a drink at a table in a quiet corner. Neither of them looked up when the door opened. It was only when a shadow fell across them that they realised they had company. Bertram Reader was relieved to see them.

'I was hoping that I'd catch you here,' he said.

'Then do join us,' invited Colbeck, pointing to an empty chair. 'Can I get you anything to drink, sir?'

Reader sat down. 'No, thank you.'

'Why did you wish to see us?'

'I may have some evidence for you, Inspector.'

'Thank goodness someone does!' said Leeming under his breath.

'First, let me give you this list drawn up by my wife. All the people on it knew that Miriam would be visiting her that day.' He handed it over. 'Now, do you still have that letter you showed me?'

'Yes,' said Colbeck, reaching inside his coat.

'May I have another look at it, please?'

Colbeck gave it to him. 'Be my guest, Mr Reader.'

'Thank you.'

Reader took out the letter and unfolded it, scanning the lines as if searching for a secret code. At length, he gave a decisive nod.

'I knew that I was right,' he said. 'It's the same hand.'

'Would you care to explain, sir?' asked Colbeck.

'My wife and I worship at All Saints' church in Northallerton. We rarely come to the church here. But when we heard that Miriam's body had been found, my wife sought a visible way to express our grief. I suggested that she might buy flowers to adorn St Andrew's this Sunday when the prayers will certainly be offered for Miriam – if not, I regret to say, for her husband.'

'That was a very kind gesture, sir.'

'It was much appreciated,' said Reader, taking a card from his pocket, 'and this was sent from the rectory in acknowledgement. As soon as I saw it, I thought I recognised the handwriting.'

Opening the card, he laid it beside the letter so that Colbeck and Leeming could compare the two. Each had the same neat, looping hand. One person had obviously written them both and the polite phrases on the card came in sharp contradistinction to the vile insinuations in the letter. Grateful for such evidence, the detectives were astounded to see the name at the bottom of the card.

It was Dorcas Skelton.

The arrival of her husband was the blessing for which Eve Doel had prayed. She collapsed into his arms, confident that he would take over and provide the commiseration that her brother had signally failed to supply. Lawrence Doel, a stocky yet elegant man of middle years, was mortified that he'd been away when tragedy had struck his family and upset that his wife had been unable to make contact with him while he was negotiating contracts with merchants in various European cities. His presence was not only succour to Eve, it had a curative effect on Adam Tarleton, who dressed and bore himself in a way more suited to the circumstances.

Mrs Withers noted the changes with approval. During a lull in what had been almost endless activity, she was in the kitchen with Lottie Pearl who was mending the tear in her dress.

'This is how it should be,' said the housekeeper. 'It's started to feel like a house of mourning at last.'

'Mr Doel seems such a capable person,' said Lottie, seated on a chair as she repaired her hem. 'You can tell by looking at him.'

'He's also a true gentleman.'

'How long will he stay, Mrs Withers?'

'They'll all be here until the funeral is over. When that is, I fear, hasn't yet been decided. They have to wait for the inquest.'

'I overheard Mrs Doel saying that the colonel wouldn't be buried in the churchyard.'

'Then you should be ashamed of yourself, Lottie,' reprimanded the other, turning on her. 'You should never listen to what's being said in private conversations.'

'I'm sorry. I couldn't help it.'

'It's one of the reasons that Ginny Hepworth had to leave. I caught her with her ear to the door of the drawing room and it wasn't the first time she'd eavesdropped. I asked the colonel to dismiss her.'

'Ginny told me it was because you didn't like her.'

'My personal feelings never came into it,' said Mrs Withers. 'The girl was hopelessly slack in her duties. She had to go.'

'Am I any better?'

'You're improving, Lottie, that's all I'll say.'

Bolstered by a rare word of praise, the girl finished her sewing and put the needle and cotton away in the basket. She stood up and let the dress fall down to her ankle. The repair was invisible and even won a glance of approval from the housekeeper.

'Is it true?' asked Lottie.

'Is *what* true?'

'What I shouldn't have overheard about the funeral.'

'There is a problem,' confessed Mrs Withers.

'No wonder Mrs Doel is so upset. I think it would be a terrible thing if the colonel is not there alongside his wife. How could he get to heaven if he's not buried proper in a churchyard?'

'Be quiet, girl. You know nothing about these things.'

'I know the Reverend Skelton likes to make up his own mind. He's told us so in the pulpit. Mother used to make me go every Sunday but I never really liked it because he frightened me.'

'Who did?'

'The rector — he makes me shiver.'

'How can you say that about a man of God?'

'I'm scared of him, Mrs Withers.'

'That means you must have a guilty conscience,' said the older woman. 'Is there anything else you've done wrong, Lottie? Is there anything else I should know?'

'I don't think so.'

'Come on, girl. You should have no secrets from me. I still haven't heard why it took you so long to fetch those eggs from Rock Farm yesterday.'

'I told you – I was chased by this horrible man.'

'That was just a story you made up.'

'It wasn't,' cried Lottie, hurt by the accusation. 'He was a pedlar and I met him near the stream. He asked me for a kiss and, when I turned away, he jumped off his cart and chased me. I wouldn't make something like that up, Mrs Withers, honest.'

The housekeeper studied her shrewdly. 'Very well,' she said after a lengthy pause. 'I believe you. But that still doesn't explain why you were held up. If someone chased you, you'd have got here faster.'

'Those eggs were broken. I had to clean up the mess in the basket because I knew you'd shout at me if I didn't.'

'Go on.'

'That's all there is to say.'

'No, it isn't,' decided Mrs Withers, taking her by the shoulders and staring into her eyes. 'You haven't lied to me but you haven't told me the full truth either. There's more, isn't there? Out with it, Lottie,' she urged. 'Holding something back is the same as telling a lie.'

The girl was in a dilemma. If she mentioned that she'd seen Adam Tarleton, she ran the risk of a stern reproach. When she'd confided to the housekeeper that Tarleton had been looking at her in a way that unsettled her, Lottie had been roundly chastised and told to curb her imagination. She did not want to repeat the experience. If, on the other hand, she maintained that there was nothing left to tell, she'd be branded as a liar. Either way, there was a penalty to pay.

Mrs Withers shook her. 'I'm waiting, Lottie.'

'There *was* something,' conceded the girl.

'I knew it.'

'But I didn't do it on purpose – as God's my witness. I just happened to be there when they rode up.'

'Who are you talking about?'

'I saw Mr Tarleton and his friend. I was behind some trees when I heard the sound of horses. They stopped quite close to me.'

'Didn't you make them aware of your presence?'

'I was afraid to do that, Mrs Withers,' said Lottie. 'It was the way they laughed. I could tell they'd been drinking.'

'That much is true,' said the housekeeper, grudgingly. 'I could smell it on his breath when he got back here. What happened then?'

'They talked for a bit but I couldn't hear a word they said. Then Mr Tarleton gave something to his friend and rode off.'

'And that's all?'

'I swear it.'

'Who was the other man?'

'I've no idea, Mrs Withers. I've never seen him before.'

'Can you describe him?'

'Well,' said Lottie, wishing that she wasn't being held so tightly, 'he was about the same age as Mr Tarleton, only thinner and with a pale face. He was tall, well dressed and he wore a hat with a feather in it. That's all I can tell you except that...'

'Go on, Lottie – spit it out.'

'If you want the truth, I thought he was very handsome.'

Mrs Withers let go of her and turned away to reflect on what she'd just heard. Lottie was dismayed, fearing another reproof for eavesdropping. She retreated to a corner of the kitchen for safety. But there was no danger. When the housekeeper turned back to her, she was calm and pensive.

'Yes,' she confirmed. 'He *is* handsome. I noticed that.'

Having toiled over his sermon for a couple of hours, Frederick Skelton was ready to practise it in front of his wife. She was an experienced and attentive listener, having heard hundreds of his speeches and homilies over the years. It was always a pleasure to listen to his well-honed rhetoric even if, as on this occasion, it was liberally spiced with denunciation. Dorcas was enthralled. Her husband had struck the perfect balance between praise and condemnation, hailing the virtues of a wife while criticising the actions of her husband. The sermon was long without being tedious, bold without being insensitive and shot through with a confidence that never lapsed into rodomontade. Had she not been in church, Dorcas would have clapped her hands.

It was not simply the words that Skelton liked to rehearse. The correct gestures were just as important to master. When the sermon was over, he went back to a certain passage and experimented with a different wave of his arm and a novel arrangement of his fingers. Satisfied that all was now perfect, he descended from the pulpit to receive a smile of congratulation from his wife. They returned arm in arm to the rectory, surprised to learn that Robert Colbeck was waiting for them in the drawing room.

'I didn't realise that you were here, Inspector,' said Skelton. 'My wife and I were in church.'

'So I understand,' said Colbeck, 'but I didn't think that the conversation we're about to have would be altogether fitting for a church.'

'May I offer you refreshment?' asked Dorcas with practised sweetness.

'No, thank you.'

She moved to the door. 'In that case, I'll leave you alone.'

'I think you should stay, Mrs Skelton. What I have to say concerns both of you.'

'Well, at least sit down while you're saying it,' said Skelton.

While Colbeck and Dorcas chose the sofa, the rector made sure that he occupied a high-backed wooden chair with elaborately carved arms. From this eminence, he looked down on the others. His air of complacency showed that he had no idea what was coming.

'If you've come on behalf of the family,' he warned, 'then let me tell you I'm resolved on the course of action dictated to me by God. I will not have a man who committed suicide buried in my churchyard.'

'That's academic, sir,' said Colbeck.

'My husband's word is final,' insisted Dorcas.

'Leave this to me, my dear,' said Skelton before flicking his eyes back to Colbeck. 'I'm not prepared to debate the matter, Inspector. Appeal to the archbishop, if you wish, but he knows that my ministry has been unimpeachable and will surely condone the stand that I've taken.'

'I respect your right to hold that opinion,' said Colbeck.

'Is that all you have to say on the subject?'

'Yes, it is – for the moment.'

Skelton rose up. 'Then we must speed you on your way.'

'Not so fast, sir – I've not finished yet. I suggest that you sit down again because this may take a little time.' The rector lowered himself down again. 'Regarding the cause of the suicide,' Colbeck resumed, 'are you aware that the colonel received several letters full of abuse and wicked accusation?'

Skelton frowned. 'I was indeed aware of it, Inspector, and I railed against the authors of such missives from the pulpit.'

'Will you accept that such poison-pen letters would have been extremely hurtful and put the colonel under intolerable pressure?'

'I'll gladly accept that, Inspector.'

'Then the people against whom you railed should surely deserve some punishment. In my view, those who skulk behind anonymity are always despicable.'

'I heartily agree with you.'

'What punishment would you advise, sir?'

'That's for the law to decide.'

'Did you issue no warnings from the pulpit?'

'I said that they should be exposed and imprisoned for their crime,' recalled Skelton. 'I'd show them no mercy.'

'Then we find ourselves in an awkward situation,' said Colbeck, taking out the letter from his pocket. 'This was the last message of hatred sent to the colonel. He died without opening it.' He proffered the envelope. 'Do you wish to read it, sir?'

'Of course I don't.'

'Is that because you know its contents?'

Skelton frothed with outrage. 'I find that remark both ill-mannered and insulting.'

'What about you, Mrs Skelton?' asked Colbeck, offering it to her. 'Would you care to read it?'

'No, Inspector,' she replied, firmly, 'I would not.'

'You seem to be playing a silly game with us, Inspector,' said Skelton, 'and I must ask you to stop.'

'Oh, it's not a game,' said Colbeck, pulling the card from his pocket. 'This was sent to Agnes Reader in acknowledgement of some flowers she kindly bought for the church. I was struck by the curious similarity between the writing on the card and the letter.'

'It's pure coincidence.'

'But you haven't seen them side to side.'

'I don't need to, Inspector.'

'I'm sure that Mrs Skelton will know why they are similar,' said Colbeck, noting the guilty blush in her cheeks. 'If I brought paper and pen, I daresay she could produce something that's also eerily similar.'

'I'm sorry,' asserted Skelton, getting to his feet, 'but I must ask you to leave. I'll not have you hurling these vile accusations at my wife. Your behaviour has been unpardonable. Dorcas would never dream of composing the kind of letter to

258

which you refer.'

'I accept that, sir. But because Mrs Skelton wouldn't dream of putting such filthy innuendoes on a sheet of stationery, it must have been dictated to her – by you.'

'How dare you!' howled Skelton.

'He *knows*, Frederick,' said his wife, quivering.

'Be quiet!'

'There's no need to berate your wife,' said Colbeck. 'After all, she was only obeying her husband when she wrote these words. You couldn't possibly do it yourself, of course, because you've often had correspondence with the colonel and he would have identified your hand at once.' He looked at Dorcas. 'How many did you send?'

'Five,' she replied.

'I told you to be quiet!' snarled the rector.

She was appalled. 'You've never spoken to me like that before.'

'Just do as I say.'

'I always do, Frederick.'

'We seem to have reached an interesting point,' said Colbeck, savouring the flash of marital dissension. 'One of you is ready to admit culpability and the other one denies it.'

'My wife admits nothing,' said Skelton. 'I speak for her.'

'Are you telling me that she wrote neither of these messages?'

'That's exactly what I'm telling you.'

Colbeck got up. 'Then it will be instructive to see if you maintain the pose of innocence when you're asked the same question under oath in a court of law.'

Skelton attempted to brazen it out, meeting his visitor's gaze with silent defiance. When he glanced at his wife, however, he saw that she was in great distress, exuding a guilt and remorse she was unable to hide. Questioned by a lone detective, she'd blurted out a confession. Under cross-examination in court, she'd be hopelessly unable to tell a succession of lies. Skelton's nerve began to fail him. One of his eyelids began to flicker and he shifted his stance. When his wife began to sob, he knew that he was lost. Putting an arm around her, he looked at Colbeck with a loathing that was edged with respect.

In a short space of time, Skelton's life had been transformed. Fifteen minutes earlier, he'd stood in his pulpit like a minor prophet dispensing wisdom to lesser mortals. He'd taken up arms in what he believed was a moral crusade and was ready to smite all who opposed him. At a stroke, he'd been deprived of his weapons and forced into ignominious surrender. Further humiliation would follow.

'What do I have to do?' he asked, dully.

'The first thing you have to do is to instruct your curate to take the service tomorrow,' said Colbeck.

'But it's *my* church with *my* congregation.'

'That makes no difference, sir.'

'I've already written my sermon. My wife listened to it.'

'I did,' she said through her tears. 'It was inspiring.'

'What you both did to the colonel was less than inspiring,' said Colbeck with quiet intensity. 'If your congregation knew the depths to which you were prepared to sink, they'd be sickened.'

'I felt impelled to do it,' bleated Skelton, grasping wildly for extenuation. 'The colonel was a man of many faults, as Miriam found out to her cost. She was blessed in her first husband and cursed in her second. He *killed* her, Inspector,' he said. 'As sure as I'm standing here, the colonel murdered his wife and it was my bounden duty to arraign him for the crime.'

'But that's not what you did, sir, was it? Not having the courage to write and sign your own letter, you passed the burden to Mrs Skelton. That's shameful,' said Colbeck with scorn. 'What sort of a husband hides behind his wife like that? What sort of a man makes a woman write foul words and coarse phrases that must never have entered her head before?'

'It's true,' said Dorcas. 'I hated writing those letters.'

'They were *necessary*, my dear,' argued Skelton.

'They were necessary for *you*, sir,' said Colbeck, 'because you had so much bile to unload. When the killer is caught – and he soon will be – you'll realise that you denounced an innocent man then tried to forbid him access to your churchyard.'

'He *mustn't* be buried here. It would be a sin.'

'As I said at the start, that's academic. The decision is no longer in your hands. It will be taken by someone with more compassion and with more knowledge of the law of the land.'

Skelton sagged. 'Will you ruin me, Inspector?'

'You brought ruin upon yourself,' Colbeck pointed out, 'and the tragedy is that you tainted your own wife in the process.'

The rector looked down at Dorcas with a mixture of apology and despair. Years of exerting unquestioned authority over her had come to an end. The woman who'd loved, honoured and obeyed him in every particular had been dragged down to a level that degraded her. He realised how it must look to a dispassionate observer. A hint of shame at last crept into his eyes.

'What will happen to us?' he asked.

'That's a matter for the archbishop,' said Colbeck.

Skelton shuddered. 'You'll tell *him* about this, Inspector?'

'That's your prerogative, sir. When you compose your letter of resignation, you must explain it how you will. I can't find the words for you,' said Colbeck with studied coldness, 'and, on this occasion, Mrs Skelton will not be able to write on your behalf.'

Caleb Andrews could not believe his ears. Though he came home to receive a welcoming kiss and knew that a tasty supper awaited him, he was stopped in his tracks by the news that his daughter had spent part of the day travelling on the Great Northern Railway.

'Inspector Colbeck had no right take you,' he protested.

'I only went as far as Peterborough and back,' she said.

'Going to King's Cross was far enough, Maddy.'

'It was such a lovely surprise.'

'Well, it's come as a nasty shock for me. I don't like the idea of you charging off to a different part of the country without a moment's notice. Inspector Colbeck should've given you more warning. For a start,' he said, 'I should have been told.'

'Robert was only in London for an hour or so,' she explained. 'Inviting me to join him was something he did on the spur of the moment. I could hardly refuse.'

'Well, no,' he muttered, 'I suppose not.'

'It was an adventure.'

'Tell him to ask my permission next time.'

'No,' she said, grinning, 'you tell him yourself.'

He washed his hands in the kitchen then ate his supper with her. It was all part of a comfortable routine that they'd settled into over the years. Andrews had accepted that it was destined to end.

'What will I do for supper when you go, Maddy?'

'Make it yourself.'

'I can't even boil an egg.'

'Then you must get your new wife to do it for you,' she said.

'*What* new wife?'

'The one you keep hinting you'll move in here as soon as I leave.'

'I haven't met her yet,' he said.

'I thought you had a whole flock of ladies interested in you.'

'Yes, I do – but I have standards. I won't take in anyone just to have companionship. I'm too old to change my ways, so any wife would have to accept me as I am.'

'Then you can abandon all hope of marriage,' she teased.

'It's a serious business, Maddy. It takes time to make up your mind. Well, look how long it took you and the inspector to come to a decision.'

'That was because of Robert's work.'

'It won't be a problem in my case,' he said, 'because I'm near retirement. I'll be here most of the time. That's another thing,' he added. 'I don't want a wife who'll be under my feet all day long.'

'The truth is, Father,' she said with an affectionate smile, 'you don't want a wife at all, do you?'

He chuckled. 'Probably not – but I'm open to offers.'

When the meal was over, they adjourned to the parlour. He saw the copy of *Cranford* on the table beside her chair.

'Did you mention what I said about it?'

'We had other things to discuss.'

'What did he tell you about the investigation?' asked Andrews. 'It says in the newspaper that it's come to a halt.'

'Reporters know nothing.'

'They must get their information from somewhere, Maddy.'

'Well, they didn't get it from Robert. He's much more optimistic. He's hoping to make an arrest before long.'

'He ought to arrest you for reading nonsense like *Cranford*.'

'It's a lovely book and much more restful than Dickens.'

'I like blood and violence,' said Andrews.

'You wouldn't say that if you had to deal with them every day as Robert does,' she told him. 'He has to see and do the most dreadful things. Take this case, for instance. How would you like to dig up a rotting corpse in the middle of the night?'

'I'd be more than happy to do so, Maddy,' he replied, cackling, 'as long as it was the corpse of the man who runs the Great Northern Railway, that is. I'd go so far as to say it'd be a real pleasure.'

While Colbeck went off to confront the rector, Leeming stayed at the Black Bull in case the visitor from Doncaster turned up. The pub served good beer but the sergeant only drank in moderation so that his mind was not befuddled. The bar was quite full and, when he heard the door open, he was unable to see over the heads of the people standing between his table and the entrance. Hoping that Kinchin had at last arrived, Leeming was perturbed to see the unlovely face of Eric Hepworth beaming down at him.

'Good evening, Sergeant,' said Hepworth.

'Good evening.'

'May I join you?'

'Actually,' said Leeming, 'I'm waiting for someone.'

'Oh – and who might that be?'

'That doesn't concern you, Sergeant.'

'If it's related to the murder – and it obviously is – then it does concern me. I live here and I don't want this hanging over us. It gives us a bad name. I want to cleanse the village. The sooner you arrest Michael Bruntcliffe, the better.'

'We have to find him first and that's proving difficult. Besides, we only have circumstantial evidence that he may be involved. The inspector is not fully persuaded that Bruntcliffe is our man.'

'Who else could have committed the murder?'

'I don't know,' admitted Leeming.

'That's why you need me. I can help. If the inspector spoke to my superintendent, I could be released from my duties to join in the search for Bruntcliffe.'

'You do your job, Sergeant, and we'll do ours.'

'But you've made no progress at all.'

'Yes, we have – though I can't go into detail.'

'I don't believe you,' challenged Hepworth.

'You can believe or disbelieve what you like,' said Leeming without rising to the bait. 'And it's not only the murder that we've been investigating. There's the series of poison-pen letters that were sent to the colonel. It might interest you to know that we've already identified one of the people who sent them.'

Hepworth was shocked. 'Who was that?'

'You'll have to wait until it becomes public knowledge.'

'Why bother about a few silly letters when there's a killer on the loose?'

'Those letters were not silly,' said Leeming. 'They were malicious and helped to drive the colonel to suicide. I read one of them. It was disgusting. The people who wrote such poisonous things need to be tracked down.' Hepworth plucked nervously at his beard. 'You talked about cleansing the village of an ugly stain. We need to cleanse a few filthy minds around here as well.'

'Yes,' said Hepworth, backing away, 'I agree. If you're expecting company, I won't intrude any longer.'

The railway policeman vanished into the crowd but his place was almost immediately taken by a dapper individual with a walrus moustache flecked with grey. Guessing that it must be Royston Kinchin, Leeming got up and introduced himself to the newcomer. Kinchin had the partly-hesitant, partly-defensive look of a man who's been summoned by the police without knowing why. When he'd bought the visitor a drink, they sat down at the table. Leeming glanced around the bar to make sure that Hepworth was not lurking nearby but there was no sign of their self-appointed assistant. The sergeant turned to Kinchin.

'Thank you for coming, sir,' he began.

'Ned Staddle said that it was important.'

'It could be. It concerns Colonel Tarleton.'

'Yes,' said Kinchin with a pained expression. 'I read about the suicide. It shocked me. The colonel always seemed such a level-headed sort of man. I'd never have expected him to do such a thing.'

'How well did you know him?'

'I wouldn't call myself a close friend but we did see each other from time to time. We had a mutual interest.'

'I had a feeling you might have been in the army, sir.'

'No, you're quite wrong there, Sergeant. I'm an engineer. I was lucky enough to be in the right place when the railways began to develop. Most of my career was spent in management. When the Great Northern extended its line, I bought a house in Doncaster.'

'Is that where the colonel used to visit you?'

'He didn't come to see *me*,' explained Kinchin. 'I met him at the station so that I could give him a lift in my carriage.'

'And where did you take him?'

'More often than not, we went to a concert. Sometimes, we simply attended a rehearsal. The colonel was one of the sponsors, you see.' Leeming was baffled. 'Evidently, you *don't* see, Sergeant.'

'What sort of concerts are you talking about, sir?'

'The colonel and I shared a passion for brass bands. When he heard that a railway band had been formed in Doncaster, he got in touch with it and offered a generous donation. That's why we were allowed to attend rehearsals,' said Kinchin. 'I, too, was a supporter of the band. We whiled away many an hour, listening to them. The Doncaster Loco Band has real quality.'

'I'll take your word for it.'

'Indeed, when I first heard of his death, I wondered if I should ask the band to play at his funeral. Then I realised that it would hardly be appropriate. The booming harmonies of a brass band have no place around a grave. On the other hand,' added Kinchin, stroking his moustache, 'if there's to be a memorial service, we might think again. The band has a wide repertoire of hymns.'

'So that's all it was,' said Leeming with disappointment. 'The colonel went to Doncaster to listen to a band. I was hoping for some information that might assist us in our investigation.'

'I'm sorry I can't be more helpful, Sergeant.'

'It's not your fault, Mr Kinchin. And at least we've now solved one little mystery.'

'Perhaps you can solve one for me in return.'

'What do you mean?'

'Well,' said the other, 'the colonel was as passionate as I am about brass band music. Neither his wife nor his friends would understand that. They preferred orchestral concerts.'

'Is that why he kept the secret to himself?'

'Probably – but it's not his only secret. This is where the mystery comes in. The colonel stopped coming to Doncaster. Without warning and with no explanation, he stopped.'

'Did you try to make contact with him?'

'Yes,' said Kinchin, 'I wrote two or three times but I didn't even get a reply. It was as if he'd cut the band out of his life altogether. It was very upsetting. To be honest, I felt like a jilted lover. I wondered if he'd taken against me for some reason.' He gave a hopeful smile. 'Do you happen to know why he lost interest so suddenly?'

'I'm afraid that I don't, sir,' said Leeming, 'but I'd be interested to find out. Can you give me an exact date when he deserted you?'

Since the rector's obstinacy with regard to the funerals had caused the Tarleton family such distress, Colbeck drove over to the house to alleviate their anxiety. He decided against giving them full details of his visit to the rectory because

269

he didn't want to add to their grief and felt that they should, in any case, wait until Skelton made a public acknowledgement of what he'd done. The family needed reassurance and that was why Colbeck was ringing the doorbell.

Lottie Pearl answered the door and let him in. They had gathered in the drawing room after dinner. Colbeck was introduced to Lawrence Doel and was pleased to see how her husband's arrival had lifted Eve's spirits. There was also a marked difference in her brother's bearing. Adam Tarleton had contrived to look as if he was bereaved. Declining the offer of a seat, Colbeck told them that he'd simply come to pass on information that it was important for them to hear.

'I've just come from the rectory,' he said. 'You'll be relieved to hear that there'll be no more squabbling over the Colonel's funeral.'

'There you are,' declared Tarleton. 'I brought the rector to heel. All it needed was a few harsh words from me.'

'There's rather more to it than that, sir, but I think the full story best left untold at the moment. If you attend church tomorrow, you need fear no awkwardness. The Reverend Skelton will not be taking the service. He's instructed his curate to take his place.'

'I'm so relieved to hear that,' said Eve. 'I was terrified that Adam would create a scene.'

'I was looking forward to it,' said Tarleton.

'Thankfully,' observed Doel, 'it won't be necessary. You always were a trifle too belligerent, Adam.'

'I got the result we all wanted.'

'Believe that, if you wish,' said Colbeck, 'but your intervention was more likely to anger him than cow him into submission. When I arrived earlier, he'd already written his sermon for tomorrow and had not relented over the proposed burial of your stepfather.'

'Then what changed the old goat's mind?'

'Listen to the inspector, Adam,' said Doel. 'He's told us all we need to know for the time being and I, for one, am very grateful. The service tomorrow should be a dignified event that's not marred by any histrionics from you. In view of the tragedies, we should expect a large congregation.'

'I think I can guarantee that, Mr Doel,' said Colbeck. 'There'll be family friends coming over from Northallerton and perhaps from even farther afield. I know that Mr and Mrs Reader will be there and I fancy you can count on Mr Everett and his wife being present.'

'Good,' Tarleton blurted out. 'I need to speak to Everett. He can give us some hints about the terms of the two wills.'

'Adam!' exclaimed his sister. 'Can't you think of anything else?'

'It means a lot to me, Eve.'

'It means a lot to everyone involved,' said Colbeck, 'but you'll have to wait until the formal reading of the wills. Having met Mr Everett, I doubt if he's a man to divulge any details beforehand.'

'All I'm asking for is a rough indication of what I'll get.'

'Then you're asking too much,' said Doel with

271

unforced authority. 'Eve is right. The last thing you should be thinking about now is the possibility of your own pecuniary gain. Apart from being indecent, it has a mercenary smack to it.'

'Let's hear no more about the subject,' decreed Eve.

Tarleton offered a reluctant apology and lapsed back into what he felt was the acceptable pose for someone grieving over the loss of parents. Colbeck was not convinced by his performance. To Adam Tarleton, he could see, the funerals were an irritating obstruction in the way of his inheritance.

'Well,' said Colbeck, 'I'm sorry to have disturbed you but I felt that my news might provide you with some solace.'

'It's done exactly that, Inspector,' said Eve.

'We can't thank you enough, sir,' added her husband.

'In that case,' said Colbeck, 'I'll take my leave. I'll be seeing you all again tomorrow at St Andrew's. It's comforting to know that there will now be no danger whatsoever of any trouble at the church.'

Moonlight filtered down through the yew trees and drew intricate patterns in the churchyard. Standing at its centre was a large, stone cross that acted both as a cynosure and as a kind of nocturnal sentry. A bird was perched on the cross but it flew away with a disgruntled squawk when somebody walked towards it through the gravestones. The man checked to see that nobody else was about then he tied a rope around the cross, securing the other end to the pommel of his saddle. Slapping his horse on the rump, he made it jump forward. At first it was checked by the solidity of the cross but a second slap made it pull with more vigour. With a resounding crack, the stone split at the base of the upright and toppled onto the grass. Undoing the rope, the man put it away in his saddlebag.

He then returned to the plinth on which the cross had stood. Chiselled into it was the name of the benefactor who had donated the money for the erection of the cross. The man lowered his breeches and urinated, taking careful aim at the name of Colonel Aubrey Tarleton.

CHAPTER FIFTEEN

Because the bar was too full and noisy to allow a private conversation, the detectives adjourned upstairs to Colbeck's room. Leeming was eager to hear about the dramatic confrontation at the rectory and sorry to have missed the sight of such an outwardly respectable married couple exposed as the authors of malign letters. Colbeck described what had happened and how the rector had been compelled to accept that resignation was his only course of action. He also told the sergeant about his visit to the house to pass on the welcome tidings that the Reverend Skelton would not be taking the service next morning. Colbeck recalled that Adam Tarleton had made no effort to conceal his selfish preoccupation with the wealth he was due to inherit.

'The young man may have a shock coming,' he said.

'Why is that, Inspector?'

'He's working on the assumption that he'll get half of whatever has been bequeathed, and that may not be so. Instead of looking to the future, Mr Tarleton should remember the past. A stepfather he consistently defied is unlikely to be overgenerous to him. Nor will his mother have looked kindly on a son who became estranged when he could no longer have such ready access to her purse. Mr Tarleton may end up with far less than he anticipates.'

'That would serve him right,' said Leeming. 'Well, it sounds as if your evening was more interesting than mine.'

He went on to talk about his abrasive few minutes with the railway policeman and how Hepworth had withdrawn rather hastily when the poison-pen letters were mentioned. Colbeck was curious about the way the man had reacted.

'Did you see any guilt in his face?' he asked.

'I didn't see a thing with that beard of his, sir. It just about covers everything. He looks like a large dog staring through a bush.'

'What was your feeling?'

'He was uneasy,' said Leeming, 'and that set me thinking. I wondered if Hepworth had also been sending the colonel some nasty, unwanted mail. Do you think we should challenge him about it?'

'There'd be no point, Victor. He'd only deny it. Mrs Withers was told to burn the earlier letters so the evidence has gone up in smoke. However,' Colbeck said, thoughtfully, 'there may be another way to find out the truth. Let's bear the egregious fellow in mind, shall we?'

'I do my best to forget him, sir.'

Leeming recounted his meeting with Kinchin and bewailed the fact that it had not provided the breakthrough for which he'd hoped.

Colbeck listened without interruption and made a mental note of the date when the colonel had abruptly ceased to visit Doncaster. He then went off into a trance for a few minutes. Leeming wondered if anything was wrong with him. Eventually, he tapped the inspector on the arm.

'Excuse me, sir.'

'Oh,' said Colbeck as if waking up. 'I left you for a while. I'm sorry about that. There was something I was trying to remember.'

'And did you recall it?'

'Yes, I did. It made me think that, in retrospect, Mr Kinchin's visit may not have been as unprofitable as you feared.'

'He told me nothing of real use, sir.'

'Yes, he did. You learnt that the colonel loved brass bands.'

'What use is that?'

'Well, it's something the superintendent didn't know about him and he was the colonel's close friend. He didn't tell Mr Tallis because he was aware – as we both are – that the superintendent hates music of all kinds. The only instrument for which he has the slightest time,' said Colbeck, 'is a church organ. The prospect of a brass band would probably make him run for cover.'

Leeming laughed. 'I'd love to see him doing that.'

'What you confirmed is what we've already found out – namely, that the colonel was very guarded.'

'He seems to have told Mr Kinchin nothing about his home life.'

'Their only point of contact was a brass band.'

'It's a very good one, I'm told,' said Leeming. 'Not that it matters. I just felt rather embarrassed at having dragged Mr Kinchin all the way from Doncaster on a fool's errand.'

'But it wasn't a fool's errand. Without realising it, the gentleman gave us a golden nugget.'

'Did he?' Leeming was perplexed. 'I didn't see any nugget.'

'The date, Victor,' said Colbeck. 'He gave us a vital date.'

'That's news to me, sir.'

'Wait until tomorrow and all will be explained. If I ask him about it when he's off duty, so to speak, I can catch him unawares. I may get the truth out of him.'

'Who are you talking about?'

'I'm talking about the colonel's banker – Bertram Reader.'

When she finally came downstairs that morning, Agnes Reader moved unsteadily and held onto the banister for support. She was in full mourning wear and had pulled down her veil to obscure her tears. Her husband was waiting for her at the bottom of the stairs.

'How do you feel now, Agnes?' he asked, taking her hand.

'I feel a little queasy.'

'You don't have to go, you know. I can represent both of us.'

'I have to be there,' she insisted. 'What would the family think if I didn't turn up at the service?'

'But it will be such an ordeal for you.'

'It will be an ordeal for all of us, Bertram.'

He nodded sadly and released her hand. She lifted her veil so that she could see herself properly in the hall mirror. After making a few adjustments to her clothing, she lowered the veil again.

'I'm not looking forward to this,' she confessed.

'Neither am I,' he said, 'though I'll be interested to hear what happened at the rectory last evening. Inspector Colbeck went off to question the rector about that letter.'

'I still can't believe that Mrs Skelton wrote it.'

'The handwriting was identical to that on the card. Thanks to your kindness in providing those flowers, two guilty people have been exposed. Not that we ought to talk about it in public, my dear,' he warned. 'The inspector was very firm on that point. People are coming to the church to honour Aubrey and Miriam. We don't want them distracted by rumours about a poison-pen letter sent from the rectory. That would really blight the whole service.'

'I won't say a word,' she murmured.

'Then promise me something else as well. If you have a change of heart on the way, it's never too late to turn back.'

'That won't happen, Bertram.'

'The option is always there,' he said. 'My concern is that the service will stir up too many emotions for you.'

'I'll pull through somehow.'

'It will be worse for Eve, of course, because she's lost two beloved parents. I'd like to say the same of Adam,' he went on, 'but we'd look in vain for any genuine sorrow there. The best that we can hope of him is that he turns up and behaves himself.'

'Adam will surely have been sobered by what happened.'

'Well, there's no hint of it so far, Agnes. After he'd been in the town to identify his mother's body, he called on Clifford Everett and more or less demanded to know what his inheritance would be. As a good lawyer should,' he said, 'Clifford told him that he was unable to disclose any details of the wills. He's bracing himself for another clash with Adam when he attends the service today.'

'I see.'

Reader opened the front door and let in a breeze that made his wife's veil dance before her eyes. When he offered his arm, she didn't take it. Instead she stayed where she was, surveying the outside world with trepidation as if not knowing whether to venture out or not.

He was solicitous. 'Is something wrong, my dear?'

'No, no,' she replied, mustering all her strength. 'Don't worry about me, Bertram. I'm fine now.'

Taking his arm, she walked towards the waiting trap.

To make sure that the rector abided by his orders, Colbeck got to the church early with Leeming in tow. They saw a knot of people in the middle of the churchyard and went over to them. The stone cross lay on the ground, its impact so strong that it had bitten deeply into the grass. Colbeck noted the inscription on the plinth.

'It's an act of God,' said one woman. 'It's because it was put here by the colonel.'

'Aye,' said another, 'God has sent us a message.'

'I think that you'll find that God confines his messages to the inside of the church,' said Colbeck. 'This was done by a human being. It was a

279

deliberate act of vandalism.'

'Clearly, someone doesn't like the colonel,' said Leeming. 'It would have needed a strong man to pull that down, Inspector.'

'He used a rope. Look – you can see the marks here.' Colbeck pointed to some nicks in the stone. 'There must have been two of them.' He explored the ground nearby and saw hoof prints. 'I was right, Victor, there *were* two of them – a man and a horse. This is where the animal stood when it took the strain.'

'Oh, yes,' said Leeming, standing beside him. 'The prints are deeper here where the horse dug in its hooves as it heaved.'

'This must have been done at night. When I went past here yesterday evening, the cross was upright. I remember seeing it.'

'At least it wasn't broken in the fall.'

'No,' said Colbeck, 'but it's already attracting far too much attention. I don't want the Tarleton family to see this. Let's put it back where it belongs.'

Removing his hat and coat, he handed them to a bystander and Leeming did the same. When he saw what they planned to do, a burly farmer offered his help, taking off his hat and coat before giving them to his wife. Getting the cross upright was relatively easy. Lifting it back onto the plinth, however, took a little more time and effort. They were fortunate. There had been a clean break so, once they'd managed to lift it between them, it was only a question of manoeuvring it back into position. It tapered outwards at the base and slotted securely back into its original position. After thanking the farmer, Colbeck used a handkerchief to wipe his hands.

'It needs to be secured with mortar,' he said. 'Now that it's back up again, I don't think anybody would be stupid enough to try to push it over.' He collected his coat and hat. 'Thank you to everybody. Could you please move away now or people will wonder what's going on?'

The small crowd drifted away, one of the women still claiming that it was an act of God. Leeming heard her.

'Well, I wish that an act of God had put it back again,' he said, pulling on his coat. 'That thing was heavy.'

'We all have our cross to bear,' said Colbeck, dryly, 'and I'm not referring to the superintendent.'

He was about to turn towards the church when he caught sight of something out of the corner of his eye. An unkempt youth was sitting on a low tombstone, playing with toy soldiers. Since he was wearing rough clothing and a crumpled cap, he was patently not a churchgoer. What interested Colbeck was that he was showing such intense concentration, moving the metal soldiers about with slow deliberation. The detectives walked across to him and had a surprise. What they had mistaken as soldiers were spent shotgun cartridges.

'Good morning,' said Colbeck, amiably.

The youth looked up at him. 'Mornin', sir.'

'Do you always play in the churchyard?'

'No room in 'ouse.'

There was no need to ask his name. As soon as they saw his face with its large, vacant eyes and

281

narrow forehead, they knew that it was the railway policeman's son.

'You must be Sam Hepworth,' said Colbeck.

'Aye, sir.'

'How old are you, Sam?'

'Sixteen.'

'That's a bit old to be playing with soldiers,' said Leeming.

'I like 'em, sir.'

'Where did you get the cartridges from?'

'Shootin' parties, sir. I carry guns.'

'You've got quite a collection here.'

'There's more at 'ome, sir. Our Dad says there's too many.'

'That would be Sergeant Hepworth, then.'

'Aye, sir.'

Colbeck felt sorry for the boy and not only because he was saddled with a father who'd browbeat him unmercifully. Sam obviously had some disabilities. His speech was slurred, his movements slow and his eyes seemed to wander ungovernably. Yet, at the same time, he was a direct link with a man about whom they had suspicions. Unlike his father, Sam Hepworth had an open face and a complete lack of guile. There was a benign simplicity about him.

'Are you going to church, Sam?' asked Colbeck.

'No, sir. Our Dad don't like rector.'

'Oh, I see. Is there any reason?'

'Aye, sir.'

'What is it?'

'Rector's too bossy, like.'

'I noticed that,' said Leeming. 'And your father

282

didn't think highly of Colonel Tarleton either, did he?'

'No, sir,' replied Sam.

'Why was that?'

'Same reason.'

'You mean that he was too bossy?'

'Aye, sir.'

Sam's attention went back to the private battle he was fighting and he moved various members of his two armies. They watched him for a while then turned to go. Sam's voice piped up.

'Sent letters, like.'

Colbeck swung round. 'What was that?'

'Our Dad sent letters, sir.'

'Letters?'

'Aye, to colonel.'

'Are you sure?' said Leeming, moving to kneel beside him. 'Is that what your father told you?'

'No, sir, it were our Ginny.'

'She's your sister, isn't she?'

'Aye, sir.'

'What did she tell you, Sam?'

'Ginny took letters there.'

'Where?'

'To big 'ouse, sir – it's where colonel lived.'

'Do you know what was in the letters?' asked Colbeck.

'No, sir – can't read.'

'Why did your sister deliver the letters? Why didn't your father take them himself?'

Sam needed time to separate the two questions in his mind. It required an effort. While he was waiting, he shifted a couple of the soldiers on the tombstone. At length, he supplied an answer.

'Our Ginny knew way there,' he said.

'I know,' said Colbeck. 'She used to work at the house.'

'No, sir – she knew secret way there.'

'What time of the day did she take the letters, Sam?'

'It were at night, sir.'

'When it was dark?' The youth nodded. 'I think I understand. Your sister had to deliver the letters without being seen. Your father didn't want the colonel to know who'd sent them.'

It was too much for Sam to comprehend. He looked bemused. Colbeck patted him on the shoulder and thanked him. Squatting on the tombstone, the youth returned to his soldiers and he was soon happily lost in the heat of battle. Leeming glanced back at him.

'Do you think it's true, sir?' he asked.

'I think it's more than likely.'

'Then the sergeant has been condemned by his own son.'

'No, Victor,' said Colbeck. 'All that Sam has done is to point the way. Against his father's word, the lad's testimony is useless. He could barely string a few sentences together.'

'What about those toy soldiers? They reminded me of the cartridges you found near the body of Mrs Tarleton. In other words,' he continued with muted excitement, 'the interfering Sergeant Hepworth may be more involved in this business than we suspected.'

'Don't rush to judgement. We need more than supposition.'

'We need a miracle, sir. Otherwise, Mr Tallis

will be coming to Yorkshire and the whole investigation will drag on for weeks. We need to pray for a miracle.'

'We've already had one,' said Colbeck, looking over his shoulder. 'His name is Sam Hepworth.'

Lottie Pearl had always been an unwilling churchgoer. The services were too long, the church was too cold and the archaic language was like a foreign tongue to her. She was therefore disconcerted when forced to join the family party. In addition to her mother's black dress, she wore a black hat borrowed from Mrs Withers and a pair of brown shoes covered in black polish. She also wore a black lace shawl. On such a fine morning, they all walked to church. Eve and Lawrence Doel led the way with Adam Tarleton at their side. Lottie and the housekeeper walked ten paces behind them.

'Why do I have to go?' asked the girl, mutinously.

'Because you do,' said Mrs Withers with unanswerable finality.

'I don't like church.'

'Your likes and dislikes don't come into it.'

'Everyone will stare at me.'

'Nobody will even know you're there. People will come to pay their respects. The family will get all the attention.'

'Ah,' said Lottie, spying some relief, 'there is that.'

'In the old days, all the servants would go to church. It was expected of us.'

'You liked the old days better, didn't you, Mrs Withers?'

'The colonel was a good master and I'd have done anything for his wife. Working for Mrs Tarleton was a joy.' She looked at Adam Tarleton's back. 'It will never be the same again.'

Lottie's fears were groundless. When they reached the church, nobody even spared her a glance. People gathered around the family to offer their condolences. She recognised Bertram and Agnes Reader because they'd visited the house when her employers were still alive. She also saw familiar faces from the village. Yet she still felt like an outsider. Everyone else seemed to know what to do. They knew how to speak in low voices and what to say. They moved with the sort of understated reverence that was beyond the girl. When they entered the church, they were completely at ease. Lottie, by contrast, was in extreme discomfort, feeling the chill in the air and wishing that the oak pew was not quite so hard. Seated beside Mrs Withers, she was afraid to say a word and could barely lift her eyes to the altar. She didn't even notice that the church was festooned with flowers.

The bell stopped tolling, the soft murmur of voices died away and the curate made his entrance. There was a grating noise as everyone rose to their feet. A few people cleared their throats. Lottie got a first glimpse of the man who was about to take the service and she actually smiled.

'It's not the rector,' she whispered.

The housekeeper's elbow speared into her ribs.

It was a sombre service and many members of the congregation were profoundly moved. Colbeck was delighted with the way that it was conducted by the curate, an earnest young man who'd been kept in the shadow of the rector and who was determined to enjoy a rare opportunity to show his mettle. The colonel and his wife were both mentioned during prayers but not during a sermon that extolled the virtues of compassion. There was an atmosphere of collective sorrow that would not have been produced by the more combative approach of Frederick Skelton. Where the rector would have sown division, the curate achieved a unity.

Once outside the church, some people broke ranks. Colbeck heard more than one of them giving vent to the opinion that the colonel killed his wife and had no right to be mourned. But the majority were too subdued to venture any comment and simply dispersed in the direction of their homes. Colbeck and Leeming waited for the chance to speak to Bertram Reader but the banker and his wife were too busy talking to members of the family. When she saw them standing there, Mrs Withers came over to the detectives.

'I thought you might be here,' she said.

'We'll be here until the murder is solved,' Colbeck told her. 'What did you think of the service?'

'It was very comforting, sir. I was touched.'

'So were we,' Leeming put in.

'I was relieved that Mrs Doel came through it. But that's not what I wanted to say,' she went on. 'When you came to the house on one of your visits, Inspector, you asked me about Michael Bruntcliffe.'

'That's right,' said Colbeck. 'Do you have any news of him?'

'I don't, sir, but Lottie does.' She crooked a finger to beckon the girl across. 'Tell them what you saw on the way back from Rock Farm.'

Lottie was nervous in the presence of the two detectives but, prompted by the housekeeper, she managed to tell her story. From the description given, Mrs Withers was certain that the person with Adam Tarleton had been Bruntcliffe. Both women were obviously frightened that they might have to suffer repercussions as a result of what they had said so Colbeck assured them that Tarleton would never know where the information had come from. After thanking him profusely, the women melted into the crowd.

'He lied to us, sir,' said Leeming. 'I thought so at the time.'

'Keep an eye on him, Victor.'

'Where are you going?'

'I want to spend that golden nugget,' said Colbeck.

Having noticed that the banker had broken away from the group around the family, he moved swiftly to intercept him. They exchanged greetings, then Reader wanted details of the confrontation with the rector on the previous evening.

'I'd love to have been a fly on the wall,' he said.

'Then you'd have been in danger of being swatted by the rector,' said Colbeck. 'He was in a vengeful mood. After I left, I suspect no ornament in the room was safe.'

'Did he confess?'

'He offered a vehement denial at first and tried

288

to send me packing but his wife broke down. Having to write such vicious things under his dictation had preyed on her mind. I put it to the rector that the only honourable thing he could do was to resign.'

'He and his wife will be indicted as well, surely?'

'Let's take this one step at a time, Mr Reader. I'll deal with them in due course. At the moment, my priority remains the arrest of the murderer and the vindication of the colonel.'

'I'll help you all I can with those two objectives.'

'Then tell me about the Leybourne Scandal.'

Reader was taken aback. 'How do you know about that?'

'The colonel was involved, wasn't he? I remember the date when the truth first came out and I have evidence that Colonel Tarleton was one of the many victims. I'm not pressing you for anything more than acknowledgement,' said Colbeck. 'Why hide the fact? If I go back to the company, they'll supply me with the names of everyone involved. Just tell me this – am I right?'

'You are, Inspector.'

'So he did invest money with Leybourne?'

Reader winced. 'He invested a great deal of money.'

'Thank you, sir. That's all I need to know at this stage.'

Colbeck had no time to question him further because he had just received a signal from Leeming. The Tarleton family were on the move. Having received kind words and commiseration from several people, they were at last ready to begin the walk home. Mrs Withers and Lottie Pearl had left ahead of them. Colbeck moved smartly to detach Adam Tarleton from the group.

'Excuse me, sir,' he said. 'Can we trouble you for a moment?'

Tarleton was brusque. 'It's highly inconvenient.'

'Nevertheless, we must insist.'

'I don't have to talk to you if I don't wish to, Inspector.'

'Of course you don't,' said Colbeck, evenly, 'but I'd advise you to humour us. If you don't, Mr Tarleton, we'll be obliged to arrest you for perverting the course of justice.'

'I've done nothing of the kind!' retorted Tarleton.

'You told us you hadn't seen Michael Bruntcliffe for years,' said Leeming, 'yet, according to one of the warders, you went to see your friend in prison not long before his release. Your name will be recorded in the visitors' book, sir, so there's no point in denying it.'

Tarleton chewed his lip. 'It's true,' he conceded, 'but it slipped my mind. You have to understand that I'm mourning the deaths of the two people I cared for most in the world. I'm consumed with sorrow. I simply can't think about anything else.'

'You thought about going for a ride the other day.'

'I had to fight with the rector about funeral arrangements.'

'That wouldn't have taken you long, sir,' resumed Colbeck, 'yet you were away for several hours. Meanwhile, your sister was moping at the house. It doesn't sound to me as if you were burdened by sorrow.'

'What are you getting at?' demanded Tarleton.

'We want to know why the man you claim you haven't seen for years – Michael Bruntcliffe – was out riding with you that day. Think before you speak,' he cautioned as Tarleton was about to bluster, 'because we have a reliable witness who saw the two of you together. It's strange that you never mentioned the fact when we talked to you later on.' He moved a step closer. 'What are you hiding, sir?'

'Nothing at all,' said Tarleton, angrily.

'Where is he?'

'I don't know.'

'Where is he?' asked Colbeck, grasping him so tightly by the arm that he let out a cry of pain. 'Where is Michael Bruntcliffe?'

'Standing outside a church is not the place to question him, sir,' said Leeming, producing a pair of handcuffs from inside his coat. 'Let's arrest him and have done with it. Then I can put these bracelets on his wrists.'

'No,' pleaded Tarleton, 'don't do that. What will everyone think? I'll tell you where Michael is but please don't arrest me today of all days. It would break my sister's heart.'

'Will you give me your word that you'll remain in the area?'

'Yes, Inspector – I must stay here. There's the inquest tomorrow, then the two funerals. After that, the wills are going to be read.'

'I don't trust him, sir,' said Leeming.

'Put the handcuffs away,' ordered Colbeck.

'If he's not in custody, he might make a run for it.'

'He's not stupid enough to do that, Sergeant. He knows that we'd go after him. Besides, Mr Tarleton has an important engagement in North-allerton that he can't possibly miss. He wants to hear the details of his inheritance.' Leeming secreted the handcuffs inside his coat. 'Now, sir,' continued Colbeck, 'where is your friend?'

'He's some distance away, Inspector,' said Tarleton.

'We can hire a trap.'

'You'd be better off on horseback. It's quite remote.'

Leeming blenched. 'Horses! I'm not happy about that.'

'We'll do whatever's necessary,' said Colbeck, eyes locked on Tarleton. 'I'm waiting, sir. Where is Michael Bruntcliffe?'

Although he was a religious man, Edward Tallis did not treat the Sabbath as a day of rest. After attending a Communion service that morning, he returned to Scotland Yard and worked through some of the files on his desk. It was almost noon when he lit a cigar, sat back and began to reflect on events in the North Riding. Convinced that his friendship with the colonel would give him insights denied to others, he longed to take an active part once more in the investigation. He found himself almost wanting Colbeck and Leeming to fail so that he had an excuse to hasten to Yorkshire in order to take charge of the case. Things were moving too slowly for his liking and he had the feeling that his detectives were holding back some of the evidence they'd so far uncovered. That was irksome. The only way to know exactly what was going on was to be in South Otterington. On the next day, he resolved, he would catch the first available train.

When he put the files away in his desk, he realised that they had been standing on the Sunday newspaper. He picked it up and sighed as he glanced at the headlines on the front page. A fire had destroyed a house in Islington and its three occupants had been burnt to a cinder. As soon as it was confirmed as a case of arson, Tallis had sent two detectives to the scene. While they had worked hard to gather evidence, they were still no nearer to discovering who the culprit had been. The newspaper article mocked them for their slowness and quoted someone who felt that a fire should be lit under the detectives to provide some stimulus. Tallis was used to ridicule in the press but it nevertheless continued to hurt, especially – as was the case here – when his own name was mentioned.

Not wishing to read any more of the article, he turned the page in search of something less infuriating. He looked up and down the columns until he saw something that caused him to stop. It was not an offensive article this time but a broadside from Yorkshire.

Now here's a murd'rous tale of woe,
See a hero misbehave.

For it shows a valiant soldier go
By railway to the grave.

Howling with rage, he tore the page out and used his cigar to set it alight, holding it between his fingers until it was reduced to a few black, curling, disintegrating wisps of paper. When the flame eventually burnt his hand, he did not even feel the pain.

On the way to the church, Mrs Withers and Lottie Pearl had walked behind the family. The situation was reversed on the return journey. Knowing that some people might be invited back to the house, they wanted to get there well in advance. Earlier that morning, the two of them had prepared refreshments and they began to set them out on trays in the kitchen. Both of them wore aprons over their black dresses. When she heard the front door open, the housekeeper put her head out to see how many guests were there. Only four people had returned with the family. The odd thing was that Adam Tarleton was not with them. Mrs Withers was about to withdraw into the kitchen when he came into the house, shot her a look of disapproval and followed the others into the drawing room.

'There are seven of them in all,' she told Lottie.

'Who have they brought back?'

'Mr and Mrs Reader – they followed in their trap.'

'Oh, I like them,' said Lottie. 'I only met them once but they were very pleasant to me. Is it true that Mrs Reader paid for all those lovely flowers in the church?'

'She's a very kind lady.'

'Who else is in there?'

'Mr and Mrs Everett,' replied the housekeeper. 'I don't know them.'

'Mr Everett is the family solicitor. He was also a good friend of Colonel Tarleton. They used to go shooting together.'

'Oh,' sighed Lottie, her face screwed up in anguish. 'I think it's so cruel, killing those poor birds like that.'

'Who cares about what you think?' snapped Mrs Withers. 'I'll go and see what they'd like to drink. And remember – when you take a tray in, hold it the way I showed you and don't tremble the way that you usually do.'

'No, Mrs Withers. I'll try.'

In fact, the girl acquitted herself well. Food and drink were served to the guests without any trembling on her part. She even earned a word of praise from the housekeeper. Once their work was done, the two women retreated to the kitchen. They were able to sit down at last and enjoy a long rest. The first thing that Mrs Withers did was to take off her shoes so that she could massage her feet. Lottie was surprised to see how dainty they were.

'Are those shoes too tight, Mrs Withers?' she asked.

'They are a little – I keep them for best.'

'It's a pity we had to walk all the way to church and back.'

'Yes,' said the other, 'and I've had no time to change them since we came home because there was so much to do.'

'You've got time now.'

'I might be needed.'

'It will only take a couple of minutes for you to slip up to your room,' said Lottie. 'I can listen out in case they call.'

The older woman was tempted. 'Are you sure?'

'Yes, Mrs Withers go on. Change your shoes while you can.'

Grateful for the offer, the housekeeper did not even bother to put the shoes on again. Instead she tripped up the stairs to the top of the house and let herself into her room. Putting the other pair away, she slipped on her working shoes and wiggled her toes. Her feet immediately felt better. She took the opportunity to straighten her dress in the mirror and to brush her hair, noting how thin it was now becoming. Then she went out again.

As she came down the first flight of steps, she was surprised to see a female figure going into what had been Miriam Tarleton's bedroom. Her protective instincts were aroused. It was not Eve Doel. She knew that. Going into her mother's bedroom had been too upsetting for the daughter. It had to be someone else and Mrs Withers felt that she simply had to confront her. She took a firm hold on the doorknob, turned it and flung the door open.

'Goodness!' exclaimed Agnes Reader, hand to her chest.

'I thought I saw someone coming in here.'

'Yes, Mrs Withers, but I'm not an intruder. I had permission from Mrs Doel. I was such an old friend of her mother's that she encouraged me to have a keepsake from her jewellery box. Oh,' she added, 'nothing expensive. I just wanted something that would have sentimental value.'

'The jewellery box is here, Mrs Reader,' said the housekeeper, picking it up from the dressing table. 'Why not take it downstairs then Mrs Doel can help you choose something?'

'What a good idea! I'll do just that.'

'Here you are.'

'Thank you,' said Agnes, taking the box from her and lifting the lid to glance into it. 'I'm afraid that it's not as full as it once was.'

'Mrs Tarleton sold some of the diamonds.'

Agnes gave a brittle laugh. 'Oh, I'm not after anything like diamonds. A simple enamel brooch will do.'

'There's a very nice one with seed pearls around the edge.'

'Good ... I'll look out for it.'

Agnes expected the housekeeper to withdraw but Mrs Withers held her ground. She gave the impression that she thought the visitor was trespassing on private territory. Closing the lid of the jewellery box, Agnes walked towards the door.

'Thank you, Mrs Withers,' she said.

Leeming was saddle-sore before they had ridden a mile. Colbeck was an accomplished horseman but his sergeant had had very little experience of riding. His discomfort was exacerbated by the fact that his bay mare seemed to have a mind of her own, disregarding his commands and neighing in protest whenever he tugged on the reins. They moved along a winding track at a steady canter. Colbeck could see that his companion was suffering and did his best to distract him.

'You're still wondering about Adam Tarleton, aren't you?'

'No, Inspector,' wailed Leeming, 'I'm still wondering if I'll manage to stay on this beast.'

'I thought you liked horses.'

'I like betting on them – not riding the damn things.'

Colbeck grinned. 'We'll make a jockey of you yet, Victor,' he said. 'But on the question of Mr Tarleton, there was no point in making an arrest.'

'But he's an accessory to the murder of his mother.'

'I don't think so. When we cornered him, he didn't react like a man with blood on his hands.'

'He wasn't the one who did the deed, sir. It was Bruntcliffe who blew that hole in her head. Tarleton paid him to do it. That servant girl saw him handing over the money.'

'Lottie saw him handing over *something*,' corrected Colbeck, 'but she could not be certain that it was money. When we meet Bruntcliffe, he can tell us what he did receive that day.'

'I'm confused,' said Leeming. 'Are you telling me that Adam Tarleton is innocent of the murder and that Bruntcliffe acted alone?'

'No, Victor. I'm suggesting that we should wait and see.'

They went through a shallow stream and the flashing hooves churned up the water. Leeming clung on grimly as he rode through the spray. It was only when they were back on dry land that he remembered something.

'You haven't told me about Mr Reader,' he said.

'I finally got the truth out of him.'

'What truth was that, sir?'

'The colonel was involved in the Leybourne Scandal.'

Leeming gaped. 'He was caught with another woman?'

'No,' said Colbeck. 'I'm talking about railways.'

'That's nothing new.'

'I know that you don't share my interest in trains.'

'I may change my mind,' said Leeming, suffering more twinges in his buttocks. 'If I had a choice between riding this horse or travelling by train, I know which one I'd prefer.'

'Let me tell you about Stuart Leybourne.'

'Who was he, sir?'

'He was two completely different people,' said Colbeck. 'One of them was a trusted employee of a major railway company who lived an apparently blameless life. The other was a cunning man who amassed a fortune by means of fraud and who ruined gullible investors. As I'd guessed, Colonel Tarleton was one of them.'

'What exactly happened?'

'Leybourne was chief clerk in the registration office. He found a loophole that allowed him to issue bogus shares and forge the transfers in the account books. With hindsight, it seems incredible that anyone could have been taken in by him but he was a very plausible man and held out the promise of good dividends.'

'Ah,' said Leeming, 'I remember the case now. Wasn't this Stuart Leybourne compared to the Railway King?'

'He was, Victor,' said Colbeck, 'except that he was even more guileful than George Hudson. The Railway King, as he was called, was the ruler of all he surveyed until his questionable accounting practices were revealed. Among other things, he'd been paying dividends out of capital to disguise the fact that one of his companies was making serious losses. His fall put an end to the years of wild speculation on the railways. Mr Hudson resigned as chairman of various companies and went abroad. Everyone said the same thing. Railway mania was over.'

'Then why could people like the colonel be taken in by this other crook?' asked Leeming, so interested in what he was hearing that he forgot his aches and pains. 'You'd have thought investors had learnt their lesson. It's not possible to make huge profits out of railways anymore.'

'Stuart Leybourne made a profit. When he was finally brought to book, it was discovered that he had a mansion both in London and in the country, a retinue of servants and a courier who went with him on his travels. In all, he defrauded people out of over two hundred thousand pounds.'

'That's amazing!'

'It explains why the colonel killed himself on the railway.'

'Does it, Inspector?'

'I think so,' said Colbeck. 'It had already killed

him financially. Walking on that railway track was a form of obituary. I had the feeling from the very beginning that he was making a statement.'

The woman still lolled in bed but Michael Bruntcliffe had put on his shirt and breeches. They were in a large cottage set on a hill that offered views across miles of beautiful country-side. Sunshine flooded in through the window to gild the woman's half-naked body. She smiled lazily up at him. Bruntcliffe sat on the bed and reached out to stroke her cheek. He was about to lean forward to kiss her when he caught sight of something through the window. Getting quickly to his feet, he stared out. Two riders had appeared in the middle distance. He watched them getting closer and closer before making his decision.

'I have to go,' he said, grabbing his boots. 'Get dressed and tell them nothing. I can't say when I'll be back.'

Before she could even speak, he'd picked up his coat and run down the stairs. Minutes later, he was mounting his horse.

Bruntcliffe was on the run.

CHAPTER SIXTEEN

Victor Leeming was in great discomfort. While Colbeck found the ride bracing, the sergeant was squirming in the saddle as he sought the position that would bring least agony. He was also sweating from every pore and struggling to keep the bay mare parallel with the other horse. They had left the track now and were making their way across an undulating plain towards the cottage on the hill.

'Are you certain this is the place?' asked Leeming.

'It has to be, Victor. It's the only dwelling for miles.'

'Mr Tarleton might have deliberately sent us astray.'

'Why should he do that?'

'To get us out of the way so that he could make his escape.'

'I've told you,' said Colbeck. 'He was not party to the murder. Had he been so, he'd have turned tail the moment that he realised that we knew he'd been in touch with Bruntcliffe.'

'He *must* be involved in the murder somehow,' argued Leeming. 'What's that Latin tag you're always quoting at me?'

'*Cui bono?* Who stands to benefit?'

'The answer is Adam Tarleton. He'll certainly benefit.'

'So will his sister but I'm not accusing Mrs Doel of killing their mother, am I? Forget them for the moment. The person of real interest to us is Bruntcliffe.'

As if on cue, a horseman suddenly emerged from the stable ahead of them, kicking his mount into a gallop and heading off in the opposite direction. Colbeck didn't hesitate. Flicking the reins and digging in his heels, he set his own horse off at full speed. Leeming was terrified to coax a faster pace out of the mare so he settled for following the others at a gentle canter. Bruntcliffe was over a hundred yards ahead of the pursuing Colbeck, stinging the horse with his whip to keep it running at full pelt. Every so often, he tossed a worried glance over his shoulder. Colbeck was slowly gaining on him, riding hell for leather and ignoring the fact that his hat had blown off. In his experience, flight was usually a confession of guilt. If Bruntcliffe had been innocent, he would have stayed at the cottage to be interviewed by the detectives. That thought made Colbeck even more resolute. He recalled the appalling state of Miriam Tarleton's body when it was unearthed in the woods. The man responsible for her death simply had to be caught, tried and hanged.

As Colbeck surged on with his frock coat flapping in the wind, Leeming was almost half a mile behind him. The gap between quarry and hunter slowly and inexorably closed. When it was down to forty yards, Bruntcliffe became desperate. Unable to outrun the pursuit, he opted for a different method of escape, wheeling his horse in a tight circle so that he headed straight at Colbeck. The inspector could see what the intention was. Bruntcliffe wanted to knock him from the saddle, take his horse by the reins and ride off with both animals. Slowing his mount with a sharp tug, Colbeck reacted instinctively. As the other man came at him with his whip raised, Colbeck slipped his feet from the stirrups and raised an arm to ward off the blow. The moment that Bruntcliffe struck, he was knocked from the saddle as Colbeck lunged across at him and tackled him around the waist. The two of them fell to the ground with a thud and rolled over on the grass, leaving the horses to run on without riders.

Both were dazed by the impact but Colbeck was the first to recover. Staggering to his feet, he took his captive by the collar and hauled him upright. Bruntcliffe was ready to fight. As his head cleared, he swung a fist drunkenly but it was easily parried. By way of retaliation, Colbeck punched him hard in the stomach then caught him with an uppercut on the chin. The resistance was over. Dazed by the blow, Bruntcliffe slumped to the ground. It gave Colbeck the time to examine the grass stains on his coat and trousers. As he hit the other man from the saddle, he'd also torn a sleeve open. That was irritating to a dandy like him. He was grateful that he'd collected a change of apparel during his short visit to London.

Bruntcliffe rubbed his bruised chin and looked up at him.

'How did you know that it was me?' he asked, sullenly.

'You gave yourself away by bolting like that.'

'What else was I supposed to do? Wait to be arrested? Adam told me that two detectives had come from London. When I saw the pair of you coming towards the cottage, I guessed who you might be.'

'I am Inspector Colbeck,' said the other, offering a hand and pulling him to his feet. 'Michael Bruntcliffe, I'm placing you under arrest for the murder of Miriam Tarleton.'

Bruntcliffe was staggered. 'What did you say?'

'I think you heard me clearly, sir.'

'I had nothing whatsoever to do with the murder. I've never even met Adam's mother. Why should I want to kill her?'

'It was in order to get your revenge on the colonel.'

'Ah,' said Bruntcliffe, sourly, 'that's a different matter.'

'Is *that* why you were running away?' asked Colbeck, thinking about the incident in the churchyard. 'You pulled down that cross last night, didn't you?'

'It was only because that venomous old bastard put it there.'

'Didn't you think of the offence it would cause?'

'What about the offence the colonel caused me?' rejoined Bruntcliffe. 'Do you know what it's like being locked up in prison for something that was simply a joke?'

'You deserved the sentence you got,' said Colbeck. 'Painting out public signs could put people in danger. If they can't read a warning, they can't exercise caution.' He grabbed him by the throat and pulled him close. 'What else did you do to get your revenge on the colonel?'

'I did nothing at all.'

'I think you did, Mr Bruntcliffe. I think you sent him some of those evil letters he received. You wanted to goad and taunt him. You wanted to make him suffer, didn't you?' He tightened his grip until the other man spluttered. 'Didn't you?'

'Yes,' admitted Bruntcliffe, baring his teeth. 'That's exactly what I did. I wanted to torment him.'

'Those letters helped to push him towards suicide.'

'Then I'm glad I sent some of them.'

'Let's see if you still feel the same when we take you to court.'

'I confess that I sent the letters and pulled down that cross, Inspector,' said Bruntcliffe with gabbled sincerity, 'but I swear, in the name of God, that I didn't murder Adam's mother. On the day that it happened, I wasn't even in the county. I was in Lincoln. That's the truth.'

He broke off as Leeming arrived, riding one horse and towing another by the rein. He had also collected Colbeck's hat and handed it to him as he dismounted.

'Thank you, Victor,' said Colbeck, releasing his prisoner.

'I'm sorry that I couldn't keep up with you, sir.'

'I managed without you this time. I've got a use for those handcuffs now,' he went on, turning to Bruntcliffe. 'This is Sergeant Leeming and he'd like you to hold out your wrists.'

Glowering at both of them, Bruntcliffe obeyed. Leeming snapped the handcuffs into place then gave a triumphant grin.

'We've finally solved the murder,' he said, happily, 'and stopped Mr Tallis descending on us tomorrow.'

'Don't celebrate too soon,' warned Colbeck. 'This gentleman has admitted freely that he committed certain crimes but murder is not one of them. I'm inclined to believe him.'

Leeming was shaken. 'But he was seen getting his blood money from Adam Tarleton.'

'What blood money?' demanded Bruntcliffe.

'You were out riding with him. When you got close to his house, he handed over your payment. We have a witness.'

'Then he must be half-blind. The only time I had money from Adam was when I came out of prison, and he was repaying a loan I'd made to him in the past. He's a good friend and the only one to stand by me when I was locked up.'

'So what did he give you that day?' asked Leeming.

'He gave me something better than money,' replied Bruntcliffe with a smirk. 'He gave me a letter of introduction to the lady who owns the cottage where I spent the last two nights. Adam told me that I'd be sure of a warm welcome there and I've no complaints. It was where he used to stay when he came back to Yorkshire without telling his mother or his stepfather.' He pointed in the direction of the cottage. 'Ask the lady, if you don't believe me.'

'We will, sir,' said Colbeck.

307

'One thing I must stress. She didn't know she was harbouring a petty criminal. She's completely innocent.'

'I question that,' said Leeming, shocked by what he'd heard. 'If the lady can permit herself to be passed so easily from one man to another, then her innocence is in grave doubt.'

'We'll talk to her before we leave,' decided Colbeck. 'Meanwhile, there's another job for you to do, Victor. Since you have such a talent for rounding up loose horses, perhaps you'd be so good as to catch that one.'

He indicated the horse that he'd been riding earlier. Having shed Colbeck, the animal had run on for a couple of minutes before jumping over a dry stone wall and slowing to a halt. It was now cropping the grass unconcernedly in the middle of a flock of sheep. Leeming studied them with misgiving.

'Well, go on,' urged Colbeck. 'They won't harm you. I've yet to hear of anyone being savaged by a wild ewe.'

About to move off, Leeming was stopped by a sudden thought.

'There's something that worries me, Inspector,' he said.

'What is it?'

'Well, in the space of a morning we've lost our two chief suspects. If neither of *them* committed the murder, who did?'

Agnes Reader bided her time until they were about to leave. Having chosen the keepsake she'd been offered – a tiny silver brooch in the shape of a thistle – she said that she would replace the jewellery box.

'No, no,' said Eve, 'let Mrs Withers do that.'

'It won't take me a second,' Agnes told her.

She went out into the hall and glided up the stairs as swiftly as she could. Letting herself into Miriam Tarleton's bedroom, she put the box back on the dressing table and crossed to the writing bureau in the corner. There was no housekeeper to interfere this time. Agnes lowered the lid of the desk and pulled out one of the little drawers. She put a hand into the space. Her fingers felt for a wooden lever and she eventually found it. When she pressed it down, a secret drawer popped out from the side of the bureau in the most unexpected place. Reaching into it, all she could find were several small keys. Relief coursed through her so strongly that she almost swooned.

'Thank God!' she murmured.

When they stopped at the cottage, it did not take Colbeck long to establish that its female owner was completely unaware of what Bruntcliffe had been doing in the name of revenge. He bade her farewell. The three men headed back towards Northallerton on horseback. Leeming was thankful that they moved at a more sedate pace and glad that they had a prisoner to show for their efforts. At the same time, he was depressed by the realisation that the killer was still at liberty and that they had very little evidence as to his identity. When they reached the town, they handed Bruntcliffe over to one of the constables and watched him being charged before he was shut away in the lock-up. Back in the saddle, Leeming passed on the fruits of his meditation.

'It has to be Sergeant Hepworth,' he concluded.

'We shall certainly take a closer look at him,' agreed Colbeck. 'What better way to conceal your guilt than by joining in the search for a woman whom you actually murdered?'

'No wonder he offered his services to us, Inspector.'

'Yes, he wanted to know exactly how the investigation went. That way, he could always stay one step ahead of us.'

'I think we should arrest him immediately,' said Leeming.

'We don't want to make another mistake, Victor. Let's be absolutely sure of our facts before we accuse him of anything.'

'But we know he sent those letters. His son told us.'

'Sam Hepworth would change his story the moment his father gave him a clip around the ear. No, we must proceed with caution. Hepworth is a railway policeman. He's familiar with the way that suspects are questioned. We mustn't show our hand too early.'

'He's our killer, sir. I know it.'

'You felt the same about Adam Tarleton.'

'What that man did was sinful,' said Leeming, bristling, 'and I was revolted that we should learn about it on the Lord's Day. How could any man hand over a woman like that to a friend? Does he have no moral scruples?'

'You didn't speak to the lady in question,'

Colbeck told him, 'but I did. Let me simply say that Bruntcliffe and Tarleton were, in my opinion, not the only guests to share her bed. Where young men are concerned, she appears to be very compliant.'

'Then I'm glad I stayed outside.'

On the ride from Northallerton, they took the identical route used by Miriam Tarleton, going past the spot where they believed the murder had taken place. They paused for a while so that Colbeck could reconstruct the ambush in his mind. Dismounting from his horse, he went to inspect the wheel marks made in the ground. After looking in both directions, he climbed back into the saddle.

'It has to be the place,' he said. 'They'd be screened from view at this point. Whoever intercepted her had to be someone she knew, someone whose presence wouldn't alarm her in any way.'

'Sergeant Hepworth.'

'It's possible.'

'It's probable, sir. Who could be less likely to alarm her than a policeman?'

Colbeck grinned. 'I know a policeman who alarms *you*, Victor.'

'I'm not talking about the superintendent. Mrs Tarleton must have known Hepworth. Everybody else does and he's not a man to hide his light under a bushel. If she met him here,' argued Leeming, 'the lady would have been reassured by the sight of that uniform.' He gave a short laugh. 'I wonder if he ever takes it off.'

'I fear that he may sleep in it,' said Colbeck.

'Hepworth must have known Mrs Tarleton would be walking that day on this particular route.'

'Yet his name wasn't on that list.'

'What list?'

'It was the one that Mr Reader gave us when he brought that card from the rector's wife. It was compiled by Mrs Reader and contained the names of all those who were definitely aware of the routine followed by the colonel's wife. Hepworth wasn't on the list.'

'That's irrelevant. He's a watcher, sir. If she'd been his target, he'd have kept her under observation for some time.'

'Yes,' conceded Colbeck, 'I can imagine him doing that.'

They continued on their way to the village. Having returned the hired horses, they went back to the Black Bull. Colbeck first washed off the dirt he'd picked up during the fight then he changed his apparel. He asked the landlord where his least favourite customer lived and they were directed to a cottage on the outer fringe of South Otterington. It was a small, low residence for a tall, bulky man and they understood why there was no room for Sam Hepworth to play with his soldiers. They knocked on the door but there was no response. When Leeming peered through a dusty window, half-hidden by ivy, he could see nobody inside. Colbeck led the way around the side of the cottage and they saw that someone was at home, after all. A red-faced girl with a mop of brown curls was pegging out some washing on a line. There was an air of morose resentment about her as if the chore were a punishment inflicted by an unkind parent. Even though she saw them over the fence, she carried on with her job.

'Are you Ginny Hepworth?' asked Colbeck.

'Could be,' she returned, cheekily.

'We know for a fact you are,' said Leeming, annoyed by her rudeness. 'We met your brother in the churchyard this morning.'

'Our Sam's always there.'

'We'd really like to talk to your father.'

'Our Dad's not 'ere.'

'Do you know where he is, Ginny?'

'Out with our Mam, like – they goes walkin' of a Sunday.'

'And they've left you to do all the work, I see,' said Colbeck. 'That was very unfair of them. This should be a day of rest. When will they be back?'

'No idea.'

'Do you know who we are?'

'Whole village knows.'

'Then perhaps you'd tell your father that we'd like to speak to him at the Black Bull. You might also tell him,' said Colbeck, adding the information by way of bait, 'that we've made an arrest.'

'I see,' she said, pegging the last item on the line before folding her arms. 'Who you got, then?'

'We'll tell your father.'

'You used to work at the big house, didn't you?' said Leeming.

'Aye – I were treated bad.'

'How did you get on with the colonel?'

'Colonel were the worst.'

'So you didn't like him?'

313

'No, I were thrown out.'

'But your father spoke up for you. He told us so.'

'Aye, that's right. Our Dad told colonel off, like.'

'And he probably wrote to him, didn't he?' Her eyelids narrowed with suspicion. 'Like any good father, he'd have wanted to defend his daughter. I'll wager that he sent a letter of complaint. I admire him for doing so. From what he said, it seems to me that you were dealt with very shabbily.'

'I were – by the colonel and Mrs Withers, at any rate.'

'Did your father get a reply to his letters?'

'No, he didn't.'

'How many did he send, Ginny?'

'Three.' She brought a hand to her mouth but it was far too late to stop the word popping out. Her cheeks went crimson. 'It were not my fault. I did as I were told.'

'We're not blaming you for anything,' Colbeck reassured her. 'And there's no need to mention this to your father. It's not something we're bothered about. It's just that he's given us some help so he deserves to know that we've got a man in custody.'

Ginny relaxed. 'When will 'e be 'anged?'

'Oh, there's a long way to go before any execution.'

'Our Dad took me to Northallerton once to see a man being 'anged there. There were a big crowd, like. We all cheered.'

'Your father should have known better,' said

Leeming. 'It's not suitable entertainment for a girl of your age. In fact, it shouldn't be entertainment at all. Did your brother go as well?'

'Our Sam stayed 'ere.'

'I'm glad to hear it.'

'Right,' said Colbeck, 'we won't hold you up, Ginny. Just pass on the message, please, and say nothing about those letters. Now that the colonel is dead, they're meaningless.'

She gave a lopsided grin and nodded her head in agreement.

In order to get everything ready in the event of guests returning to the house from church, Mrs Withers and Lottie had got up an hour earlier than usual. They had toiled away before and after the service and were unable to rest until the four visitors had finally departed. Eve and Lawrence Doel had eaten the refreshments in lieu of luncheon, leaving Adam Tarleton to have a full meal on his own in the dining room. While his sister and her husband stayed in the drawing room, he went off to the library to read for an hour. The servants were able to contemplate a short period when they, too, could rest. Lottie chose to sit on a chair and put her aching feet up on a stool. Mrs Withers preferred to withdraw to her room.

Once inside, she locked the door and crossed to the bed. Lifting up the mattress, she felt under it for something she'd hidden there earlier. It was the first chance she'd had to scrutinise it. She sat in the chair by the window so that she caught the best of the light then she undid the pink ribbon

315

around the little bundle. Unfolding the first letter, she began to read it. The housekeeper did not get far. Within the first paragraph there were enough surprises to make her heart beat at a furious rate and to make her whole body burn with embarrassment. Unable to read on, she clutched the letter to her chest and began to sob. Mrs Withers wished that she'd never seen such disturbing words. They pressed down on her brain like so many hot bricks, making her feel as if her head was about to burst into flames. After all the years of devoted service she'd given, she now felt utterly betrayed. It was unnerving. The concept of loyalty suddenly took on a whole new meaning for her.

For their meeting with Hepworth, the detectives withdrew to a private room at the rear of the Black Bull. Colbeck placed pen, ink and paper on the table. Leeming was puzzled.

'What are they for, Inspector?'

'I want to give Hepworth a fright.'

'How will you do that?'

'I'll ask him to write something for us so that we can compare it with the letters received by the colonel.'

'But we don't *have* any letters.'

'*You* know that,' said Colbeck, 'but the sergeant doesn't.'

Leeming was surprised. 'Are you going to lie to him?'

'I'm going to use a little fiction to establish some facts. Without any of those letters he wrote, we could never secure a conviction in court.

What we can do, however, is to unsettle him so much that he'll lower his defence when we ask about the murder.'

'Mr Tallis might not approve of your methods,' said Leeming.

'Mr Tallis wants results,' said Colbeck, blithely. 'With a man like Hepworth, this may be the only way to achieve them.'

They didn't have to wait long. Only half an hour after their visit to his cottage, the railway policeman entered the pub with his usual swagger. When the landlord pointed to the other room, Hepworth banged on the door before pushing it open.

'Good afternoon, gentlemen,' he said, closing the door behind him. 'You sent for me, I hear.'

'Come and sit down, Sergeant,' invited Colbeck.

'Thank you, sir.'

He lowered himself into the chair opposite them, grinning broadly like a new confederate admitted to a conspiracy. Rubbing his hands, he waited to be let in on the secret.

'Your daughter can obviously deliver a message,' said Leeming.

'Ginny is a clever girl.'

'What about your lad?'

'She had most of the brains. Sam had what little was left.'

'We've made an arrest,' Colbeck told him.

Hepworth cocked an ear. 'Was it Michael Bruntcliffe?'

'Yes, it was.'

'I thought it would be. Where did you find him?'

317

'He was staying in a cottage the other side of Bedale. He made a complete confession. He's locked up in Northallerton now.'

'So the murder is solved now, is it, Inspector?'

'Oh, no, we're still hunting the killer.'

'But you've just arrested Bruntcliffe,' said Hepworth, confused.

'That was on two lesser charges,' said Colbeck. 'In the course of last night, he slipped into the churchyard and, with the assistance of his horse, he toppled that large stone cross paid for by the colonel. Luckily, we got there early enough this morning to put it back into place with the help of a farmer.'

'It was like a ton weight,' recalled Leeming.

'Most of the congregation were unaware of what had happened. I had a quiet word with the curate afterwards and he promised to get a mason to secure the cross at its base. Incidentally,' said Colbeck, 'we met your son in the churchyard. He was playing with toy soldiers.'

'Except that they were actually cartridges,' said Leeming with a meaningful glance at Hepworth. 'Sam told us he collects them.'

'That's right,' admitted Hepworth, warily. 'It keeps him occupied. He wants to join the army one day but I doubt if they'd take him.' When he leant forward, his beard touched the table. 'Is that all you charged Bruntcliffe with?'

'Causing damage to church property is a serious offence,' said Colbeck. 'He's bought himself a ticket straight back to prison. His sentence will be lengthened when he pleads guilty to a second offence.'

'What's that, Inspector?'

'Sending anonymous letters to the colonel, full of libellous material and designed to cause him distress. In short, helping to unbalance his mind and drive him to take his own life.'

'I thought you'd already arrested someone for that.'

'We have,' said Colbeck, 'but he wasn't the only correspondent. There were a number of evil-minded people who got pleasure from kicking Colonel Tarleton when he was down, as it were. What's your opinion of such individuals, Sergeant Hepworth?'

'They're despicable,' insisted Leeming, 'and they should be prosecuted with the full rigour of the law.'

'I agree,' said Hepworth, half-heartedly, drawing back in his seat. 'It's a spiteful thing to do.'

'It's spiteful and it's cowardly,' Colbeck went on. 'If someone had an accusation to hurl at the colonel, they should have done so to his face. Well, that's what *you* did when he dismissed your daughter.'

'I did, Inspector. He deserved it. I didn't beat about the bush. When I had that argument with him, I came straight to the point.'

'And you did the same in your letters to him, didn't you?'

Hepworth tensed. 'What letters?'

'The letters you never signed.'

'It's an arrant lie!' yelled the other. 'I didn't send any letters.'

'Then the girl must have been mistaken,' said Colbeck, making it up as he went along. 'Lottie

319

Pearl sleeps in an attic room at the top of the house. She swears that she saw your daughter, Ginny, sneak up to the house at night and post a letter through the door.'

'Lottie was seeing things.'

'Then we'll have to rely on the testimony of Mrs Withers. She knows that secret path from the village to the house. According to her, Ginny emerged from it one night with something in her hand.'

Hepworth snarled. 'How could they see anything in the dark?'

'That's a fair point, Sergeant, so it would be wrong to accuse you on the basis of what they claim. Besides, it's not necessary. We still have the letters in question. All we have to do,' he went on, indicating the writing materials, 'is to ask you to pen a few lines that we can compare with the handwriting on those particular letters.' He turned to Leeming. 'How many were there, Victor?'

'Three, sir.'

'Of the people who wrote, this anonymous author was the only one who charged the colonel with having improper conduct with his house-keeper.' He smiled at Hepworth. 'Wasn't that the very claim you made in our hearing, Sergeant?' He pushed the inkwell in front of him. 'Write something for us, please.'

'You can't make me do this,' said Hepworth, defiantly.

'It's true – we can't force you. But, then, we don't need to.'

'What do you mean?'

320

'We simply have to speak to your employers,' said Colbeck. 'You no doubt send in regular reports so there'll be plenty of examples of your handwriting. When you are sentenced in court, the judge will take into consideration the fact that you refused to cooperate once your subterfuge had been exposed.'

'You didn't even have the courage to deliver the letters yourself,' said Leeming with derision. 'You implicated your own child.'

'Ginny offered,' said Hepworth, reeling back in horror at his unintended confession. 'Look,' he went on with a nervous laugh, 'why don't I buy you a drink and we can forget all about this? The colonel is dead. Nothing that anyone wrote about him can hurt him now.'

'It can hurt his children,' Colbeck pointed out. 'It can disgust his friends, Superintendent Tallis among them. Let's have the truth, Sergeant Hepworth, or it will be the worse for you. You've more or less admitted that you wrote those three letters, didn't you? That's what you can write on the paper.' He put a sheet in front of him. 'If we have a confession, it will save a great deal of time in court and spare you from further humiliation.' He held out the pen. 'Take it. Write something that you're actually brave enough to sign.'

Hepworth was in a panic. 'Don't take me to court,' he begged. 'I've got a wife and children to support. Ginny can't find work and, if you've met Sam, you'll have seen that he's something of a halfwit. Yes, I confess that I did dash off a few lines to the colonel but only because I was still angry at him. We all write things on impulse that

321

we regret afterwards.'

'Not three times in a row,' said Leeming.

'I'm a policeman – one of your own.'

'You'd never get into the Metropolitan Police Force.'

'I've got a position here,' said Hepworth. 'I'm respected.'

'Not by me, Sergeant.'

'Nor by me,' said Colbeck. 'Someone who sends poison-pen letters to a bereaved husband doesn't deserve respect. You're a disgrace to that uniform.'

'I'm sorry,' bleated Hepworth. 'I didn't mean to do it.'

'Think of the searing pain your letters gave to the colonel.'

'It was wrong of me, Inspector. I feel so guilty about it.'

'I haven't seen any signs of guilt.'

'Give me a chance, I implore you.'

'You'll have a lot to do to redeem yourself.'

'I'll do anything you say,' promised Hepworth, 'only please don't ruin me. I couldn't bear it if you sent me to prison.'

'Your brother's a warder there, isn't he?' said Leeming, enjoying the man's discomfort. 'You'll be able to see him more often.'

'Think of my wife – think of my children.'

'You should have done that, Sergeant.'

'I never imagined anyone would find out,' howled Hepworth with his head in his hands. 'I thought it was safe.'

Having got him thoroughly rattled, Colbeck turned to the subject he really wanted to discuss.

He stood up and pointed.

'What were you doing on the day Miriam Tarleton was killed?' he demanded. 'Where were you at the time of the murder?'

Hepworth raised his head in alarm and started to gibber.

Sunday afternoon tea with her aunt and uncle was always a pleasant occasion for Madeleine Andrews, even more so when her father was there. He often spent the Sabbath at work but not this time. He'd been able to put on his suit, attend church with her and forget all about driving a locomotive. Andrews enjoyed changing out of his working clothes and shedding the abiding smell of the railway. As he and Madeleine strolled back home through Camden, there was a spring in his step and his hat was set at a rakish angle. He was reminded of many long-lost Sunday afternoons when his wife had been on his arm. Nostalgia swelled up inside him.

'I wish your mother was here,' he said, involuntarily.

'So do I, Father.'

'Your aunt looks so much like her.'

'She ought to,' said Madeleine. 'They were sisters.'

He chuckled. 'I'll let you into a secret,' he confided. 'She never liked me when I was courting your mother. She thought I was too forward. But I won her over in the end. I charmed her, Maddy.'

'I'm not sure that I believe that.'

'I could do it in those days. I was young once,

323

you know. I wasn't always so crotchety.'

'I know that, Father.'

He tipped his hat to a passing woman. 'She'd have been so proud of you,' he went on. 'Your mother, I mean. Who'd have thought that we had a budding artist in the family? The only thing I could ever draw was a fire. You've got a talent.'

'Only because Robert encouraged me to develop it,' she said.

'Your mother would have been impressed by that as well. We both thought you'd marry a railwayman like me, but you've done so much better for yourself with Inspector Colbeck. He's a proper gentleman.'

'I'd be happy with Robert whatever he did. He enjoys his work but the person he envies is you.'

'Me?' he asked with a laugh.

'Part of him had always wanted to be an engine driver.'

'Then he can thank the Lord above he never became one. He'd have had to put up with hard work, long hours and being out in all weathers. I'm not sure that he'd be able to stand it.'

'He stands it already,' she pointed out. 'He works hard, has long hours and is out in wind, rain, fog, snow and ice. I know there are accidents on the railway, but Robert faces far greater danger when he comes up against desperate criminals. So does Sergeant Leeming, for that matter – he's been badly beaten more than once.'

'He lived to tell the tale,' said Andrews with feeling. 'When I was attacked, I very nearly died. I was in a coma for a long time.'

'You don't need to tell me that. I was sitting

beside you.'

'My suffering was your gain, Maddy.'

'I wouldn't put it that way.'

'I would,' he said. 'If the train hadn't been robbed that day, and if I hadn't been knocked unconscious, you might never have met Inspector Colbeck. Something good came out of it all.'

'The best thing was that you survived, Father.'

'Well, someone has to give you away at the wedding.'

She laughed. 'You sound as if you want to get rid of me.'

'To be honest, I do,' he said, cheerily. 'You obviously didn't see the way that Mrs Hodgkin was smiling at me in church this morning. She's been widowed for three years now. I knew her husband when he worked for the LNWR. He was always boasting what a wonderful cook his wife was. And she's still a fine-looking woman.'

Madeleine didn't know if he was serious or merely joking. She was also uncertain about her own feelings on the subject. Her father had been so distraught at the death of his wife that Madeleine never thought he'd recover. It had never occurred to her that he might one day think of a second marriage. Yet he'd raised the possibility a number of times recently and she found it oddly worrying. It was almost as if she wasn't ready to part with him to another woman. Madeleine had looked after him for so long now, she had become possessive. She tried to fight against such emotions. Since she would be starting a new life when she married, there was no reason why her father shouldn't be allowed to do the same. In fact, on reflection, she felt that it might be a good thing for him. Because he wouldn't be an easy man to live with, she knew that the secret lay in choosing an understanding wife.

'Do you really mean it, Father?' she asked.

'Mean what?'

'That remark you made about Mrs Hodgkin. One minute you tell me that you intend to get married, and the next you laugh at the idea. Are you simply teasing me?'

'Only up to a point, Maddy,' he said. 'When I first mentioned it, I suppose that I was teasing you a little, but I'm starting to like the idea. The house will be very empty when you've gone. Maybe it's time for me to find another wife before I lose my good looks.' They laughed together, then he became quite solemn. 'It's not the same for you and the inspector. You're young and have a whole lifetime ahead of you. I don't, Maddy. But, even at my age, I can still love and be loved.'

'Of course,' she said, squeezing his arm.

'It will be a different kind of love, that's all.'

Colbeck's interrogation was so unremitting that he almost reduced Eric Hepworth to tears. Gone was the overweening arrogance of the railway policeman. In its place was a whimpering submission. For all that, the detectives had not caught a murderer. Hepworth had been working on the day that Miriam Tarleton had been killed and could call on several witnesses to prove it. Having decided that Hepworth was the killer,

Leeming was depressed. Colbeck was less dismayed because he'd kept an open mind. In his view, the meeting had been of positive value. It had eliminated a suspect. It had also had such a sobering effect on Hepworth that he would behave with more humility in future. There was one flash of his old self.

'If I'd wanted to kill anyone,' he'd said, rearing up in his chair, 'then I'd have shot the colonel not his wife. I'd have blown his head off.' He calmed down and shrugged an apology. 'That's all in the past now. I'd rather forget it.'

'Then we'll forget the impulse that made you write those letters,' said Colbeck. 'Guard against such wicked feelings next time.'

'Oh, I will, I will, Inspector.'

'Go to church and cleanse your mind,' advised Leeming.

'Yes, yes, I'll do that as well.'

Overcome with gratitude at being – as he perceived it – let off the hook, Hepworth rose to his feet and shook hands with each of them. Then he snatched up his hat and left the room swiftly. Leeming was dejected.

'I felt certain it was him,' he said. 'It would have given me such pleasure to arrest that buffoon.'

Colbeck was more philosophical. 'We exposed him as the author of those wounding letters,' he said, 'even though we had no evidence beyond the words of his children. That will have shaken him up. I think that our interview with Sergeant Hepworth may have done the whole village a good turn.'

'But it's left us chasing shadows, Inspector.'

'We made a mistake, that's all. We've been looking for a man who killed Mrs Tarleton in order to get revenge against her husband. What we really needed to search for was someone who had a motive to kill the colonel's wife. Yes,' he added as Leeming was about to speak, 'I know that she was, by common report, such a harmless and likeable woman but even the nicest human beings can sometimes excite hatred.'

'We've lost three suspects in a row,' complained Leeming.

'And we may lose a few more before we're done, Victor.'

'Superintendent Tallis will have some harsh words when he sees how little we've achieved.'

'That's unjust,' said Colbeck. 'We helped to put a stone cross up in the churchyard. We arrested the man who pulled it over in the first place and who had an additional crime to his name. We extracted a confession from Hepworth with regard to those letters he wrote, and we've sent him out of here a reformed man. I don't think that's a bad record for a Sunday.'

'We still haven't caught the man we're after, sir.'

'Then we must look at the other potential suspects.'

'There *are* none,' said Leeming.

'What about the list that Mr Reader gave us?' asked Colbeck, taking it from his pocket and laying it on the table. 'Since his wife went to the trouble of drawing it up for us, we ought to use it.' He tapped the piece of paper. 'Everyone on here knew that Mrs Tarleton would be walking to Northallerton that day. The chances are that the killer's name is right under our noses.'

'Well, it certainly isn't Mrs Reader herself, yet her name is at the top of the list. In fact,' Leeming went on, 'I'd cross off the names of all the women on that list.'

'Some women are capable of firing a shotgun, Victor.'

The sergeant gasped. 'You think the killer was female?'

'I think that we should rule nothing out.'

'I still fancy that Adam Tarleton is involved somehow. Why don't we go and talk to him again?'

'There's no point,' said Colbeck, getting up. 'Besides, it would be wrong to disturb a house of sorrow. It was very brave of Mrs Doel to attend church this morning but I could see that it was a strain for her. She and the rest of the family should be left alone.'

Leeming rose to his feet, 'Very well, sir.'

Picking up the list, Colbeck took a last look at it before slipping it into his pocket. He then opened the door and went out. Seconds after he did so, Mrs Withers entered the bar. She was panting hard and her face was lined with anxiety. When she saw Colbeck, she lurched gratefully towards him.

'Could I speak to you in private, please?' she begged.

'Yes, of course,' he replied. 'Step in here, Mrs Withers.'

As she went past him into the empty room, he could see that she was in a state of considerable distress. He gestured to Leeming who gave an understanding nod. Colbeck went into the room after her and helped her to a chair. Beneath her black hat, he noticed the perspiration on her brow.

'Get your breath back first,' he advised.

'I ran part of the way,' she gasped.

'Then it must be important. The sergeant is getting something for you so there's no hurry now. You can relax.'

'I don't think I'll ever be able to do that again, Inspector.'

She produced a handkerchief and dabbed at her face. Her shoulders were heaving and there was a look of desperation in her eyes. Leeming had ordered a glass of brandy in the bar. When it was handed to him, Colbeck closed the door and crossed over to his visitor.

'Take a sip of this, Mrs Withers,' he said. 'It may help.'

'I need something,' she admitted.

'It's brandy. Drink it slowly.'

She took a first sip and it seemed to steady her nerves. Though her panting slowly eased, she was afraid to meet Colbeck's eyes. He sat opposite her and waited. After a second nip of brandy, she found the courage to speak.

'Mrs Tarleton trusted me,' she began. 'She said that she'd never manage without me.'

'That's praise, indeed.'

'It's how I came to know about the bureau, you see.'

'What bureau is that, Mrs Withers?' he asked.

'It was in her bedroom. She used to write letters and to store things in. When it first arrived, she showed me that it had a secret compartment. You'd never guess that there was one there.'

'Actually, I might,' said Colbeck. 'My father was a cabinetmaker and so was my grandfather. They showed me all the tricks of the trade. But do go on,' he said. 'What was in this secret compartment?'

'Mrs Tarleton told me she kept her keys in there – the keys to the wardrobe, the chest of drawers and various other places.'

'That sounds like a sensible idea.'

'I had no need to look into the compartment until today...' Her voice cracked and she used the handkerchief to stem some tears. He put the glass to her lips and she took another sip. 'I'm sorry,' she said. 'I just wasn't prepared for such a shock. I still haven't got used to it.' She took a deep breath. 'It all started when Mrs Reader went upstairs. I saw her go into the bedroom and nobody was allowed in there when Mrs Tarleton was alive. When I went in after her, she was standing beside the bureau. Mrs Reader said that she'd been told she could have a keepsake from the jewellery box but that was on the other side of the room. I gave it to her and told her to take it downstairs so that she could choose something while Mrs Doel was there.'

'That seems reasonable.'

'It worried me, Inspector,' she said. 'It worried me that she was going to open the bureau. I wondered if she knew about that secret compartment and was after the keys. So, after she'd gone...' The tears had to be kept at bay again. 'Oh,

I know that I shouldn't have done what I did. It wasn't my place to do it but I felt that Mrs Tarleton's privacy was being invaded. I felt responsible.'

'You were right to do so,' he told her, trying to spare her the ordeal of giving a full explanation. 'I think that you wisely decided to check that the keys were still in the secret compartment. Is that what happened?' She nodded. 'And were they there?'

She nodded again then dissolved into tears of shame. He got up to put a consoling arm around her and to coax her into taking another sip of brandy. When she'd finally dried her eyes, he spoke again.

'You found something else in there, didn't you?'

'I wish to God that I hadn't!' she cried. 'If I had my time over again, I'd never go near that bureau. I shouldn't have found out what I did, Inspector. I shouldn't *know*.'

She opened her bag and took out a bundle of letters written on pink stationery. Handing the bundle to Colbeck, she lowered her head in embarrassment. Colbeck undid the ribbon and opened the first letter. Like all the others, it had been written in a graceful hand by Agnes Reader. He read it through without comment then looked at each of the others in turn. He tied the ribbon around the bundle once again.

'May I keep hold of these, please?' he asked.

'Oh, yes!' she said. 'I never want to see them again.'

'I can understand that, Mrs Withers, but you

mustn't blame yourself. In finding these, you've done Mrs Tarleton a great service because you've provided me with a clue that will almost certainly lead to the arrest of her killer.'

'I've never heard of such a thing, Inspector. I keep thinking of the poor colonel. Do you believe that he could have known?'

'I hope that he didn't,' said Colbeck, softly. 'Have you told anyone else about this?'

'I'd be too ashamed to do that, sir.'

'Please keep it to yourself for the time being. When you've finished that brandy, I'll get Sergeant Leeming to see you back to the house.' She was still profoundly disturbed by her discovery and in need of reassurance. 'You did the right thing, Mrs Withers. One day, you'll come to appreciate that.'

Agnes Reader was so overcome with sadness when they returned home that she took to her bed. Unable to sleep, she lay there brooding for a few hours. When her husband looked in on her, she was still wide awake. He was attentive.

'Is there anything I can get you, my dear?'

'No, thank you.'

'Shall I have a pot of tea sent up?'

'I'd just like to be left alone, Bertram,' she said.

'Then you shall be,' he told her, backing away. The doorbell rang down below. 'We're not expecting anyone, are we?'

'No ... and whoever it is, I don't want to see them.'

'You won't be disturbed, Agnes, I promise.'

Reader left the room and padded downstairs.

He was taken aback to see the maid showing Colbeck into the drawing room. After dismissing her with a wave, he went in to meet his visitor.

'Good afternoon, Inspector,' he said.

'I'm sorry to intrude on you again, Mr Reader,' said Colbeck, 'but I really need to speak to Mrs Reader.'

'She's not available at the moment, I'm afraid.'

'Then I'll have to wait until she is available, however long it takes. Perhaps you could convey that message to her.'

'My wife is asleep.'

'I'll still be here when she wakes up.'

Colbeck was polite but purposeful. The banker could see that he wouldn't leave the house until he'd spoken to Agnes.

'May I know what this is all about, Inspector?' he asked.

'That's a decision only your wife can make.'

'I don't like mysteries.'

'I love them, sir,' said Colbeck. 'Solving them always gives me a sense of deep satisfaction.'

'Couldn't this wait until tomorrow?'

'No, Mr Reader. It needs to be resolved before the inquest.'

The banker stared at him and there was a silent battle of wills. Determined not to bother his wife, Reader was at the same time curious to know why Colbeck was there. For his part, the inspector was inscrutable. His non-committal smile gave nothing away, except the fact that he intended to stay indefinitely. In the end, Reader weakened and edged towards the door.

'I'll see if my wife has woken up yet,' he said.

'Thank you, sir. I'd be most grateful.'

Reader went out and was absent for a long time. Colbeck was able to take a good look at the room. Its paintings and ornaments had dazzled Leeming but Colbeck was more interested in the furniture. Coming from a family of cabinet-makers, he had an eye for superior craftsmanship. He was admiring a Jacobean court cupboard when Reader finally reappeared with his wife. Agnes was composed.

'I believe you wish to speak to me,' she said.

'That's right, Mrs Reader. It's on a private matter. You may or may not wish your husband to remain.'

'My wife has no secrets from me, Inspector,' said Reader.

Agnes studied the visitor's face. 'In this instance,' she said, sensing what might have brought Colbeck there, 'I think I would like you to leave us, Bertram.' He was clearly hurt. 'I'll tell you everything that passes between us.'

'If that's what you wish, my dear, that's how it will be. But I won't be far away. Should you need me,' he went on, tossing a glance at Colbeck, 'you only have to call.'

Crossing to the double doors on the other side of the room, he opened them wide and stepped through into the library. Colbeck waited until he heard the doors click shut once more. Agnes pointed to the sofa and he sat down. Eyes never leaving his face, she chose an armchair. She looked calm and poised.

'Certain letters have come into my possession,' he said, quietly.

'You had no right to read them,' she protested. 'That was a private correspondence.'

'It also happens to be evidence in a murder investigation, Mrs Reader. That being the case, I had every right to examine them.'

'It was that bitch of a housekeeper, wasn't it?'

'That's immaterial,' said Colbeck. 'The fact is that I read the letters and they were able to fill in a number of blank spaces for me. When I heard that Mrs Tarleton used to visit Edinburgh to see her cousin, I assumed that she stayed at the cousin's home. That was not always so, was it? On at least three occasions, you and she shared a room at a particular hotel.'

'There's no need to repeat it,' she snapped. 'And if you expect me to feel guilty about it, you'll be disappointed. Miriam and I had a very special friendship. Talking about it the way you do only serves to cheapen it.'

'I make no moral judgement, Mrs Reader, and I think you'll find that you can rely on my discretion. I came here for two reasons. First, I wanted to see if you'd resort to denial.'

'That would be an insult to both of us, Inspector. Why deny something that was so beautiful?'

'I respect that.

'You said that there were two reasons.'

'The second one is perhaps more important. Who else knew about your friendship with Mrs Tarleton?'

She was firm. 'Nobody knew,' she said. 'We were extremely careful. The colonel was too bound up in his own affairs and my husband allows me complete freedom.'

'Presumably, Mrs Tarleton wrote you letters?'

'You're not going to see those, Inspector.'

'I don't wish to do so.'

'They're very precious to me. Nobody else will ever see them.'

'I've brought your letters with me,' he said, patting his pocket. 'You're welcome to have them back with my assurance that I'm the only person to have read them.'

'What about Mrs Withers?'

'She was too shocked to see more than half a page.'

Agnes weighed him up with a shrewd glance, wondering how much she could trust him. She was thankful that he'd come alone and not brought the sergeant with him. Discussing the matter with one man was a trial. To have had the two of them there would have been insufferable. Colbeck had spoken gently and without comment. She felt that he understood her position.

'Could I please ask you to destroy those letters?' she asked.

'I'll burn them as soon as I leave here.'

'Thank you, Inspector.'

'You might like to know that I haven't shown them to Sergeant Leeming nor confided anything of their contents.' He looked towards the library. 'The question now arises as to what you tell your husband when I go.'

'Leave that to me,' she said, complacently. 'I'm used to making up stories for Bertram. He believes everything I tell him.'

'That's not true!' yelled Reader, flinging open the double doors and standing there with a pistol in his hand. 'I stopped believing you months ago, Agnes.'

'Bertram!' she cried, jumping up. 'Have you been listening?'

'I heard every word.'

'Put that pistol down, sir,' said Colbeck, rising slowly to his feet. 'We don't want to have an unfortunate accident.'

'It won't be an accident, Inspector. It's something I should have done long ago.' A pleading note dominated. 'I tried so hard, Agnes. I hoped that when Miriam died, we could start afresh and put all this behind us, but that's never going to happen, is it? Alive or dead, she'll always be there between us.'

'I'm sorry,' she said, watching the pistol with alarm. 'You weren't supposed to know. I wanted to spare you that pain.'

'You gave me more than enough pain as it was,' he said, waving the weapon at her. 'Is it too much to ask of a woman I marry that we live as husband and wife? Is it too much to ask of someone for whom I've done everything that she's mine and nobody else's?'

'Please, sir,' said Colbeck, going towards him with an extended hand, 'let me have the pistol.'

'Stand back or I'll shoot,' warned Reader, turning the weapon on him. Colbeck came to a halt. 'I had a feeling that you'd catch me in the end. You're like a dog with a bone. You never stop. Well, now you know the hideous truth.'

'It isn't hideous,' cried Agnes. 'I was proud of what I did.'

'How do you think that makes *me* feel? When I

338

paid a private detective to follow you to Edinburgh, I couldn't believe what it said in his report. There had to be a mistake. Surely, no wife of mine would ever betray me in that unspeakable fashion.'

Agnes was indignant. 'You spied on me?' she said, vehemently. 'How dare you do something so awful!' She rocked back on her heels as she finally realised the truth. 'It was *you*, wasn't it? You weren't in Darlington that day, after all. That was just an excuse. You killed Miriam! You killed the only person I ever truly loved.'

'Yes,' he confessed. 'I did and I enjoyed doing it. I thought that, if I could remove the woman who'd poisoned our marriage, you'd come back to me. But you haven't and you never will. I made an error,' he went on, levelling the pistol at her. 'I shot the wrong woman. Instead of killing Miriam, I should have killed *you*.'

Colbeck flung himself in front of Agnes and held out his arms to screen her. He could hear her sobbing and feel her shivering against his body. Reader took a step closer so that he was only six feet away.

'You'll have to shoot me first, Mr Reader,' he said.

'Get out of the way, Inspector!'

'It won't be so easy this time, sir. I'm not a docile woman who'll turn her back on you unsuspectingly so that you can put that sacking over her head. I'm looking you in the eye,' he continued, 'and I can see the doubts swirling about in your mind. Even from that distance, you're not sure of killing me, are you? You're not a marksman like the colonel or Mr Everett. You're a banker with no real interest in firearms. Look, your hand is shaking. You could miss altogether, couldn't you? Have you considered that?' He offered his hand. 'Now give the pistol to me, please. It's all over, Mr Reader. An intelligent man like you must know that. It's all over.'

Reader's hand was trembling so much that he was in danger of dropping the pistol. Colbeck watched him carefully, waiting for a moment when he could dive forward and wrest the weapon from him. Agnes, meanwhile, was cowering behind the inspector's back, praying that he wouldn't be shot dead by her husband. Seeing the hesitation in the banker's eyes, Colbeck tried to reason with him.

'What will be achieved by killing someone else, sir?' he asked. 'You already have two deaths on your conscience.'

'*One* death,' said Reader, 'and it's not on my conscience.'

'The murder of Mrs Tarleton may not trouble you but, when you killed her, you also killed her husband. He loved his wife so much that he couldn't live without her. Doesn't that fact prey on your mind?' he went on. 'Do you feel no guilt at having sent a close friend on that fatal walk along a railway track?'

'I wasn't to know that that would happen.'

'But it did, sir, and you were responsible.'

'Be quiet!'

'Can't you bear to hear the truth?'

'I simply wanted that woman out of our lives.'

'Murder is never simple,' said Colbeck, one eye

on the pistol. 'There are always unseen consequences. Because of the way you killed Mrs
Tarleton, you subjected her husband to the most
unendurable torment. Those vicious letters he
received were only a component of the misery
that drove him to take his own life. *That's* what
you did to the colonel, sir. You put him through
agony.'

'And what about *my* agony?' wailed Reader.

Colbeck's reply came in the form of a sudden
leap. Diving forward, he grabbed the wrist of the
hand holding the pistol and twisted it away. As he
grappled with the banker, Agnes took cover
behind the sofa and put her hands over her ears
to block out the expletives that her husband
began to hurl at her. Reader was soon silenced.
In the course of the struggle, the pistol went off
and the bullet shattered a glass cabinet, sending
shards flying everywhere. Dropping the pistol to
the floor, Reader used both hands in a vain
attempt to push the detective away. Colbeck was
too fast for him, sticking out a foot to trip him up
and shoving him hard in the chest.

As the banker tumbled to the carpet, Colbeck
snatched up the pistol and used the butt to knock
him unconscious with one strike. By the time
that Reader eventually came to, he found that his
wrists had been handcuffed behind his back.

The inquest into the death of Miriam Tarleton
was able to record a verdict that named her killer.
Sitting through it with his detectives, Edward
Tallis had the satisfaction of seeing the murder
solved and the reputation of his old army

comrade restored. Colbeck had spoken to the coroner beforehand with regard to Wilf Moxey's evidence. The farm labourer was relieved that he was not pressed to account for his presence in the wood during the night. After its interruption, his romance with Lorna Begg could now continue. Eve Doel, her husband and her brother sat through the proceedings in a daze, stunned by the revelation that a trusted family friend had been the killer. Agnes Reader did not appear at the inquest, having already fled to stay with friends in Norfolk. Mrs Withers was also missing. Still trying to cope with the enormity of what she'd discovered, she was now looking forward to quitting a house that had held such a dark secret. Lottie Pearl was blissfully unaware of the true facts of the case.

Tallis remained in Yorkshire to attend the funerals, allowing Colbeck and Leeming to return to London. On the train journey back, they were fortunate enough to have a carriage to themselves. It enabled the sergeant to express his full horror.

'How can any woman do such things?' he asked, incredulously. 'It's against nature.'

'Yet it's not against the law.'

'In my opinion, it should be.'

'It's not for us to question what they did,' said Colbeck, tolerantly. 'The two ladies in question found in each other the love that was lacking in their respective marriages. The tragedy is that it led to the brutal death of one of them.'

'Mrs Tarleton is the one who surprises me, sir. I mean, she bore children. She did what women are put on this earth to do. It's what the Bible teaches us.'

'Agnes Readier had an alternative theology. She married to disguise her inclinations and had no intention of having a family. At first, Mrs Tarleton and she were just friends. Without realising it, the colonel drove them into each other's arms.'

'How did he do that, Inspector?'

'By making a disastrous investment in the railways,' said Colbeck. 'His lawyer advised him against it – so did his banker – but the colonel had the single-minded approach we've seen in Mr Tallis. Nothing could hold him back. The prospect of earning a fortune was too enticing. He not only lost most of his own money,' he concluded, 'he persuaded his wife to venture her wealth as well. Thanks to Stuart Leybourne, they were defrauded out of every penny.'

'Any wife would have been embittered by that,' said Leeming.

'It's my belief that Mrs Tarleton turned to her friend for comfort. I'm sure that Mrs Reader was extremely sympathetic. One thing led to another with the result that we now know.'

'It makes my blood run cold, sir. It's so *abnormal*.'

'You should read some ancient history, Victor.'

'Oh, I know what those Greek women are supposed to have done but that was a long time ago. You don't expect that kind of thing to happen in this day and age – least of all in Yorkshire.'

Colbeck laughed. 'What's so special about Yorkshire?'

'People there seem so straightforward and

343

down to earth.'

'Sergeant Hepworth wasn't very straight-forward.'

'He was the exception to the rule.'

'And so was Michael Bruntcliffe, not to mention the rector.'

'You know what I mean, sir,' said Leeming with exasperation. 'Country folk are more open. That's what I found, anyway. I suppose that's what makes this all the more revolting.' He shook his head. 'I don't know how I can tell my wife about it.'

'Do you always confide details of our cases in Estelle?'

'I do most of the time.'

'Did you tell her about some of the brothels you raided when you were in uniform? Or what a corpse looks like when it's been in the Thames for three weeks? Or what that peer of the realm we arrested had been up to with his valet?'

'Oh, no,' replied Leeming. 'That would only upset her.'

'I think it would have upset *you* even more,' said Colbeck with an avuncular smile. 'Why not spare your wife the distress and save yourself the embarrassment?'

'I think I might do just that, Inspector. What about you?'

'Me?'

'Are you going to tell Miss Andrews about those two women?'

'Only if Madeleine asks me,' said Colbeck, 'and I have a strong suspicion that she will.'

Thrilled to have him back in London again, Madeleine had pressed for details of the investigation. She saw it as both an insurance against the future and a form of education. If she was to be the wife of a detective inspector, she wanted a forewarning about the kind of life she would be sharing. At the same time, she found it instructive to learn about the criminal underworld in which Colbeck spent most of his time. Madeleine had been actively involved in some investigations but was completely detached from this one. When he told her about the relationship between Agnes Reader and Miriam Tarleton, her first reaction was to blush. Having met neither of the women involved, she just couldn't comprehend the strength of feeling between them. It was something entirely outside her experience.

Though she didn't flinch from any of the details, she was glad when Colbeck had moved on to discuss their own relationship. He admitted that he had prevaricated for too long and he promised her that, when the superintendent returned, he would tell him about the engagement at the earliest opportunity. It was a final hurdle that needed to be cleared. As she prepared breakfast that morning, she glanced up at the clock on the mantelpiece and felt a glow of pleasure at the thought that Colbeck would be breaking the news to Tallis later that same day. Having heard so much about the superintendent and his hostile attitude to marriage among his detectives, Madeleine was alive to the irony of the situation. While she knew that he'd never accept her with any enthusiasm, it was only when he'd been told about her existence that she'd feel wholly accepted by Colbeck. She would be a recognised feature in his life and not something that had to be kept hidden from his superior.

When Tallis came back to work that morning, Colbeck was waiting for him. He noticed how uncharacteristically subdued the superintendent was and put it down to grief. It made him think twice about the promise he'd made to Madeleine and he wondered if he should postpone his declaration until another time. After consideration, however, Colbeck decided that he couldn't let her down again. It was time to grasp the nettle and explain his situation.

'There's something I must tell you, sir,' he said.

'I don't wish to know any more,' warned Tallis. 'Whatever you read in the dreadful letters from that woman is no concern of mine. I'll simply cherish the memory of two wonderful friends. They were buried side by side, you know.'

'I hoped that they would be, sir.'

'The funerals took place after nine o'clock in the evening. It was a very moving occasion. Miriam was accorded the rites of a Christian burial while her husband was denied them. But they were together,' he emphasised, 'and that was what the colonel would have wanted.' He took a cigar from the box and rolled it gently between his palms. 'We have you to thank for that, Inspector. If you hadn't exposed the rector for the villainous hypocrite he was, we'd still be arguing about when and where the funerals would actually take place. I'm sorry to have missed

346

seeing the rector and his wife in court. I'm grateful to you for putting them there.'

'Mr Reader deserves some of the credit, sir.'

'Don't mention that man's name,' said Tallis, sharply, 'and, whatever you do, don't bring his wife into the conversation.'

'I understand,' said Colbeck. 'Did you have the opportunity to speak to Mrs Doel and her brother about their plans?'

'I found it more useful to talk to Mr Everett. He knows what the children are set to inherit. He hinted to me that Eve will receive the bulk of the estate while Adam will have only a token sum of money.'

'That will upset him.'

'It's no more than he deserves,' said Tallis. A fond smile then lit up his face. 'Mr Everett was kind enough to inform me that I'd been remembered in the colonel's will. I was very touched.'

He went off into a reverie and Colbeck saw his chance. He waited until the superintendent came out of his daydream then he plunged straight in.

'There's a personal matter I wish to discuss, sir,' he said.

'Is there?'

'I haven't had the opportunity to tell you this before but now, I feel, is the right moment to do so.'

Tallis was worried. 'You're not going to *resign*, are you?'

'No, no, it's nothing like that.'

'Good – you're the best man I have, Colbeck.'

'Thank you, sir,' said the other, not stopping to savour the compliment. 'The fact is, Superintend-

347

ent, that I recently became engaged to be married.'

'Yes, I know.'

Colbeck was astonished. 'You *know?*'

'For obvious reasons, I don't read that sort of thing in the newspapers but the commissioner does. He saw the announcement and mentioned it to me. He sends his congratulations, by the way.'

'Thank you, sir.'

'Is that all you have to say?'

'Yes,' said Colbeck, amazed that he'd escaped the lecture and the condemnation he'd feared. Overcome with relief, he reached for the tinderbox on the desk. 'Let me light your cigar for you, sir.'

'This is not *my* cigar, man – it's for you.'

Colbeck took it from him. 'That's very kind of you.'

'It's in lieu of the congratulations I'm unable to extend. There's no need to explain why,' said Tallis, taking a second cigar from the box. 'For a man like you, marriage will be an unmitigated disaster. It will weaken your resolve, slow your responses, impede your readiness to work away from London, divide your loyalty and act as a permanent distraction. Well, you only have to look back over the last week to realise the damage that ensues when you take a woman into your life. Not that my strictures will have an effect,' he went on, creating a spark to light his cigar. 'Marriage is madness.' He puffed hard until there was a glow at the end of the cigar then he beamed at Colbeck.

'I want you to do me a favour, Inspector.'

'What's that, sir?'

'Prove me wrong.'

It was a long time since Madeleine had been able to spend a whole evening in Colbeck's company and she was determined to make the most of it. Since he was taking her to the theatre, she spent much longer than usual in front of the mirror on her dressing table. He arrived in a cab to pick her up and marvelled at her appearance. Only one thing was on Madeleine's mind. As soon as they settled into the cab, she turned to Colbeck.

'Did you tell him, Robert?' she asked.

'Tell who?'

'This is serious. Did you speak to the super-intendent today?'

'I spoke to him several times.'

'Don't tease me,' she said. 'Did you or did you not tell him?'

'I suppose the truthful answer is that I didn't,' said Colbeck.

'Robert ... you promised!'

'I know and I did my best but it was totally unnecessary. He already knew. Mr Tallis had been told by the commissioner.'

She was angry. 'Have I been suffering all this time without really needing to?' she asked. 'Why didn't the superintendent tell you that he already knew about the engagement?'

'That's the sort of person he is, Madeleine.'

'You mean that he deliberately made no comment?'

'I mean that this kind of behaviour is in the

nature of the beast.'

'That's one way to describe him,' she said with a laugh. 'Are we going to invite him to the wedding?' She saw the look of absolute horror that he shot her. 'I thought not.'

'Mr Tallis knows and disapproves yet he nevertheless gave me one of his cigars by way of celebration. That's all we need to say on the subject,' decreed Colbeck. 'We're going to put my work completely out of our minds and enjoy an evening at the theatre. Is that agreed?'

'Yes, Robert. What are we going to see?'

'It's a play called *Money* by Edward Bulwer-Lytton. I've seen it before and I think you'll find it very amusing.'

'What's it about?'

'Something that both of us will endorse,' he said, pulling her close. 'It's about getting married for the right reasons.'

The publishers hope that this book has given you enjoyable reading. Large Print Books are especially designed to be as easy to see and hold as possible. If you wish a complete list of our books please ask at your local library or write directly to:

Magna Large Print Books
Magna House, Long Preston,
Skipton, North Yorkshire.
BD23 4ND

This Large Print Book for the partially sighted, who cannot read normal print, is published under the auspices of

THE ULVERSCROFT FOUNDATION